Tequila Tuesdays

Palm Springs Poolside Book 2

J. L. Brannick

Tequila Tuesdays Copyright © 2023 by J. L. Brannick

www.jlbrannick.com

Published by Smart Mouth Publishing LLC

Paperback ISBN: 979-8-9879188-5-2
Ebook ISBN: 979-8-9879188-4-5

Chapter 1

Bending over, I rested my hands on my knees, heaving in and out. Sweat dripped off my chin. I glanced through the volleyball net at the opposing team and was relieved to see they also looked winded.

It was time to substitute Jaime out. He was so tired, he'd shanked his last two serves.

"Frankie, you're in," I called. "Jaime needs to catch his breath. And do a little cardio once in a while."

Jaime had a handsome tan face, jet-black hair, and a big white smile. He also hated exercise. Frankie was in her early twenties. She had long dark brown hair and a slight build. From the back, it was hard to tell whether she'd hit puberty yet.

Flashing me a shit-eating grin, Jaime made smoochy kisses as he walked backward off the court. Tattoos climbed up his neck, and gang symbols covered his knuckles.

"I love you too, Harley!" Jaime yelled.

I shook my head. "Do some cardio."

My palms still rested on my knees, and I flipped him off by tucking in all but my middle fingers. He smiled even wider.

I stood up and waved Frankie in to replace him. She stared at me with wide eyes like I'd lost my damn mind. Frankie usually flinched whenever the ball came near her, but by some miracle, she served these beautiful, unpredictable floaters. The opposing team usually had to scramble to figure out where her serves were going to land.

The score was tied at fifteen all. I was hot, tired, and annoyed. If my old college coach could see me now, he'd chew me out for my sorry state.

I was sweating everywhere—under my boobs, down my back. Even my kneecaps were wet. My entire team was a pathetic, tired mess. But they were *my* pathetic mess, by God.

Strands of sweaty hair clung to my neck. Before every match, I braided my long wavy blonde hair into thin braids, then pulled them back in a high ponytail. It was the best way I knew to keep my hair out of my face, and I thought it looked intimidating.

We'd gotten the ball back after Jaime had subbed out, and Josh was up to serve. Josh sported thick black gauges in his ears, and his face was pocked with scars. I'd been able to teach Josh enough to get the ball over the net, but he didn't have a strong serve. The opposing players shifted around intently, ready to take advantage.

The one I'd secretly labeled "Dimples" grinned at me through the net. He was tall, muscular, and confident. And he had a distracting dimple in his cheek. His thick, dark blond hair looked like he combed it with his fingers.

He was also a competitive bastard, and his team was good. It took everything I had, and maybe a few underhanded tricks, to sometimes squeak out a win.

One of their players who looked like an ex-football player and had a wicked serve, straightened up and rubbed the back of his neck.

"All right, you lazy assholes," he called to his team. "If we keep this up, it'll be dinner time before we get done with this match."

"Yeah, and what Valkyrie over there said about cardio goes for a few of you." Dimples looked around. "Not you, Johanna."

Johanna smiled and preened a little. "Thanks, Damien."

Her perfect hair and makeup, and her expensive volleyball outfit, made her look like she was modeling athletic clothing instead of sweating through a city rec league volleyball game. I wore generic spandex shorts and a sports bra under my jersey that I'd probably owned in high school.

Dimples and his huge friend had tried to recruit me when I first started playing in the league, but I quickly shot them down. My team wasn't typical, and they were here for reasons that went beyond winning.

Dimples stood on the other side of the net, looking me up and down. "You've put up an impressive fight, Val. But you're playing with a team who looks like you rounded them up in a Walmart parking lot."

My eyes narrowed and I straightened. "Walmart parking lot?" I repeated slowly.

He nodded. "And you're looking slow and tired. I don't think you're gonna be able to pull a rabbit out of your ass this time."

Last season he and his large friend had started calling me Valkyrie, I assumed after one of the blonde Viking war goddesses, and then Val for short. It wasn't the first time someone had given me a nickname, and I'd heard a lot worse. What Dimples didn't understand is that I thrived on smack talk. It was a sweet rush of adrenaline to my system.

What he *really* didn't understand is my "Walmart parking lot" team had more grit and determination than any team I'd ever played with. I went from annoyed and tired to furious and laser focused. No one fucked with my team.

I stood up straight and looked him in the eye. "Watch me."

Nodding at Josh to serve the ball, I bent my knees and got ready to play. He served it underhand to make sure it got over the net. The ball went to Johanna on the other side who bumped it from the back row. Her bump was too close to the net to give their setter a chance to get under it, so Dimple's friend tipped it over onto our side. Right to Frankie.

"Move," I clipped as Frankie squeaked and instinctively got out of my way.

I dove under the ball and pancaked my hand out just centimeters from the dirt, hitting it up. Then I rolled up fast. Kevin got under the ball and gave me a decent set not too close to the net.

I bent my knees, pumped my arms, and engaged my quads. My vertical leap this one time was almost as good as it had been in college. I rotated my arm back and spiked the living shit out of that ball—right into Dimple's face. He instinctively flinched, but the impact jerked his head back, and the ball bounced off the side of his nose and rolled off the net.

He wiped his hand under his nose and gazed down at the blood. Then he looked up and stared at me.

His teammates froze for a couple of seconds, then swarmed around him. I stood impassively with my hands on my hips, watching them fuss over him. Johanna glared at me.

The big player—I think his name was Zach or Zeke—glanced at me and smirked, then grabbed a towel off one of their bags.

He tossed it to Dimples. "Here."

"Damien, are you okay? Your nose is bleeding!" Johanna fluttered around him.

One of their players with green shorts on shook his head in amazement. "Holy shit, man! That spike was like a rocket—right to your face. Good thing you turned your head. That was an amazing jump."

Dimples gave him an exasperated look.

The green-shorts guy shrugged. "What? It's true." He looked over at me, his eyes traveling up and down my legs. I gave him a bored look.

Dimples pulled the towel from his face and watched me. A sluggish drop of blood oozed out of one nostril. "Anyone have any tissues? I need to stop the bleeding so we can finish."

His friend cocked his head. "What're you thinking? You gonna to pack your nose and keep playing?"

Dimples looked at me. "Yeah."

"I've got tissues," Johanna volunteered. Of course she had tissues.

He took the package from her but kept staring at me. I watched as he efficiently stuffed his nostrils. Then we got back into position, and we resumed play. We traded three more points back and forth, fighting to the death for every return.

We were finally up by one, but my team was breathing hard and fading fast. It was now or never. Finally, after a volley that seemed to last forever, Frankie put up a decent set—probably her first one of the season.

"All right!" Josh shouted in approval.

It wasn't perfect, but I could work with it. I drew on the last of my reserves, jumping high and swinging my arm back again. Their front line froze for a millisecond, probably remembering my last spike. I pulled the hit at the last second and tapped the ball softly to the side of their left blocker. It landed inbounds with only centimeters to spare.

My team, who minutes before had been winded and tired, erupted into celebration.

"We won! We won! We won!" someone chanted.

Josh grabbed Frankie and spun her around.

"*Gracias Dios*!" Jaime muttered and flopped down on the grass.

Frankie looked shell-shocked. When Josh finally put her down, the others swarmed around her, patting her on the back and congratulating her.

"Nice work, lanky Frankie." I gave her a hard slap on her ass and patted her shoulder. She smiled up at me with the most beautiful smile I'd ever seen.

While my team celebrated, I looked over at Dimples. He watched me carefully.

"Walmart parking lot," I mouthed at him.

He tilted his head as if trying to understand what I'd said.

His big friend came up to him and patted his shoulder. "I think she mouthed something about Walmart."

The noise from our side quieted down a bit, and Dimples walked over to the net in front of me. "Nice fake, Val. I'll see you next season."

"Yeah, you will." I started to turn away, but turned back at the last second. "You can shit-talk me all you want. But don't fuck with my team, Dimples."

Josh came over and smacked my shoulder, and I turned back to celebrate with my jubilant, mismatched team.

Chapter 2

I f I'd known who was going to be at my neighbor's pool party that Monday night, I would have stayed home. I could have finished binge-watching the South Korean series about a brilliant autistic attorney who loved whales. Or maybe cleaned my house.

But Ava, my mother, came over on Sunday morning and convinced me to go.

"Harley, I need you to go with me tomorrow night." She'd bustled through my house into my backyard without knocking. Gary, my small gray and white rescue mutt, lay on the loveseat with his head in my lap. Ava scowled down at him.

Ava still had nice curves, and she was shorter than me by at least six inches. She turned heads with her Scandinavian complexion, blond hair, and clean bone structure. I'd inherited a few of those traits, but my height and lean frame came from my dad.

"Why?" I leaned back and studied her.

"Grace and Sheila want you to come, and I'm calling *quid pro quo.*"

My little house sat on the left side of her larger one. When she found the house she wanted, she'd begged me to buy the little rundown home next to hers when it had gone up for sale.

So after finishing law school and landing a job, I took out a mortgage loan. I bought the little house for a great price, but it needed a lot of work.

I loved my place now. However, Ava living next door was the fly in the ointment. I called her Ava instead of Mom for good reasons.

"You need to knock. How many times do I have to tell you? What if I was having sex on the couch?"

She paused and cocked her head. "You haven't dated in years, so the chances of that are miniscule. Your vagina probably has cobwebs in it by now."

"Ava! Geez. Just knock, okay? And why are you calling *quid pro quo*?"

Dad often talked to us in legalese, and some of our family conversations still sounded like we were negotiating a legal contract.

"Grace and Sheila are hosting the Martini Monday party tomorrow, and they specifically invited you."

They lived two doors down and across the street from me. They'd also just completed a major remodel on their Spanish revival home.

"Okay. What favor do I owe you?"

"I picked you up from the oil change place and took you to lunch last week when it was taking too long," Ava replied.

"Yeah, you picked me up because you wanted a couple of margaritas with your lunch, so you needed someone to drive you home afterward," I shot back. "And should you be drinking?"

She ignored my question. "True, but you used my car for the rest of the day. So *quid pro quo*."

I shrugged. "Okay, if you want to use it for that. Deal." I leaned back and smiled smugly. "That was a bad deal. I would've gone anyway since I want to see how their house turned out."

She narrowed her eyes. "Why didn't you just say so?"

"You started it, Ms. *Quid Pro Quo*. And I knew you were saving the oil change to spring on me."

She huffed and sat down. "I'll remember that for next time. Your hair looks greasy. You need to wash it."

"You don't have any room to talk. Most of the hair on your head isn't even yours."

She sniffed but had no comeback.

The ladies across the street were funny and friendly, and I liked them. So it wasn't a hardship to go. Grace worked as a paralegal at a well-known law firm in town, and she'd helped me out a few times when I started working as a new attorney. She and Ava also golfed together several times a week.

"What's a Martini Monday party?" I asked.

"It's a little get-together to socialize and meet people on Monday evenings. And of course, drink martinis. A lovely woman started it years ago."

I set my computer aside. "Who usually goes?"

"Whoever's invited and a few regulars. Her niece is continuing the tradition along with Ramone and Jonathan, Grace's bosses. Sometimes the parties have themes. Those are my favorite."

"What kinds of themes?"

"Fern, the lady who started them, hired a jazz band one time and had a Mardi Gras party with dancing, beads, masks. The whole nine yards. That was before I moved here. And a few years ago, she held it on New Year's Eve at the Avalon Hotel when it fell on a Monday. It went on all night."

I raised my eyebrows. "That sounds expensive."

Ava sighed. "It was amazing. I may have had a little fling with a much younger hotel server that night."

I gagged a little. "Why do you tell me things like that?"

Ava smirked. "I hate to say it, but you're a prude. The love of my life might be gone, but he wouldn't have wanted *my* lady parts to atrophy."

"Thanks for putting that image in my brain."

"Harley, you have the personality of a stale cracker. It's sad that your fortyish-year-old mother has a more exciting life than you do."

I rolled my eyes. "It's not sad, it's kind of creepy. And fortyish? Is that like the new sixtyish now?"

Ava smacked my arm, then picked up her quart-size coffee mug and magazine and stood up. She had a deep and abiding love for caffeine these days. Whatever helped her cope.

"So? Are you coming?"

I sighed, loud and long. "Yeah, I'll come."

"Good. Have a nice day. Grace and I are going golfing this afternoon."

Ava had moved to Palm Springs not long after my younger sister graduated from high school. I'd been relieved and grateful when Grace and Sheila befriended her.

"Wash your hair," she threw over her shoulder as she walked away.

I watched her go and shook my head.

"Hello, neighbors! Harley, thanks for coming tonight." Sheila met us at their front door on Monday evening. Sheila also liked golf but wasn't as fanatical about it as Grace and Ava.

I walked in and looked around. "Your house turned out beautifully. Ava said it's been a major pain, but the results are stunning."

She grimaced. "Maybe in a year or ten I'll look back and think it was worth it. It's still too soon, though."

Over the last year, I'd watched their renovation from my front yard. I understood how painful it could be. My little property included a small house and a tiny yard with a back patio and a spool—a small pool that was a cross between a spa and a pool. Even that small space had been a major headache to clean up and remodel.

Their renovation had taken three times as long and a lot more money, but it looked wonderful. The old wood beams and refinished wood floors in the living room gleamed. They'd stayed true to the Spanish revival style of the home, and it had a nostalgic and charming feel to it.

After giving us the tour, we walked out to their backyard. They'd redone the landscaping around their pool area to make it look like a natural lagoon.

Soft string lights hung around the perimeter, and rose bushes climbed the red brick and white stucco wall surrounding the yard. Their fragrance, along with the orange tree blossoms, scented the air. The whole backyard was enchanting.

Ava saw one of her golf buddies and excused herself, and I turned to Sheila. "Grace said she has a friend who just graduated from law school she wants me to meet."

Sheila pointed to a woman with long dark brown hair about my age who was talking with Grace. "That's Laurel. She transferred from back East when she found out her aunt had breast cancer and finished her degree in Las Vegas. Her aunt Fern passed away last Spring and left her a house over in the Deepwell estates area."

"That's too bad about Fern. I didn't know her, but Ava liked her."

Sheila sighed. "Fern was a fabulous woman, inside and out."

"She sounds fascinating."

Sheila smiled. "Laurel takes after Fern in a lot of ways, but Laurel's father is a first-rate bastard."

"That's too bad. Does she have any family besides her father?"

"Young twin half-brothers. Ramone's pretty much adopted her—you know how Ramone is."

I smiled. "He kind of adopted me, too."

Sheila looked at me. "I'm not surprised. How?"

"About a month after I started at my old firm, one of the partners dumped an ugly divorce case on me. The estranged husband and his snake of an attorney were filing motion after motion, and all these unnecessary discovery requests on my client."

Sheila grimaced. "It sounds ugly. And expensive."

"It was, and I had no idea how to help my client. I mentioned my dilemma to Grace one day. And the next thing I knew, Ramone called me to discuss the case at no charge. He hates the opposing counsel, so that helped."

"If anyone could help you, it would be Ramone. What'd he tell you to do?"

I grinned. "He introduced me to the vexatious litigant doctrine, which is someone who files repetitive, burdensome, and frivolous motions just to be an asshole. After researching the statute, I filed a motion and had the opposing party deemed a vexatious litigant. His attorney fees tripled due to all the hoops he and his attorney had to jump through. Not long afterward, the case settled, thank God."

She patted my arm. "Nice job."

"So yeah, I know all about Ramone and his ways. I love that man."

Sheila smiled. "I'll introduce you."

When Sheila went to help Grace at the bar, I turned to Laurel. "I hear you're going to work at Lewis and Clark. I love those guys."

She smiled. "I love them too."

Ramone Lewis and Jonathan Clark owned the law firm where Grace worked. They'd been married for years, and I thought the coincidence of their last names was charming.

"I hear your aunt started these parties."

Laurel nodded. "Fern wanted them to have a 1950s Hollywood-style pool party feel. She would have loved this." She gazed around Grace and Sheila's backyard.

We decided to try the martinis. When she asked Sheila for a dry martini, I grimaced.

She laughed. "If you don't like martinis, have a cosmopolitan instead."

Laurel and I found a place to sit and sip our drinks. We talked for almost an hour, and I invited her to the Friday potluck lunch my office partners and I usually held. She'd like my office partners, and it would be a good way for her to network.

Laurel reached over and squeezed my hand. "Thank you. For coming tonight to meet me and for helping me meet other attorneys."

"You're welcome. Ramone and Jonathan did it for me."

We'd just swapped contact information when Laurel glanced behind me and started waving. I turned around and noticed two tall, good-looking men walking into the backyard. I studied them briefly, then did a double take.

One of the men had dark blond hair and a distinctive dimple. He also sported a little stubble. Dimples didn't have a volleyball jersey on and his nose wasn't bleeding, but I'd recognize his face anywhere.

"Aw, fuck," I muttered.

Chapter 3

I tried to grab Laurel's arm and get her to stop waving. But it was too late. They walked over to us, and Dimples gave Laurel a hug and looked at me without recognition. He and his friend were both still as muscular as ever, and I mentally cringed.

I thought about my volleyball team, and what shape they were probably in a few weeks before the new season started.

Laurel introduced us. "Damien, this is Harley Emerson."

Captain Dimples' name was Damien. Good to know. My ears rang, and I missed some of what they were saying.

Damien introduced his friend. "This is Zeke Deegan. He's our other partner."

So the big guy was Zeke. It sounded like they were also friends and business partners with Sebastian Mendoza.

I could also tell by the funny, expectant look on Zeke's face that he knew exactly who I was. He seemed to be patiently waiting for Damien to recognize me as well. I didn't hear most of what Laurel and Damien said to each other; I was too busy quietly freaking out.

Damien turned his dimpled grin on me. "Hello, Harley Emerson. How do you know Grace and Sheila?"

Should I tell him who I was, or pretend ignorance? Zeke would probably tell him if I didn't.

I crossed my arms. "You don't recognize me, do you?"

Damien cocked his head, and his expression sharpened. "Should I recognize you?"

"Yeah. Because I almost broke your nose last fall."

I saw the second he placed me. His flirty smile slid off, and he instinctively reached up to touch his nose. Then he stepped closer to me. "Valkyrie," he drawled. "I didn't recognize you without your Viking braids and spandex shorts."

Zeke leaned over and started laughing. "Do you still think she's beautiful?"

Damien must have said something while I'd been freaking out.

"Shut up, Zeke." He didn't take his eyes off me.

I watched him cautiously, and he stared back at me.

Laurel broke the silence. "Okay. Someone needs to tell me this story because it sounds like a good one."

Neither of us said a word, but Zeke was still laughing.

Laurel persisted. "A broken nose? Viking braids? Come on, someone tell me."

Zeke finally took Laurel's arm and walked away while Damien and I glared at each other.

I carefully set my drink down and put my hands on my hips. "Stop scowling at me, I didn't do it on purpose. Quit being such a baby. You kept playing."

He folded his arms. "You spiked the ball right at my face as hard as you could. How is that not on purpose?"

"You were being a putz, and you shouldn't have gotten your face in my way."

"In your *way*?" He leaned into me. "You could have hit that ball anywhere you damn well wanted to, and we both know it. Your ball placement is freakishly good."

"I didn't break your nose, and you kept playing for God's sake."

"The only reason you *didn't* is because I jerked my head to the side at the last second."

I shrugged. "Probably."

He stared at me incredulously and took a step closer. "Probably?"

"You want me to lie and make you feel better? Yeah, if the ball would have hit your nose head-on, it probably would have broken it."

He pinched the nose in question. "And you still don't give a fuck, do you? You never apologized or said shit to me."

I glared at him. "That's not true. I said shit to you. I told you not to fuck with my 'Walmart parking lot' teammates."

He froze at my comment, and his hand slowly lowered.

I pointed my finger at his sternum. "And *you* never apologized for making such a biased, shitty comment."

His eyes narrowed again. "Don't give me that bullshit, Val. You and some of your teammates, who looked like prison inmates from San Quentin, make more smartass remarks than any other team in the league."

"Thanks, Dimples." I took his comment as a compliment. "But I think your Barbie and Ken team gets the prize in that category.

It's too bad Sebastian doesn't play anymore. He's the only one who wasn't a preppy jerk. And maybe Zeke."

"None of us are preppy, for fuck's sake."

I held up a finger. "Johanna."

He stopped and rubbed his forehead. "Okay, maybe Johanna. And how do you know Sebastian?" He watched me intently. "He's Laurel's boyfriend."

"Huh. I never would have put those two together, but I can somehow see it. It would be hard for even him to be a jerk to her."

He stepped closer to me. "How do you know Sebastian?" he asked again.

It was a strange question, and I squinted at him. "From Grace and Sheila. And his company helps a few of us who live on this street with maintenance and repairs."

"That's it?" he asked.

"Noooo," I dragged out like he was stupid. "From volleyball too. And even though he was a bit of an ass, he never said mean things about my teammates. I liked him."

Damien folded his arms. "Yeah, you would."

I had to look up at Damien when I talked to him. It annoyed me since I could look most men straight in the eyes. I stepped back.

"Let me give you a little advice, Ken with dimples. You don't want to call my teammates Walmart parking lot rejects or San Quentin inmates to my face again unless you want another hard spike to your face. Or a knee to your balls."

"My name's Damien, Val. And it's hypocritical when you get pissed off at me for accurately describing your team. I recognize a couple of them from my time as a police officer."

When I opened my mouth to retort, he put up a hand and continued. "But if some of my comments offended you, I apologize."

His apology took all the wind out of my sails. I let out a long, loud sigh and some of the tension drained out of me.

I reached up and touched the small scar on my cheekbone. "My name's not Val. Or Valkyrie. It's Harley. And I accept your apology." I didn't sound happy about it.

He blinked at me as if waiting for something. "And?"

"And what?"

"And you apologize for smashing the ball in my face and almost breaking my nose."

I stared at him but kept my mouth shut. I didn't like to lie.

"Right?" He glared at me.

My gaze slid away.

"So you're not sorry?" He searched my face like he really wanted to know.

I sighed again. "Not really, all right? I think you hurt Jaime's feelings. And Frankie's been working on her self-esteem issues." I picked up my drink.

He stared at me for a few seconds, like I'd surprised him. His head tilted. "Where'd you meet your teammates?"

My eyes slid away from his. "Around."

He put his hands on his hips. "Who organized your team?"

"People," I muttered.

He studied me. "Jaime has gang symbol tattoos."

I studied my feet. "Huh."

"And you think I hurt his feelings," he said slowly.

I paused and thought about it. "He wouldn't tell me if you did, but maybe. His wife works at Walmart."

"Huh," he mimicked.

He was too perceptive. I decided to end the conversation. "You can talk crap to me all you want. And you can make fun of my teammates' shitty volleyball skills because God knows it wouldn't hurt them to practice a little. But leave their other issues alone."

He kept staring at me but didn't say anything,

I started backing away. "I'm going to find Laurel. Have a nice evening."

He nodded slowly. "I'll see you in a few weeks then, Harley Emerson."

Sheila looked up when I walked back to the bar. "Do you want another cosmopolitan?"

She eyed my half-full glass and then looked at Damien. I could almost feel his stare burning into my back.

I sighed. "Do you happen to have the ingredients for a margarita?"

She smirked. "Coming right up." She reached for a bottle and poured me a shot. "And in the meantime, here's a shot of tequila."

Taking the glass, I threw the shot back. The earthy flavor hit my tongue, and the alcohol burned down my throat. "Thanks. I needed that."

Chapter 4

That Friday, Laurel came to our law office for our weekly Friday potluck lunch. My two office mates and I had opened our law firm almost a year after I'd moved to Palm Springs.

We were all busy with our own lives and practices, so we held a potluck lunch almost every Friday so we could catch up a little and decompress.

Laurel brought double chocolate caramel brownies, and my partners instantly loved her.

I introduced everyone. "This is Yun and Sariah, my fellow office partners."

We ended up talking and laughing for over two hours. Laurel told us about her aunt, and the house in the Deepwell neighborhood she'd inherited. Yun and Sariah also knew the law office where Laurel would be working.

Sariah grinned. "I adore Ramone and Jonathan."

"I refer clients to them all the time," Yun added.

I smirked. "I don't. My clients are criminals, juveniles, or both. Not their typical clientele."

Sariah told Laurel about how we became office mates when we'd left the law firm where we used to work.

"The firm specialized in commercial contracts and real estate law, with a little criminal law on the side." Sariah shook her head. "A few months after Harley started, I got passed over for a partnership position."

"She got screwed," Yun added. "The partnership went to a younger, less competent male attorney who also happened to be related to one of the partners."

Sariah bit into her brownie. "It still ticks me off every time I think about it. Even though it worked out for the best."

Yun nodded. "And not long after that I approached the partners, all middle-aged men with children of their own, about working from home a couple of days a week so my husband and I could start our family."

She leaned over and pointed her fork at Laurel. "I'd been working there for six years, and I was one of the most productive and profitable attorneys they had on staff. Those assholes turned me down."

I remembered that day well. Yun had found Sariah and me and herded us into one of the conference rooms. Then she told us if we left the firm, she wanted in.

Grinning at the memory, I turned to Laurel. "So that Friday evening we met at George's Bar. You know that speakeasy-style bar and restaurant on Vista Chino Road in that rundown strip mall?"

Sariah sipped her drink. "I love that place. It's wedged between a dispensary and a vape shop. And the signage and front windows give off the impression it's a generic, seedy little dive bar."

Laurel looked dubious. "It doesn't sound that awesome, the way you guys describe it."

Yun laughed. "Right? And it was the first time I'd been there. When I first saw it, I thought these two were having a good laugh at me. And then I walked in."

Sariah nodded enthusiastically. "The inside of the restaurant is the antithesis of its outside. It has this magnificent floor-to-ceiling, wall-to-wall mahogany bar with a gleaming granite countertop."

I smiled. "And there are hundreds of colorful backlit liquor bottles lining the shelves. The room has this intimate, relaxed feel to it. And George, the owner, usually works behind the bar creating these delicious, elaborate cocktails."

Laurel grinned. "I adore a good cocktail."

Yun waved her hand. "Anyway, we hatched our plan and just over two months later we quit the law firm, found this small but kickass office space, and hung out our sign."

Our office was located on the north side of Palm Canyon Drive. The building had a red tile roof and a quaint courtyard with a fountain in the middle. There were flowering trees and a garden with rosemary bushes that let off an earthy, sweet fragrance.

Sariah smirked. "We heard through the grapevine the law firm took a big hit when a lot of our clients followed us over. I like to think it's karma."

We finally wrapped up our lunch, and Laurel invited us to Martini Monday at her house. Yun and Sariah both had husbands and a child at home, but I told Laurel I'd be there.

When Laurel left and I got ready to head home for the weekend, I looked around the office and realized I was flourishing professionally. But my life outside work was not. Yun and Sariah both had families and other friends, and I often spent weekends with just my dog, Gary.

My sister, Olivia, was busy with school and lived thousands of miles away. Ava and I were civil to each other, but not close, and I missed my dad and my deceased fiancé, Ryan, fiercely. They'd been my best friends and confidants, and I wished sometimes it didn't feel like half my heart had been ripped out and buried with them when they died.

On Monday evening, I drove to Laurel's house. Her lovely mid-century modern home was located in one of my favorite neighborhoods in Palm Springs.

Several of the houses were perfect examples of mid-century modern architecture, and some were just pure quirky Palm Springs.

I also loved all the colorful front doors. I'd passed a few houses in her neighborhood with bright turquoise blue doors, a couple of pink doors, and an orange one.

Her desert landscaping was mature and well-tended, and it contrasted nicely with the long bougainvillea hedge running the length of the yard. But my favorite aspect was the life-size skeletons scaling the palm trees in the front yard.

When I walked in, Sebastian and Laurel stood behind her bar with cocktail ingredients laid out in front of them. There were also a few strange-colored martinis lined up in front of them, and Laurel was dressed for Halloween.

I knew Sebastian and appreciated his quiet, slightly pissed-off demeanor. We were both introverted and seemed to understand we basically wanted to be left alone.

Laurel smiled, then promptly warned me Damien was coming.

"Who?" I asked innocently.

She gave me a look. "The guy whose nose you almost broke? The one with the dimple?"

I sighed. "I didn't break his nose."

"It's interesting you remember he stuck tissue up his nose and kept playing, but you can't remember his name," Laurel said innocently.

I stared at her. "What can I say? I thought it was disturbingly hot."

Laurel's lip twitched and she looked over my shoulder. A throat cleared behind me. Goddamn it, I knew who I'd find when I turned around. Damien and Zeke both grinned at me.

"Disturbingly hot?" Damien asked, his gray eyes crinkling at the corners.

Zeke chuckled.

I turned to Laurel and crossed my arms. "You knew he was there."

"Maybe?" She looked at Damien. "You owe me."

Rolling my eyes, I turned to Sebastian at the bar. "Which one of these strange, florescent Halloween drinks is the strongest? And sweetest?"

Sebastian pointed at the bright green one. "This one has lime gelatin in it, so I can't recommend it."

Laurel lightly socked his arm. "Hey! That's the flying monkey martini."

I raised my eyebrow. "That name doesn't make it sound any more appetizing."

Sebastian motioned to another drink. "There's a blood orange martini with the black spiderweb." He looked down at all the ingredients in front of him. "I also have the ingredients for a classic black Manhattan. That's what I'd recommend."

"I'll try one of those."

Zeke sat down on a barstool and leaned back. "I'll have the blood orange one. It reminds me of when Harley beat the shit out of Damien's nose."

I sighed, then looked at Zeke and rubbed my forehead with my middle finger. He laughed.

Sebastian started preparing my black Manhattan. "I'm fucking sorry I missed that."

We chatted and laughed for the rest of the evening. We discussed the George Bar and a few other great spots in town. They also talked about the issues Laurel was having with her father, who sounded like a complete asshole.

It had been a fun evening, and by the end of the night, it felt like Laurel and I had been friends forever. And I also wanted to beat Damien and Zeke's volleyball team more than ever.

A couple of weeks later, I walked into my new gym. When I first moved to Palm Springs, I kept my old gym membership out of habit. It was a low-budget chain, and there was a branch in Palm Springs. But the gym was overcrowded and worn out.

So I upgraded and found a nice locally owned gym closer to my house. Kurt, the owner, usually brought in his golden retriever named Jack to the gym.

I walked in around six, which was earlier than usual for me. But I'd resolved to make my mornings more productive since my caseload kept getting bigger.

Kurt nodded at me as I scanned my pass, and I bent down to give Jack a rub and a scratch behind his ears.

"Hey, Kurt. How's it going? Hi, Jack, how're you doing this morning, my favorite handsome boy? Huh?"

Kurt shook his head. "I wish my boyfriend talked to me like that every morning."

I smiled. "He's probably fast asleep when you leave for work."

Kurt nodded. "Good point. Have a good workout." I waved and headed over to the cardio equipment section.

Usually, I started on the treadmill or bike before doing some weights. Working out was a holdover from playing organized sports in high school and college. It was also excellent therapy, and I usually felt better afterward, but I struggled sometimes with consistency. I looked up and noticed Sebastian running at a nice clip on one of the treadmills.

"Hey, Sebastian." I walked over to the same stationary bike I usually used.

"Harley." He nodded. "Didn't know you used this gym."

I adjusted the settings, then started peddling. "This place is less crowded and has better equipment. And there's Jack. I switched a few months ago."

"Laurel said you guys are planning a camping trip."

I grinned. "We are. We've also been discussing work. She's going to apply for a juvenile court public defender contract when she gets sworn in."

"She mentioned it."

I pointed my finger. "Your surly, sore-loser friend with the dimple told me you two are pretty serious. Be nice to her. I know that'll be hard for you."

He smirked. "I will. I'm not stupid. What's with you and Damien?"

I jerked my shoulder and peddled a little faster. "Nothing." I sounded defensive.

"I'd be pissed if you smashed a volleyball in my face."

I sighed. "Yeah, I'd probably be mad too."

"So you're ready to apologize, then?" I jumped a little and lost my rhythm. Damien stood right behind me.

"Goddamn it, quit sneaking up on me."

He folded his arms and grinned. "I didn't know you worked out here, Legs. Are you training for volleyball season? Because you should know, it's not you, it's the rest of your team who needs the training." Damien got on a treadmill next to Sebastian. He was already sweaty. He must be one of those people who did cardio last instead of first.

"No shit, Sherlock. I'm well aware of that. Their main motivation isn't to win though..." I stopped talking.

"What is it?" He ran while he talked to me.

"Other things."

Damien gave me an exasperated look, but he didn't push.

Sebastian slowed down and walked for a minute, then got off the treadmill. "I'm done. See you at the office." He walked out.

I adjusted the bike settings. "He's not much of a talker, is he?"

Damien smirked. "Nope. He talks to Laurel though."

"Pretty sure they do more than talking."

"Pretty sure you're right."

We exercised for a few minutes in silence, then I wound down and got off to go get some strength training in.

"What *is* your team's motivation if it isn't to win?" Damien asked as he pounded away on the treadmill.

"To just make it through another week. One day at a time. See you in a couple of weeks." I absently rubbed the small scar on my cheekbone.

As I lifted weights, I thought about my volleyball team and an annoying, tenacious man with gray eyes and a dimple. I was blissfully unaware I'd soon have to swallow my pride and ask Damien to use his tenacity to help me with a case.

Chapter 5

The next Tuesday afternoon, I walked out of court and ran right into Dimples. Again.

On the second and fourth Tuesday of every month, Judge Perez held a juvenile drug court staffing meeting followed by the review hearing. All the professionals who made up the juvenile drug court team came together and discussed the kids' progress and issues before the hearing, which was held with the kids and their parents. I'd taken over as the juvenile drug court public defender last year.

The minors in drug court usually had serious substance abuse issues and had been charged with drug-related offenses. I represented them as they worked through treatment and drug testing in return for a plea in abeyance, which meant if they completed treatment and stayed clean, their charges were dismissed at the end of the program. That was the hope anyway.

But my clients were young, hormone-driven teenagers with addiction issues. I never knew what they were going to do from one week to the next.

Wendy Wood, the DCFS worker, sat on my right during the staffing meeting. Wendy had dark red hair and several tattoos, and the minors adored her. Christian Yates, the prosecutor assigned to the juvenile drug court, sat on my left. He had a nice, dry wit and reasonable expectations. He also had a deep and abiding passion for fishing that I didn't pretend to understand.

Pauley Wilson, the drug treatment supervisor, sat across from us. He was my least favorite person on the drug court staffing team. I wasn't sure why he even worked in juvenile court because he had a short temper and he wasn't very patient. And most of these kids required a lot of patience.

Judge Perez looked through the progress reports for each minor. He let out a drawn-out sigh, and I knew he'd just gotten to my client, Darla Jensen's report.

"Well, I can't say there weren't signs. But a marijuana grow box in her closet, with commercial-grade HID lights? Where did she get all the supplies?"

Wendy looked over her notes. "I called her mom and talked to her yesterday. Her dad works in landscaping and thought it was nice Darla seemed to be interested in gardening."

I sat back. "He didn't know the lights and box were for marijuana. The high-intensity discharge lights should've tipped him off though." It was amazing how naive some parents were.

Christian shook his head. "If she spent half as much time and effort on her treatment and homework, she'd be a straight B student and through with the treatment program by now."

Pauley clucked his tongue. "Judge, she needs a felony distribution charge along with the possession and paraphernalia charges. And she should spend a few days in jail. Darla isn't taking this seriously and never has."

I mentally rolled my eyes. If I had a nickel every time Pauley said one of my clients "wasn't taking this seriously and never had," I could die rich. They were teenagers, for God's sake. Most of them didn't take anything seriously—except maybe their social media.

I tried not to let my annoyance show. "I don't agree that a felony distribution charge is warranted. It was a small grow box, and according to the photos she only had three scraggly little plants."

"She had a grow box in her closet. And lights," Pauley countered.

"Darla didn't have enough product, and it's not reasonable to assume she planned to distribute."

Pauley scoffed. "She's growing marijuana in her closet."

I fought not to grind my teeth. "Her drug of choice is—big surprise, marijuana. It's reasonable to infer she was growing it for herself."

Judge Perez cut in. "Does anyone have any suggestions or ideas? She can't pay fines because her mother won't allow her to work, and incarceration isn't recommended."

I thought about what devious punishment my dad would've come up with in these circumstances. He believed in natural consequences. I'd hated it while growing up, but neither my sister nor I had criminal records and we weren't working a pole, so it must have been somewhat effective.

Turning to Judge Perez, I pointed at Darla's report. "She wants to 'garden' so much, maybe that would be an appropriate sanction. She could mow lawns and landscape with her dad. Do a little manual labor."

"She could also work to pay her dad back for the supplies he gave her. And maybe she could continue afterward and earn some money if it works out," Wendy added.

Judge Perez smiled. "I like it."

I walked out of the courtroom that afternoon with Wendy. Besides Darla's grow box, my kids seemed to be doing well for the moment. Roland, my biggest repeat offender, had gotten another shoplifting charge. But in the scheme of things that was an improvement for him. Baby steps.

Someone called my name, and I looked up and saw Damien walking through the metal detectors. Butterflies erupted in my stomach. I needed to get this attraction or whatever it was under control.

"What're you doing here?" he asked, gathering his things off the conveyor belt.

Wendy stopped next to me, blatantly eavesdropping. I loved the woman, but she was nosy, and she couldn't understand why I didn't date or even use Tinder, or Match, or whatever the newest hookup app was.

"Stuff," I answered vaguely.

Wendy snickered.

"Okaaay. What kind of stuff?" Damien asked.

"Legal stuff."

He smirked. "What kind of legal stuff?" He seemed to be enjoying our game.

"Boring legal stuff."

Wendy broke in. "Lord, woman. It shouldn't be this hard for you to have a normal conversation." She turned to Damien and stuck out her hand.

"Hi, my name's Wendy. And you are?"

He grinned and shook her hand. "Damien Andreasen, but Harley calls me Dimples."

That asshole was purposefully giving Wendy the wrong idea. I glared at him.

Wendy smiled even wider. "Aw, that's a cute endearment. And I can see why she calls you that. Nice to meet a friend of Harley's." She glanced at me. "She tries hard not to have any."

"That's not true—" I started to say.

She ran right over me. "She's here today as the juvenile drug court public defender. And I'm the DCFS worker."

Damien's eyes swept down, and took in my dressy black heels and slim charcoal suit. I tugged a little at the pencil skirt. My sister gave me the suit last year for my birthday, and I thought I looked decent in it.

"Hello, Wendy. Any friend of Harley's is a friend of mine."

"Suck up," I muttered.

He ignored me. I could smell his masculine, spicy scent. It annoyed me that I liked it.

"You said you're a DCFS worker?" he asked her.

Wendy nodded but seemed mesmerized by his dimple.

"I bet you have some interesting stories. I used to be a detective before I became an investigator. I've worked with a lot of social workers over the years."

He still held Wendy's hand, or she held his—it was hard to tell.

"You said Harley's an attorney, and she's here today as the juvenile court public defender?"

Wendy seemed to shake herself and finally let go of Damien's hand. "She's a criminal defense attorney. And she does a little adult public defender work too. Her clients seem to love her. I don't know why though."

She leaned into Damien like she was telling him a secret. "Harley can be a little abrasive sometimes."

Damien's eyes widened. "Really? I never would've guessed."

Wendy kept flapping her big mouth. "But some attorneys see it as a challenge. She doesn't date. *Ever.*"

Wendy finally noticed I'd crossed my arms and was tapping my foot. I glared at the two of them.

"I'm standing right here." I turned to Damien. "If you want to know something, ask *me*, nosy."

He grinned unrepentantly. "That doesn't seem to work, Legs." He looked back at Wendy. "I see what you mean now about her being abrasive sometimes. What else does she do?"

I rolled my eyes and kept tapping my foot.

Wendy wasn't intimidated at all. "She's one of the adult felony drug court public defenders in Judge Hansen's court. Oh, and she helps with the Addicts to Athletes program in the Coachella Valley. She's the volleyball coach."

Damien raised his eyebrows and turned slowly to me. "Huh. Mystery solved. Everything makes sense now." He folded his arms and studied me.

I shifted uncomfortably. "It isn't a big deal. I like sports and I've had experience with addicts. It was a natural fit. What are *you* doing here?"

Wendy cut in. "I wish I could stay and watch Harley squirm, but I have a family team meeting." Wendy pointed at me. "You're going to tell me everything the next time I see you."

"Don't hold your breath. See you Thursday."

"*Everything*," she mouthed. Then she waved and strolled off.

I turned to him. "Why are you here? Is it anyone I know?"

My gut tightened. Bad luck seemed to follow the people I knew.

He lost his grin. "Laurel's dad assaulted her stepmom and little brothers yesterday. Laurel's flying them in from New York, and I'm dropping off some paperwork regarding a protective order."

Worry flooded me. "Oh God, are you kidding me? Are they okay?" I made a mental note to call her later today and see how I could help.

Damien rubbed his neck. "I think so. She's doing what she can to protect them."

"She'll be putting herself in his crosshairs. I'd do the same thing, but she needs to be careful." I grabbed his arm without thinking. "Her poor little brothers."

Some people didn't understand or care about the long-term impact on a person's mental and emotional health when they experienced domestic violence as a child.

"We're putting in live surveillance cameras, and we'll monitor them. Sebastian plans to keep an eye on her." He stared down at me and abruptly changed the subject. "You're a mystery, Harley, but I got a few clues today."

I didn't know where he was going with this. "I'm an open book, Andreasen."

He snorted. "What did Wendy mean when she said you never date, and you're considered a challenge?"

I shook my head and tried to look sincere. "I have no idea. You need to drop off your paperwork. I'll see you later."

I started to walk off, then paused. "Will you let me know if there's anything I can do? And keep me posted?"

Damien nodded, watching me as I walked away. I needed to stay away from that man. He was too nosy and astute for my peace of mind.

Chapter 6

The following week a new public defender client sat across from me, squirming in her seat, and lying through her teeth. Shanda had just turned eighteen two months ago, and she looked young and scared.

I sighed heavily and leaned back in my chair. "Let me recap what you're telling me. The two eyewitnesses *and* the victims in the vehicle he hit—" She open her mouth, but I put my hand up. "Excuse me, in the vehicle *you* allegedly hit, all either lied or their memory was faulty, and they somehow thought Jason was driving."

"Yes. That's what I'm saying." Shanda's eyes slid around the room, and she bounced her leg and chewed on her thumbnail. I idly wondered whether she was high or just nervous. It was only nine in the morning, but that didn't mean much.

She'd dyed her hair orange at some point, but her dark blond roots were showing. The orange color hadn't been a good choice with her skin tone. Shanda wore ripped wide-leg jeans, a short black pullover, and combat boots. And then there were her piercings.

Shanda must've gotten a discount when she'd gotten her ears pierced because I counted at least seven hoops in each lobe—not counting her septum piercing. I wouldn't have thought twice about them, except it looked like one of her ear piercings and the nose piercing were becoming infected.

"You probably think you're protecting Jason by lying for him and taking the blame for the accident. But this is serious, and you both could get charged with obstruction of justice and lying to a police officer."

"Why would I lie? I'm not." She was absolutely lying, and she looked a little panicky.

"Shanda, what you tell me is confidential. That means what we discuss doesn't go outside this room unless you permit me to discuss it. But for me to help you, I need to know what happened."

"I *told* you what happened. I was driving and the other car pulled out too soon," she insisted.

"The driver is still in the ICU, and both you and Jason had meth in your systems." I looked at the documents that had been emailed over to me listing their drug test results. "There was also meth and paraphernalia found in the backpack behind the driver's seat." I glanced at her. "And Jason also tested positive for heroin."

He looked mean and unhinged in his mug shot. I saw her body go still for a split second, but she stayed silent and focused on the wall behind me. Then her eyes started darting around the room again.

Since she wasn't talking to me, I decided to tell her what I thought happened. "I think Jason tried to make the light but ended up T-boning the Honda Accord with the couple in it."

She glanced at me but didn't say anything. "After the accident when he got a look at the occupants and saw their injuries, he told you to lie for him."

Her knee bobbed furiously. "You don't know shit."

I continued. "He knew he'd test positive for meth *and* heroin, and he probably told you he might go to prison if you didn't lie for him. I bet he also threatened you."

Her gaze jerked involuntarily back to me, and it was a dead giveaway. "That's not what happened. You don't know anything." She started shaking her head.

"I've seen his criminal history. He has over two dozen assault and drug-related charges and multiple convictions. And a conviction for giving false information to a police officer."

"That doesn't have anything to do with this case." She stood up and shoved her chair back. "I want another lawyer. You're supposed to be helping me, not... accusing me of lying, then lying yourself!"

I shook my head. "You can't pick and choose your public defender, Shanda, just because you don't like what I'm telling you. And why would I lie?" I held up both hands. "But I'll make you a deal. Sit down and listen—please."

"I'm listening. But I still want another lawyer." She didn't sit down.

"If you don't change your mind after I show you a couple of things, I'll try to help you get another attorney myself. Okay?" I pulled out a document. "Here's Jason's criminal record. I know those charges and convictions are all his because they match his full name, Jason Carter Ulrich. And his birthdate as well."

I handed her the five-page report. She took it reluctantly and scanned through it. The record included everything from aggravated assault to small claims and petty theft. And drug charges—so many drug charges.

"This doesn't prove anything." She quickly flipped through the document, then set it down on my desk.

"Maybe not. But this does." I turned my laptop around so the screen faced her. She slowly sank back into the chair. Then I hit play and showed her the short video clip an insurance investigator had emailed me two days ago. It was a grainy video taken from someone's cell phone.

The wreck happened at the intersection of Ramone and Cathedral Village Drive. It was a busy intersection with shopping centers on both sides. Dust and smoke still hung in the air when the video started. Both cars were smashed and dented from the impact, and glass and debris littered the ground.

A driver-side door opened not long after the video started, and Jason stumbled out of his car. Shanda followed a few seconds later, clearly getting out on the passenger side.

Jason put his hands on top of his head and shouted what sounded like "Ah, fuck" over and over. He was medium build and still handsome even though he looked like he'd lived a hard life. He had lines on his face and looked gaunt and unhealthy.

Jason stumbled around and seemed dazed at first, then he limped over and looked at the passengers in the vehicle he'd T-boned. He backed away as other people rushed over to help. The clip ended there.

I knew a video couldn't convey the smell of burning rubber, the sounds of screeching metal, or the feel or velocity of the impact. Or the aftermath.

Shanda sat in silence for several seconds, then slowly started shaking her head. "No." She rocked back and forth. "No, no, no."

Her reaction surprised me, and I looked closely at her. I'd expected her to bluster a little bit, then cave and blame Jason for making her lie. But she'd gone pale, and her hands were shaking. That fucker *had* threatened her.

Rubbing my neck, I leaned forward. "It's going to be okay. You're scared."

"You think?" she snapped and continued rocking.

It was good to see she had a little backbone. "What did he say to you?"

She turned her head away and her lip quivered.

"I know he made threats. Listen, you can blame me. I was the one who showed you the video and forced you to tell the truth. I told you that you'd both be facing felony obstruction of justice charges."

She silently cried, and her nose and mascara started running. I pushed the tissue box I kept on the corner of my desk toward her. She needed to do something about the redness around her septum piercing.

"You don't know him. You don't know what he'll do." She blew her nose, then sniffed noisily. "He's fucking scary, and crazy as shit."

"Well, then tell me. I have a better chance of helping you if you're honest with me. I need to know what kind of threat he made."

She took a few breaths and wiped her nose, then got herself together. "I need to think about it." She gnawed at her thumbnail again.

"All right. Let's schedule another appointment for next Wednesday at noon. That'll give you plenty of time to think it through."

I pulled out a business card and wrote the date and time on the back, then slid it over to her.

"Okay." She pocketed the card.

"Now we're going for a little walk to get coffee and a bagel. And stopping by the pharmacy on the way there. My treat." I pointed to her nose and ear. "Two of your piercings look infected, and you need to do something about it before your nose or ear swells up to the size of a lemon."

Her eyes went wide, and her hand flew to her nose. "I've never heard of that."

I stared at her. "I've seen it before and trust me, it's not pretty."

She cringed, then nodded reluctantly.

Shanda and I walked to a small pharmacy nearby and picked up some sterile saline solution and antibiotic ointment. Then we went to my favorite coffee shop called Paws for Coffee. They had great coffee and smoothies and a nice patio area out front that allowed dogs. Gary and I came here sometimes on the weekend.

"Use them a few times a day until the redness goes away," I told her while we doctored our coffees and waited for our bagels. "The solution will clean out the piercings, and the ointment should treat any infections."

"Okay. Why are you helping me?"

I shrugged and pointed at her nose. "Because it looks painful, and that could become serious. As for the coffee, that's self-explanatory." I took a sip and sighed blissfully.

We found a seat near the counter and waited in silence for our food. Shanda fidgeted next to me. I didn't think she was high, just nervous.

She finally turned to me. "I have a baby sister. She's almost two now. My mom's an okay parent, well, at least she tries. But my stepdad... he's friends with Jason."

"Okay." She was trying to tell me something.

"Jason knows I have a little sister." She didn't say anything else.

I understood what she was telling me, and I felt a little sick. Our number was called, and I got up and picked up our food and set it on the table in front of us. We both just looked at it for a minute.

"What's your little sister's name?" I asked softly.

"Roberta." She wrinkled her nose a little.

I took a drink of coffee. "That's... nice."

Poor kid. It would take a while for a baby to grow into that name.

"It's a stupid name for a baby. It's my step-grandmother's name. She lives in Detroit and hasn't even seen Bertie."

Shanda finally pulled her cinnamon toast bagel toward her and started eating. She took a huge bite and kept talking with her mouth full.

"I've never met her either," she mumbled around her food.

"Bertie's a great name." I unwrapped my bagel and started eating.

"I know. I'm the one who came up with it." She smiled for the first time, and even with her mouth full, her orange hair, and her inflamed nose piercing, she was beautiful.

We didn't say anything for a few minutes while we ate.

"Did he threaten you and Bertie?" I asked when we'd both finished.

She pushed a glob of leftover cream cheese around on her wrapper but didn't answer.

I continued. "It doesn't matter what your story is at this point. The video speaks for itself."

She kept her gaze on the glob of cream cheese. "Bertie's only two."

"Does your stepdad know Jason threatened Bertie?"

She finally wadded up the wrapper and looked at me. "I don't know, but I can't chance it. She's the only innocent person in this whole fucking mess."

"What exactly did Jason say to you about Bertie?" I asked carefully.

She glanced at me then glanced away. "We have that confidential thing, right? You told me you can't tell anyone what I say."

"That's true unless you give me the okay. I *can* discuss the case within reason with the prosecutor to try and get a plea deal or resolution."

"Okay. I need to think about it. And I need to tell my mom and stepdad and see if maybe they can get Jason off my back."

"All right. We have an appointment already set." I didn't think pushing her at this point would help.

Shanda looked at me for a moment with a solemn face. She looked about ten years older right then. "Jason's crazy, like not right in the head crazy. And he's fucking scary."

I nodded. "I understand. Please keep in touch with me. How are you getting around?"

She shrugged. "I manage."

"The public defender office has some bus passes if you need one. I can get you one if you want."

She shrugged again. "I've been scrounging up rides when I need to."

I could tell she was ready to go. "Okay. Let me know if you change your mind about the bus pass."

"Okay. I'm gonna take off."

I nodded and pointed to the pharmacy bag on the table. She grabbed it and quickly walked out.

Chapter 7

Later that week, I made chocolate chip cookies and dropped a plate off at Laurel's house for her little brothers. I'd taken them brownies and ice cream when they first got into town, but I heard they were still having a rough time.

Martina, Laurel's good friend and roommate, was the only one home when I dropped them off. She was friendly, loud, and a little crazy.

"Tell me exactly what's happening with Laurel," I demanded when Martina opened the front door.

She motioned for me to come inside. "I'll fill you in." We sat at the bar and split a cookie. I rearranged the plate so the hole didn't show while she told me what had happened.

Martina bit into her cookie. "Laurel's father came here looking for his wife, and ended up assaulting Laurel."

My body jerked upright. "What!? You're kidding me."

She nodded, then pulled out her phone and showed me the video she'd taken of the incident.

"She did it to get dirt on him, didn't she?" I asked after I watched it.

She studied me. "Sometimes I forget you're an attorney. Absolutely, and it worked. Except she didn't tell Sebastian or Ramone what she was planning."

I winced. "I bet Sebastian was pissed." Ramone was a big softy, except when it came to his job. But Sebastian was another story.

When I left, the half-cookie felt heavy in my stomach, and I was disheartened and sad that Laurel and her little brothers had such a narcissistic asshole for a father. Ava was certainly less than perfect, but at least I knew she loved me in her own way.

My dad had also been my best friend when I was growing up. For some reason, I thought of Shanda and her hard mother and meth-head stepfather. I didn't know where her biological father was. Probably dead or in prison with that girl's luck.

Late Thursday afternoon, my team had its first volleyball practice of the season. Unfortunately, it would probably be our last. Our first match was on Saturday morning, and while my teammates usually showed up for our matches, they rarely showed up for practices.

This time I'd promised them pizza and birthday cake, and I told them we were celebrating Frankie's birthday afterward. I figured a little bribery and guilt might work.

Frankie was the first to show up. She looked a little thinner and more tired than the last time I'd seen her. I fervently hoped it was from not getting enough sleep.

Frankie was one of those unlucky people who'd grown up in a house with an active drug-using parent. Maybe that's why I had such a soft spot for her. But she had a kind heart and was one of the sweetest people I knew.

She walked up and hugged me. "I got your text about practice and celebrating my birthday. My birthday is eight months' away."

"Yeah, I know." I awkwardly patted her back.

"You know? Then why did you tell everyone we're celebrating my birthday?"

I grinned. "Because we are. We're just not celebrating it right on that *day*."

"Or that month. I hope they're not mad."

"I figured your birthday would get more people out. Everyone loves you."

She seemed surprised. "Really? That's a nice thing to say."

"It's true. Now if I'd told them it was Kevin's birthday, that would be a different story."

When Kevin had first started drug court and treatment, he'd complained about everything and blamed everyone but himself for his shitty life. At the time, I'd mentally given him a low chance of succeeding in drug court.

But after the first few rocky months, he seemed to turn a corner and started responding to treatment. Nothing was certain, but he'd come a long way. He was still a jerk though.

"He's gotten better though," Frankie said charitably.

We looked over and saw Jaime pull up, and Josh and Kevin came not long after that. Tiana was another woman on the team, and she'd let me know she couldn't make it.

Jaime and Tiana weren't in drug court anymore, but they still played on our team. Neither of them had been my client, but we'd gotten to know each other through the Addicts to Athletes program.

"Okay everybody, let's warm up. We're going to run around the field twice, do a few reps of calisthenics, and finish up with burpees before we get our hands on the ball."

Several of them groaned about the burpees.

"My wife got her hands on my balls last night," Jaime volunteered.

Josh grinned and gave him a fist bump.

I shook my head. "Thanks for sharing, and putting that disturbing image in our heads. Okay, let's get the run out of the way."

We started jogging around the field. Josh and Kevin tried to keep up with me for the first lap, then fell behind when I picked up speed on the second one. Frankie ran at a slow but steady pace for both laps. And Jaime shuffle-walked for the first lap and picked it up when I threatened to lap him. Then he cut across the field for the final lap and called it good.

"I hate push-ups," Kevin muttered as he dropped to his knees.

They finished the rest of the workout, most of them grumbling under their breath.

"Why do we always have to do burpees?" Jaime complained as he threw his hands above his head but didn't jump up.

"Because your vertical is nonexistent. In fact, I think it's a negative number."

"What's a vertical?" Josh asked.

"It's basically how high you can reach minus your jump reach," I told him as I did another burpee.

"Whatever the fuck that means," Kevin muttered, giving a pathetic little hop.

I shook my head. "Kevin, you're like a big black sprinkle on a rainbow cupcake."

"I'd still eat it," Jaime huffed.

"Was your vertical good?" Frankie asked.

Remembering those days, I smiled a little. "Yeah. Back in college, it was pretty good."

"If it was anything like that final game last season, it was fucking awesome," Josh said. He'd finished his last burpee and stood there panting.

"They're called sets, not games," I told them for the millionth time. They all ignored me.

Jaime grinned. "Yeah, did you see that motherfucker who called us the Walmart crew get his face rearranged when you smashed the ball into it?"

Frankie shuddered. "Oh my God, there was so much blood."

"And we fucking won," Josh added. He and Jaime high-fived each other. They were still savoring that win.

"I thought he was pretty cool about it," Kevin said. I looked at him in surprise.

"What? He was. And he shoved tissue up his nose and kept playing. That was pretty dope."

I shrugged because it was true. "Yeah, he was decent about it. He still wants me to apologize though." I grinned.

Frankie looked at me curiously. "Have you run into him?"

"A couple of times." I didn't know why I felt embarrassed. "I saw him at the courthouse once, and he's friends with some of my neighbors."

They all studied me curiously, and Jaime smirked.

I clapped my hands. "Okay, let's practice."

We practiced bumping and setting, then they served to each other. I sighed as I watched them goof around and half-heartedly practice. There hadn't been much improvement since the end of last season. A few of them seemed to have gotten worse.

Toward the end of practice, I confirmed the pizza order was on its way and grabbed the cake and picnic supplies out of my vehicle.

Josh helped me carry the stuff over to a couple of picnic tables we'd dragged together. "You know it's not Frankie's birthday, right?"

"What?! I can't believe she lied to me."

He looked alarmed, and I laughed and smacked his arm. "I'm kidding. Yeah, I know. But we needed to practice at least once this season, and I figured since everyone likes her, we'd get a better turnout."

"You're kind of scary. But we did get cake and pizza out of it, so it's all good."

I'd splurged and ordered from B.O.B.'s Pizza. The three huge boxes smelled delicious when the delivery guy laid them on the picnic table. The pizzas were twenty-four inches each of pure heaven.

"Har, if I weren't already married to a hot momma, I'd marry you," Jaime joked as he dug into the meat lovers' pizza.

Frankie grabbed the half veggie half Hawaiian box, and we all dug in. We cracked open a twelve-pack of seltzer water since beer was off-limits.

I popped a can and grabbed a slice of greasy pepperoni. Because why mess with perfection? Dusk was settling in, and it had cooled down a bit. The evening was perfect for having a picnic in the park.

I looked around at my teammates and grabbed my cell phone to snap a few photos of us together. It was a good night. Later when I thought about that impromptu fake birthday party, it would remind me of that Brad Paisley song "Last Time for Everything."

Chapter 8

On Saturday morning, our first volleyball match didn't go exactly as planned. We had the earlier start time, and only one female player showed up for the opposing team. They didn't have enough players to make up a coed team, so we mixed up the teams and played a few sets for fun.

A local cannabis shop sponsored this team, and a few players had sampled the inventory before the game. I could detect the distinct skunky, herbal smell of marijuana wafting off a few of them.

When one of the players missed the ball entirely when he tried to serve, a few players got the giggles. It took a good five minutes for them to settle down enough to resume play.

Kevin watched them through the net. "They're fucking morons. I hope I was never that stupid when I was high."

I patted his arm. "You're too mean to get the giggles. You'd be more likely to start a fight or stab someone."

He smiled. "That's true."

My teammates were happy because we'd technically won, but I felt vaguely cheated because the friendly game hadn't been competitive at all. It'd been a fun morning though.

"You and Frankie need to come play with us next season," Carl said while we were gathering up our things after the last set. Carl was their head coach, and he owned the cannabis shop. "I'll give you a discount at my shop and design team jerseys just for you."

"Thanks, that's a generous offer. But we like our team and we've got history."

He looked my teammates over, probably wondering how we'd all met. His team was a fun, cheerful group, and they told us they'd put a team together mostly so they could hang out away from work.

"If you change your mind, just swing by my shop." He pointed to his jersey. It read Buddy Boyz Cannabis Shop in dark green letters with a stylized cannabis leaf logo, and "photosynthesis" written below. I had to admit, it was a great jersey.

On Monday morning, I visited a client in jail, and while I was there I found out Laurel's father was being released. I called Laurel and Sebastian to let them know just in case the jail hadn't contacted them yet. Neither one of them answered, so I sent Laurel a text and called Damien's work.

"Hello, Harley. Did you call to finally apologize?" I could hear the grin in his voice.

"No. And don't hold your breath."

"I'm patient, I can wait. What can I do for you?"

I smiled in spite of myself. "I'm just walking out of the county jail. The front desk clerk did me a solid and let me know Laurel's father is getting out today."

"Fuuuck," he growled. "I was hoping he'd be in there longer. Did you call Laurel or Sebastian?"

I rolled my eyes. "No, I called you first because I can't get enough of your charming personality and incredible wit. Of course I tried to call them first. They probably already know, but just in case. I also texted them."

"Okay. I'll see if I can track them down."

"Thanks." I was silent for a moment. "Martina showed me the video of what happened. It was hard to watch."

Damien let out a breath. "I know." We were both silent for a moment, then I heard someone talking to him in the background. "I've got to go. See you tonight."

I didn't know what he was talking about at first. Then I remembered Ramone and Jonathan were hosting the Martini Monday. Anxiety and butterflies rolled around together in my stomach. Damien would be there, and I was looking forward to seeing him. And that worried me.

The theme for Martini Monday that week was comfort food. Jonathan decided to have people bring their favorite comfort food to go along with the drinks since it had been such a long, crappy weekend for them.

I made fried macaroni and cheese balls, and Martina baked a tres leches cake even though it wasn't anyone's birthday. Damien brought fried chicken from Dan's Hot Chicken, and Sebastian plunked a six-pack of Fat Tire beer down on the counter.

I looked at his offering and snickered. "It was a toss-up between fried mac and cheese balls or Coronas with lime wedges."

Sebastian nodded in approval.

Luckily, Grace and Sheila brought a veggie and fruit board, so the spread that night wasn't completely made up of alcohol and greasy food.

Laurel walked in, and I saw the fading purple and yellowish bruises on her neck. Sheila had been right; her dad was a bastard.

"How's your team looking this season?" Damien asked, distracting me from staring at Laurel's neck.

I sighed. "We held a practice last week. I think they've actually gotten worse."

"That's too bad. Maybe we'll pull out a win this time."

Over my dead body. "Mm-hmm. Sure."

He grinned, and I knew we understood each other.

I'd snagged a dirty martini since I'd never tried one before. I took a sip and made a face. "I'm just not cut out for martinis. I'm more of a margarita person, I guess."

"Is that a dirty martini?" he asked. "Because the olive juice is a no-go for me."

"Ah. That's what I was tasting." I set the drink down on the bar.

He laughed and held out his beer bottle. "Do you need something to wash it out?"

It seemed like a dare, so I grabbed the bottle and took a swig. "Thanks."

"You're welcome." He studied me. "Are all your teammates current or former clients?"

"No. Anyone who's successfully graduated from a drug court can join too. But some of them are."

"Are you worried about getting too close to them?"

Damien made me nervous and twitchy. "Maybe. I'm working on staying objective."

I started edging away, and Damien casually grasped my elbow. "Do you work for a firm around here or are you a solo practitioner?"

His touch stopped me. The heat from his hand traveled up my arm, and his masculine scent seemed to envelop me. "It's kind of a hybrid situation."

"What do you mean?"

I explained my current setup with Yun and Sariah. "It was a good change for all of us. Sometimes being a female attorney is difficult."

His gaze sharpened. "In what way? Did something happen?"

The conversation was getting too personal, so I changed the subject. "You used to be a police officer, didn't you? Did you make detective before you resigned?"

"Yeah." He took a drink.

Damien seemed to like asking personal questions but didn't like answering them. "Why'd you quit?" I asked anyway.

He rocked back a little. "Several reasons. Money, burnout, and having to answer to someone else. The usual." The shadows in his eyes told a different story, and suddenly I wanted to know the real reasons.

Chapter 9

Shanda didn't make her afternoon appointment that Wednesday. I was disappointed but not too surprised since a fair number of my public defender clients missed appointments and court hearings sometimes.

I tried the number she'd written down on her intake form, but she didn't answer. I noticed her address listed the same apartment complex as her mother, but not a unit number. When Shanda still hadn't contacted me a week later, I decided to make a house call and see if I could find her.

The apartment complex sat just off Rosa Parks Road on the north end of Palm Springs. The neighborhood was a checkerboard of small but decent homes with fenced yards, smaller rundown homes, and even a few homes that were abandoned and boarded up.

Most of the apartment complexes in the neighborhood were two-story squat cinderblock buildings. I was relieved to see the old apartment complex Shanda lived in still looked like it was being maintained at least. I pulled into a visitor parking spot and noticed a few men milling around the open courtyard area smoking and talking.

They stopped talking and watched me approach.

"Hello. Does anyone know where Charlene Briggs lives?" I didn't give Shanda's name.

One of them finally turned to me. He had on a yellow flannel shirt and track pants. He was an older man who looked like he hadn't seen a razor or a comb in a while, and his hairstyle reminded me of the mad scientist in *Back to the Future*. But his clothes looked clean.

He looked me up and down. "What do you want with Charlene and Mikey, anyway? Nothing good goes on in that apartment."

"I need to talk with someone who lives there."

"Are you a bill collector? Or child welfare?" he asked.

I decided being vague wasn't getting me anywhere. "No, I'm a public defender, and I'm looking for Charlene's daughter. She missed an appointment with me a few days ago."

The other two men he'd been talking with shifted back a little. "I'll see you later, Walt," one of them said as the other flicked his cigarette butt on the ground. They both walked away.

Walt assessed me. "You talking about Shanda Briggs?"

I nodded and his mouth tightened.

"Have you seen her lately?" I asked.

He looked across the playground. "I heard she got into a mess not long ago. She and my granddaughter used to be friends."

"Why aren't they friends anymore?"

"Shanda's stepdad started selling drugs out of their apartment a while back." He glanced over his shoulder.

"Will you answer a few questions for me?"

He looked around again. "I thought I was already doing that."

I smiled wryly. "A few more questions then."

"I don't want my name mentioned. I live here with my daughter and granddaughter, and we don't want trouble."

"Fair enough. Shanda said she has a little sister. Who watches her?"

He looked at me. "You sure you're not from DCFS?"

I shook my head and pulled my California State Bar card out of my little backpack and showed it to him.

"I'm just a public defender. But I know Shanda's worried about Bertie. And I'm worried about both of them."

He seemed to relax a little. "Her mom, Charlene, works at the corner Arco gas station part-time, and I think Mikey is supposed to be watching the baby when Charlene's gone. But it's usually Shanda who babysits."

"What does Mikey do?" I asked.

He scratched his ear and grimaced. "I'm pretty sure he sells drugs when Charlene's gone. I think she knows though because they've had some loud fights lately."

"But he's still living there."

Walt blew out a breath. "Yeah. Shanda brought Bertie over to our place a few times when Charlene was working. But then Shanda came over high one day. And it wasn't marijuana. I told her she couldn't come back."

I put my hand on his arm. "I get it. You need to protect your grandchild first."

He swallowed then nodded. "They live in apartment thirteen B. I think Charlene is still home, but it seems like she usually works evening shifts." He looked me up and down. "I'd be careful about going over there, especially at night."

"Okay. Do you know where Shanda would be if she's not home?"

"Maybe the park or the community center north of here a few blocks." He pointed in that direction.

"Desert Highland Park?"

"Yeah."

"Okay, thanks." I started to turn away but stopped.

"Can I give you my card in case you see or hear anything? I swear I won't tell anyone I talked to you. I understand about not getting on anyone's radar." I pulled a business card out of the side pocket of my backpack.

"Yeah. But pretend you don't know me if you come back and I'm around, okay?"

"Absolutely." I wrote my cell number on the back of the card and handed it to him. He nodded and walked away.

Their unit was on the second floor. I heard a TV playing and rang the doorbell, but no one answered. After a minute, I rang the doorbell again and knocked on the door.

"Are you going to get that or what, Mikey?" I could hear a lady's voice inside say.

"No, 'cause it ain't for me." It sounded like he was sitting right inside the door.

"You lazy fucker, I'm changing Bertie's diaper. You wanna do that instead?"

"Fuck no," the man answered.

"Then get the goddamn door!"

A shorter man who appeared to be in his mid-forties opened the door. He had on a stained white t-shirt, and he was thin and sallow with a few sores on his face.

"Hello. My name's Harley Emerson, and I'm Shanda's public defender. Is she around?"

"Shanda's attorney is at the door!" he yelled, looking up at me. "What do you want me to tell her?"

I looked over Mikey's shoulder and saw Charlene walking out of one of the back bedrooms with Bertie on her hip.

"Nothing. Just get out of the way." She waved her hand at him.

Mikey shrugged and sat in front of the TV. The coffee table had at least three takeout meals' worth of trash on it.

"Yeah? What can I do for you?" she asked. Bertie had on a little sunflower dress and her hair was in a pigtail on top of her head.

"Shanda missed an appointment with me last Wednesday, and I haven't heard from her since. Is she here?"

"No. I haven't seen her for almost a week, but that's nothing new." She eyed me. "Do most public defenders go to their clients' apartments? 'Cause none of the ones I've had ever did that."

"No, but I got worried about her. She's barely eighteen."

Charlene huffed. "She's fine. If I had a nickel for every time she hasn't come home, I'd be fuckin' rich."

"Okay. Do you have a way to get a hold of her? Or do you know where she is? Her court appearance is coming up, and I need to talk to her."

Mikey piped up from his spot in front of the TV. "She's a fucking adult now. She needs to go use the stupid CBD license she got in school last year and move the hell out."

Charlene frowned at him. "Mind your business, Mikey."

"It'd be one less fuckin' mouth to feed," he muttered under his breath.

I cocked my head to the side. "A CBD license? I didn't know an eighteen-year-old could get one of those."

Charlene smirked and stepped outside next to me, then closed the door behind her. She absently bounced Bertie on her hip. Bertie stared at me with lovely hazel eyes. I smiled at her and waved. She waved back. Shanda was right, she was adorable.

"So tell me about this CBD license," I said, trying to break the ice.

"It's a CNA license. He's a fucking moron. And probably on drugs on top of being born stupid."

She said it so nonchalantly I wondered for a second if I'd heard her correctly.

She rolled her eyes. "You think I didn't know? I'm pretty sure you knew less than a second after he opened the door. He has fucking sores on his face."

"Yeah, those were kind of hard to miss, and I'm a public defender. So..."

She sighed. "I don't know where Shanda is, and she hasn't answered her phone. But she's fine."

"All right." I pointed at her apartment. "Aren't you worried about your baby and Shanda being around him if he's using?"

"Yeah, but what the hell can I do? I threatened him with his life and his dick if he ever did it inside the apartment."

"Are you here all the time?" I asked carefully.

"No," she clipped. She knew what I was thinking.

"Huh. Anyway, do you know where Shanda could be?"

"She has an older boyfriend who comes around sometimes. She might be staying with him. Jared, I think?"

"Jason?"

"Yeah, that's it. I've only met him a couple of times."

Either this woman willfully ignored what was staring her right in the face, or Mikey was a better liar than anyone gave him credit for. I'd bet my bar license Jason was using Shanda as a cover for coming around here. And probably other things.

"Please let Shanda know I came by. And tell her to call me so we can talk before her hearing."

"Kay."

Bertie started jabbering, and she held her hand out to me like she wanted a high five.

"Geez, she's too cute. What's her name?" I held up my hand close to hers, and she slapped it. I didn't see a point in telling Charlene I already knew about Bertie.

Charlene smiled a little, and she looked like a different person.

"Roberta, but we call her Bertie." She gave me a half-assed wave and stepped back into the apartment. "I need to get ready for work, but whenever Shanda pulls her head out of her ass and comes home, I'll tell her you were here." Then she closed the door in my face.

I turned and walked slowly back down the stairs, wondering why I was more concerned about Shanda than her own mother. It was time to call in some help.

Chapter 10

That weekend, we played the oldest volleyball team in the league. It was a group of retired teachers, and the match had been friendly and civil. There hadn't been any flair-ups or arguments. Not even any smack talk.

Their coach came over and congratulated us on our win afterward. "You guys are so eclectic and interesting! That was a fun game, even if Stan threw out his hip trying to return your serve." She pointed at me.

Jaime chuckled. "You couldn't even be nice to the geriatric crowd."

"They're all in better shape than you," I muttered under my breath.

Frankie laughed and patted Jaime on his shoulder. "I still love you, Jaime."

On Sunday, there was a birthday lunch celebration for Jonathan I'd been invited to, but I had the morning free.

I needed to check in on Ava, so I walked over to her house after showering. I knocked on her front door and rang the doorbell, but she didn't answer. Gary looked up at me and I shrugged. When I rang the doorbell a third time, I grew concerned and started having flashbacks.

Not long after my dad died, I sometimes found Ava high or passed out somewhere in the house when her opioid addiction hit a bad stretch. Once, I found her passed out wet and naked lying in her bathtub. It had scared the shit out of me.

The old fear and resentment reared up, but I tamped it down and put in the code to her front door lock. No use borrowing trouble. I walked in and could hear her TV playing in her meditation room. She sat in front of it on a yoga mat with her eyes closed.

Ava had decorated the room in a vaguely Zen style, complete with a fish tank and mood lighting. She had yoga mats and some exercise paraphernalia artfully stacked in a corner. But she mostly used the room to watch golf meditation videos.

A *Golf and Life Meditation* video played on the screen. The scene was an idyllic green golf course, and a smooth, soothing generic female voice intoned golf and life affirmation statements. New-age ambient music played softly in the background.

"You are a focused golfer. You are a confident golfer." The female voice paused, then continued. "You are a consistent and calm golfer."

I rolled my eyes. My mom was *not* a calm golfer.

"You improve every single day." Ambient music continued to play in between pauses.

I leaned on the door jamb and listened.

"You have steady, focused breathing. You can visualize your swing." The voice paused again for a few seconds.

The ambient music continued playing, but the rhythm slowed down.

"Now repeat in your head; I am a focused, confident person. I am consistent and calm. I visualize contentment and happiness."

My own breathing and heart rate slowed a little as I listened. Maybe there was something to meditation. I still thought the golf affirmation thing was a bit odd, but I knew plenty of athletes who used visualization and affirmation techniques. Whatever worked.

The music slowly faded, and Ava picked up the clicker and turned off the TV. I cleared my throat, and she startled a little.

"I rang the doorbell a few times and got nervous, so I let myself in."

She flinched slightly but nodded. She knew why I'd gotten nervous. My mom had an opioid addiction, and she'd fallen apart after my father died. She left me to care for her, my little sister, and the house. I'd been fifteen at the time.

"I watched a good segment of that." I nodded toward the TV. "Maybe it's not as Age of Aquarius and 'out there' as I thought."

She smiled and tilted her head. "It would do you good. What're you doing here? I usually have to hunt you down to see you." Besides my twice-weekly scheduled check-ins with Ava, I didn't come around a lot.

"Laurel invited me to Sunday brunch at Willa and Fran's Cafe around noon. It's Jonathan's birthday. Do you want to come?"

She perked up. "I'd love to."

"I think Sheila and Grace will be there."

She looked at me carefully. "You don't mind?"

"I wouldn't have invited you if I minded. Just don't throw food or chew with your mouth open this time, okay?"

She shook her head. My mom usually had impeccable manners, unless she was high or upset. Then all bets were off.

I turned to walk out, and Gary stood up to follow me. "I'll drive. Come over a few minutes before noon."

She looked down at Gary. "Have you fed him already?"

I stopped short, then mentally sighed. "Yeah, he ate after we got back from our hike this morning."

She hadn't fed Gary in almost two years, and he'd lived with me full-time not long after she brought him home from the animal shelter.

One day Ava had decided she wanted a pet. So she went to the shelter and picked one out. When she first brought him home, I noticed she didn't take him on walks or play with him.

But when I saw that his water bowl was dry on more than one occasion and he was losing weight, I'd stepped in and re-homed him––to my house. It had taken Ava three days to realize he was missing.

Ava nodded jerkily. I guess her morning meditation session hadn't calmed or centered her all that much after all.

I wasn't going to have this argument with her again for the millionth time, so I walked out, and Gary followed me. Ava came over a little before noon, and we drove over to the restaurant in near silence.

Willa and Fran's Cafe was located in an orange building in the middle of Palm Canyon Drive. They had an extensive brunch menu, but their Sunday buffet was the draw.

When Ava and I got there, Jonathan and Ramone were already seated at the front of the table. Laurel and Sebastian, as well as Martina, were just sitting down. I said hello to everyone and gave Laurel a long hug. The bruises on her neck were finally almost gone, thank God.

Damien and Zeke sat at the other end of the table. Grace and Sheila hadn't made it yet.

I patted Jonathan's shoulder. "Happy birthday, counselor." I slipped him a birthday card with a gift certificate to a men's boutique that sold the bright aloha short-sleeved print shirts he liked to wear.

"Thanks, Harley." He pulled out the card and noticed the gift certificate. "You didn't need to do that, but I'm glad you did. This is one of the few places I like to shop."

"Let's see what you got." Ramone leaned over and noticed the name on the gift certificate. "This is what makes you an exceptional attorney." He tipped his mimosa at me. "You pay attention to the details."

I smiled. "I texted you to find out his favorite store."

"See? Details."

Laughing, I gave Ramone a one-armed hug, then shuffled down the table to introduce Ava to anyone who hadn't met her. Zeke and Damien were last.

"This is Ava, my mother." I turned to my mom. "And these two are Damien and Zeke. They're friends and business partners with Sebastian."

Damien and Zeke stood up and shook Ava's hand. I started edging back up the table to sit further away from Damien, but

Ava plopped herself down in front of them and set her purse on the table. I reluctantly sat down next to her.

Damien smiled, clearly knowing I didn't particularly want to sit by him. He'd probably ask me to apologize, or start asking me personal questions again.

"So," I said awkwardly.

Damien's eyes crinkled in the corners. "So," he repeated. He had a light scruff, and his hair was a little damp. He looked good, and I had to work to keep from staring.

Grace and Sheila walked in just then and sat down next to us.

"You still up for our afternoon tee time, Ava?" Grace asked as she settled in her seat.

Ava nodded. "Of course. Sheila, are you coming today?"

"No. You two ladies have fun without me."

Grace leaned around my mother. "You coming, Har?"

"No, but thanks for inviting me."

Damien leaned back in his chair and looked at me. "Do you golf?"

Grace nodded. "Yes, she does. Ava told me she wanted Harley to play golf instead of volleyball in high school." Grace had no idea about the can of worms she'd just opened.

Ava looked at me with that same old hurt expression. "But Harley wanted to play volleyball, just like her father, as usual. Even though she was one of the best female golfers."

My back started itching between my shoulder blades. "I like volleyball more than golf." I turned to Damien and Zeke. "How's your rec team doing this season?"

"We've won both our matches so far. How about you?" Damien glanced at Ava quizzically.

"We have too. But one was by forfeit, so I can't count it."

"Was that to the Buddy Boyz?" Zeke asked.

"Yeah. I take it they didn't have enough females on their team when you played them either?"

Damien leaned back and put his arm across the back of the empty chair next to him. He had nice shoulders and triceps. "They didn't have *any* show up that day, but they didn't give a shit."

I smirked. "They're a mellow group."

Zeke chuckled. "Yeah, a few of them came high. At nine in the morning. We played anyway, and it was still fun."

"We did too. Their coach asked Frankie and me to join his team next season, and offered us a discount to his cannabis shop and specially designed jerseys."

Damien tilted his head. "He doesn't know your team is part of the Addicts to Athletes program, I take it."

I shook my head and grinned. "He'll probably feel bad if he finds out."

"Well, shit. I didn't know that either." Zeke leaned back in his chair. He turned to Damien. "That explains a lot."

Damien nodded. "I told Harley the same thing when I found out."

Just then, one of the hosts came over to the table. She was pretty and had on a white linen dress with cute tan sandals. Her long brown hair hung in loose curls and her makeup was understated and dewy. She walked over to Damien and Zeke's side of the table.

"Damien Andreasen, I haven't seen you since... well, you remember." She smiled and squeezed his shoulder.

Damien looked at her blankly for a minute, then recognition seemed to dawn.

"Hey..." His eyes flicked down to her name tag. "Samantha. It's nice to see you."

Samantha slid over to stand next to Damien and opened her arms for a hug. Damien stood up a little reluctantly and gave her a stiff one. He smiled down at her, and his dimple popped, but I could tell he wasn't excited to see her. He patted her on the back, then sat.

"You never called me back after Chrissy's party."

I leaned back and avidly watched the interaction. Samantha was now running her hand up and down his shoulder and bicep. She had good taste, I'd give her that.

Damien tilted to the side and looked up at her. In the process, he dislodged her hand.

"I know. I've been busy with work, but it was nice to see you again." She stared down at him and lost her big smile. She blinked, and I got the impression she rarely got the brush-off. Samantha swallowed, and her hand hovered over his shoulder as if she didn't know what to do.

The silence was awkward. I stood up and leaned over the table with my hand outstretched. "Hi, Samantha. I'm Harley. We're here for our friend Jonathan's birthday." I pointed over to where Jonathan sat.

She blinked at me. "Oh, okay."

"Toward the end of the meal, will you ask the server to come sing a birthday song to him? We'd like to embarrass him a little."

Samantha stared at me, then slowly reached over, and shook my hand. "Hi, Harley. It's nice to meet you too." She sucked in a breath and glanced down at Damien, then back at me.

"Yes, for sure. You guys have a good lunch." She turned and quickly walked away.

Damien gazed at me, and I gave him a small shrug and sat down.

Grace leaned forward and started talking again. "Anyway, Harley started the Addicts to Athletes' volleyball team a couple of years ago. I think she needs to start an Addicts to Athletes' golf team."

I thought about it. "Hmm. I like that idea. I don't want to be the coach, but I'll pass it on to the program director."

"Why don't you ever play golf with me anymore?" Ava said.

I mentally cringed. Every so often she got in these woe-is-me depressed moods, and she didn't seem to care who was around or what she said.

"I play with you all the time," I answered. That technically wasn't true. I played with her when I couldn't get out of it. "But I have some things to do this afternoon. And besides, you and Grace have more fun without me."

"Is it because I broke your favorite driver?" she asked.

My hands clenched involuntarily. She had to remind me. "No. And that was years ago. I've gotten over it." She'd run over my clubs when she'd been high and broken my driver in the process. Ryan, my fiancé, had given me that driver. Okay, I'd *mostly* gotten over it.

Ava heaved a big sigh and turned to Damien and Zeke. "How do you know Jonathan?"

Zeke folded his arms. "We're friends, and our offices are in the same building across the hall. We also do work for their law firm sometimes."

"What kind of business do you have?" Ava asked.

"Security systems and investigations. Sebastian's our partner. I think we put in a security system at your house a couple of years ago."

Ava nodded. "That's right, you did. When Harley decided she wanted to be a criminal defense attorney full-time."

Zeke tilted his head. "Why'd that make you decide to put a system in? I bet she usually doesn't invite clients home." I decided I liked Zeke.

Ava ignored Zeke's subtle jab. "Have you seen some of the clients she works with? And she lives with me."

Damien silently pushed his full mimosa over to me.

I looked at him and he leaned in. "I don't like champagne. And I think you need it more than I do."

Grace and Sheila glanced at each other. They'd seen Ava like this a few times.

"Ava, honey, didn't you ask Harley to buy the small rundown house next to yours?" Sheila asked.

"Well, yes," Ava admitted.

"She owns her own home, and there's a fence between your properties," Sheila continued. "So I think you're pretty safe. And you both have Gary."

I cringed inside. Gary was not a good topic to bring up. I grabbed the mimosa and took a big swallow.

Grace tried to salvage the conversation. "You did a marvelous job with your remodel, Harley. Your place looks great now."

I smiled tightly. "Thanks, but your house is on a scale all its own. Doesn't their house look great, Ava?"

Ava ignored me. "Even though Harley's dad was a commercial real estate attorney, and she started with a real estate firm, she decided to be a criminal defense attorney instead."

I needed to shut her up. "I don't think anyone wants to hear this."

She continued to ignore me. "I lost my husband, then she lost her fiancé whom we all adored. And I struggle with a life-threatening illness. But she decided after all that, she's going to practice criminal law."

Damien looked at me with a troubled expression. The table had gone quiet.

"And she won't date. It's been almost five years since Ryan died." She turned to me. "And you won't date. You won't go out, and you don't have sex."

I'd had enough. She didn't get to violate my privacy like that. "Not another word." My voice was low, and it vibrated with hurt and anger.

She opened her mouth, but I put my hand up. "Not. One. Word."

When she opened her mouth again, I leaned in and hissed at her. "Or I'll tell everyone what your 'life-threatening illness' really is."

Her head jerked back, and her eyes got wide.

"You're ruining Jonathan's birthday lunch and embarrassing yourself. And me."

Ava finally looked around and realized everyone was watching us. She shrank back in her seat and looked like she was going to cry. But I had no patience or sympathy for her. The silence was painful.

Damien cleared his throat and leaned toward me. "Harley, does everyone know what your nickname for me is? And did you tell them all how we met?"

"You have a nickname for him?" Laurel asked after a few seconds. She bent forward and looked down at us.

Damien grinned. "Yeah. She calls me Dimples. And I'll be damned if I'm not starting to like it."

Laurel turned to me and wiggled her eyebrows.

"How *did* you two meet?" Jonathan asked curiously.

Martina started to laugh. "This is a great story."

"Oh, Lord," I muttered under my breath. But there wasn't any fire in it. Damien had deflected an ugly situation when he could've easily just sat back and watched. I downed the rest of his mimosa. Damn it all, I was starting to *like* the man.

Chapter 11

On Monday, I called one of the private investigators who worked with the public defender's office to see if they could help track down Shanda. I was really worried about her.

"Dickie speaking." Martin Dixon answered on the fourth ring. He sounded rough.

"Hey, Martin, this is Harley Emerson. You sound terrible." Dickie's first name was Martin. Most people called him Dickie, but he reminded me more of a Martin.

"Hi, Harley." His voice was wheezy and raspy. "I have bronchitis, fuck me. I'm pretty sure my nephew gave it to me."

"That's too bad. Any idea when you'll get back on your feet?"

He started coughing again, and I winced in sympathy.

"My doctor said it usually lasts a few weeks, and the coughing can go longer. I'm planning to take a month off just to be safe," he wheezed.

"Glad to hear you're taking it seriously, and I hope you feel better soon. How's your nephew doing?"

He cleared his throat. "The cute little shit is doing better than me. James goes to daycare, and I swear that place is a biohazard site. Do you need help with a case?"

"Martin, I'll see who else is available. You shouldn't worry about work right now."

"I'm bored out of my mind and sick of hearing myself cough. Just tell me what you've got," he whined.

"Okay, but let me know when you've had enough. I don't want to overtax you."

He sighed. "I've been cooped up in bed for five days. Lay it on me."

So I told him about Shanda's case and her disappearance.

"Hmm. I've heard of Jason Ulrich. Do you remember Ernie's big case last year? The one involving the shooting at that shitty bar in Indio?"

"Yeah. Vaguely."

Ernie was also a public defender. He was a great criminal defense attorney and had a lot more experience. He usually got the high-profile cases. "Wasn't it over someone's girlfriend or something like that?"

"Kind of. I think the shooter—his name was Chauncey—was looking for one of his meth buyers who'd found another supplier. I doubt he went looking for his buyer to put two bullets in his head."

"Yeah, that'd be bad for business. So why did he?"

"The buyer was at the bar cuddled up with Chauncey's girlfriend."

"Ah. What an idiot."

"He's a dead idiot now." Martin coughed again. It sounded deep and raspy. "Anyway, allegedly the new supplier was Jason Ulrich."

I sat up straight. "You think Jason is a major supplier now?"

"Ernie was more focused on his case, and the detective only had what the girlfriend overheard, so I don't think anything came of it."

"That's not good." My stomach clenched. "I need to find her. Do you know any investigators you could recommend who'd be able to track her down?"

"If the PD's office has the budget for it, I'd use MAD Investigations *if* you can get them to take the case."

I buried my head in my arms. "Why?" I asked myself softly.

"Harley, you there?" Martin asked.

I sat up. "Yeah, Martin. I know Damien and Zeke. I'll see if the PD's office will approve it. Damien and I... have a little history."

"Oh, really? Did you used to date him or something?" he asked.

"No! Nothing like that. I may have put his nose out of joint with a volleyball one time."

Martin started laughing. "That was you?"

"What do you mean? How did *you* hear about it?"

He kept chuckling. "I heard from one of his colleagues he got hit in the face with a volleyball by this blonde Viking warrior who had a face that... Well, anyway."

I got up and started pacing my office. "What, Martin? Tell me."

He sighed, then coughed. "They said it, not me. Okay?"

"Said what?"

"You have a face that makes men want to... spank their meat."

I paused and pulled the phone away from my ear for a second. "What does that—oh."

He laughed again, then started coughing.

Some men were such pigs. "I wish you wouldn't have told me that."

"Hey, you asked." He continued laughing and coughing.

I shook my head even though Martin couldn't see me. "We're going to pretend we never had this conversation."

"You don't have to ask me twice. Damien's one of the best investigators I know. He's smart and methodical."

I stopped pacing. "Do you know why he's not a detective anymore?"

"I do." He didn't elaborate.

"And?"

"It's not my story to tell." He started coughing again. "I gotta go, I can feel a coughing fit coming on, and I need to clear out some phlegm."

"Gross. Okay, feel better soon."

Martin had given me some good information, even if he couldn't take the case. I looked up Damien's email address and sent him an official work email, explaining that Martin had recommended him and what I needed.

Then I shook off my worry about Shanda and started working on another file.

Damien called while I was in juvenile drug court and left a voice-mail. "Hey, Harley. I got your email. It was so professional and business-like, I forgot for a minute how we met. Come by my office after you're done with work, and we'll discuss your case. And save my phone number in your contacts so you don't have to keep calling the office or using email to get a hold of me from now on."

After I listened to his voicemail, I added his name and number to my contacts and checked the time. It wasn't quite five, so I took a chance and swung by his office. Ramone and Jonathan also had their offices in the same building, and it was a nice area in downtown Palm Springs. When I walked into the foyer of MAD Investigations, a pretty receptionist greeted me. She eyed me a little warily when I walked in.

"Hello. Do you have an appointment?"

I approached the high counter. "No. But Damien left me a voicemail and said to come by if I could make it before closing. I'm here about a case."

She smiled in relief and glanced at the clock on the wall behind the counter. "Give me your name and I'll let him know you're here."

I nodded. "It's Harley Emerson. I appreciate it."

She headed back to the offices, and I looked around the reception area. It had a clean, contemporary feel with nice signage behind the counter and framed black and white photographs on the wall. I studied them while I waited for Damien. Someone was a talented photographer, and I recognized the San Jacinto mountain range with a few big horn sheep in the foreground.

Damien walked over and stood next to me. "Laurel took those."

I looked at him in surprise. "Wow. They're great." I scanned the one on the far right a little closer and pointed to two sheep in the background. "Are those two…?"

Damien grinned down at me. "Fornicating? Yes. You're only the third person to notice."

I laughed. "Laurel has a wicked sense of humor."

The receptionist came out of the back with her jacket and purse. "Damien, I forwarded you two messages, and neither are urgent. I'm taking off. Will you lock up?"

"Yes. Thanks, Kara." Damien turned and studied my clothes. "You look different in a suit and without your Viking warrior braids and spandex shorts." I had on a navy suit and a violet-colored shell. He reached over and took my laptop case. "Very professional. But you're the only person I know who looks *less* intimidating in a suit."

I smiled. "I'll have to start wearing my volleyball uniform to work, I guess."

"You might cause a riot."

I cocked my head. "Why?"

His lips twisted. "Because you look a little *too* good in those spandex shorts."

My face heated. I'd worn those spandex shorts most of my life. Every female volleyball player did.

He grinned. "Why do you think I call you Legs?"

"Because I have long legs?" I answered.

Damien grinned. "That's part of the reason. But I digress, and we need to discuss your case. I didn't eat lunch and I'm starving. Would you mind if we grabbed some dinner and talk while we eat?"

My stomach jumped a little. He was doing me a favor by taking my case, and I realized with a start that I enjoyed being around him, and the way we teased and ribbed each other.

I nodded. "Sounds good. What are you hungry for?"

He looked me up and down. "You're pretty dressed up for fast food or Mexican. Do you want to go home and change first?"

"I'm fine. We could walk over to one of the restaurants along Indian Canyon Drive. There's a good Italian or Asian fusion restaurant. Or the oyster bar along Tahquitz Canyon."

He raised his eyebrow. "I'd like to watch you slurp down oysters. But that restaurant might be a little loud if we're going to discuss the case. How about the Italian restaurant?"

"Italian it is."

I waited for him to lock up his office, and then we walked outside. It was already starting to get dark, and he put his hand on the small of my back as we walked.

"How's Dickie doing?" he asked.

"He sounds horrible. He has bronchitis, but he's bored, and he still wanted me to tell him about my case. He had some useful information."

Damien shook his head. "I'm not surprised. He smokes and drinks like a fish, but he'll probably outlive us all. Tell me about your case."

So I told him about Shanda and her little sister, and I outlined what I knew about Jason.

"You're worried about her?" he asked.

I nodded. "She just turned eighteen two months ago, and she's been missing for almost two weeks. Her home life is horrible."

We made it to the restaurant, and the host seated us in a booth by the window. The restaurant wasn't fancy or pretentious, but it was cozy, and the food was fresh and delicious. I loved the flowers in the pots at the entrance and the arched gate with orange trumpet vines. I ordered a glass of the house red wine and shrimp linguine, and Damien ordered the oven-baked sea bass.

When the server left, I took off my jacket and pulled my hair out of the French twist, then rubbed my scalp with my fingers. I hummed a little in pleasure. "I've been wanting to do that all day."

He leaned back in his seat and watched me with hooded eyes. His look felt intimate and made my insides tighten. This almost felt like a date or a romantic evening with a lover. It wasn't either of those things, and I needed to rein it in.

I straightened up. "Let me tell you a little more about the case."

The server came by with my wine, and I took a sip. Then I told him about the car accident and the video I'd shown Shanda. We also discussed Jason's extensive criminal history.

I took another sip of wine. "Shanda was genuinely scared when I called her out on her lie. Then we walked over to the coffee shop, and she finally told me about her little sister and how worried she was."

Damien's mouth tightened. "You think that fucker threatened her little sister."

I nodded slowly. "I'd bet a large amount of money on it. The last thing she said to me was Jason is crazy and fucking scary. Her words, not mine."

He reached over and grabbed my hand. "We'll find her. Give me whatever you can about her, and I'll send out a few feelers and see if I can track her down on social media."

He ran his thumb across the back of my knuckles, and my insides clenched at the soft contact. The server came with our food just then, and Damien let go of my hand. We ate in companionable silence, each lost in our thoughts.

"You want a taste of my sea bass?" he asked, scooping up a forkful and bringing it across the table to my lips. It looked good, so I opened my mouth and took the bite.

"Thank you. That's delicious." I used my spoon and fork to roll some linguine, then leaned over and put it on his plate along with a couple of shrimp.

"Thanks, Legs." He smiled and his dimple popped. My vagina spasmed, and I clenched my thighs together and grabbed my wine glass to take another sip. I needed to stay away from this man. I just didn't want to anymore.

Chapter 12

On Thursday morning, Damien was waiting for me when I got to the gym.

"I thought we could get sweaty together this morning and strategize about Shanda's case."

Heat rolled through me at the thought of getting sweaty with him in other ways. I gave him a quick once over as he stood there in his workout shorts and a black moister-wicking muscle shirt. My cheeks started burning, and I looked away.

"Sounds like a plan. What do you have for me?" I asked, finally looking up at him.

He grinned. "I have a lot of things for you, Legs. But getting back to the case, I think the best way to track her down is through her social media."

We walked toward the treadmills together. I was hyper-aware of him, and I'd never been so distracted during a workout. Even after we finished, he still looked and smelled so good.

His hair was damp and curled a little, and his biceps glistened. I used work as an excuse to take off right after we got done, but my mind was distracted, and I kept thinking about Damien the rest of the day. I was in so much trouble.

Sheila and Grace invited Ava and me over for Thanksgiving dinner the following week. I was grateful for their invitation, but I would have been happy to skip Thanksgiving.

It was my least favorite holiday, and this year I dreaded it even more because Olivia, my sister, wouldn't be there to act as a buffer. She planned to come home at the end of the semester in mid-December, but she couldn't get away for Thanksgiving. I called her again on Wednesday evening just to complain.

"Ollie, come home," I whined as soon as she answered the phone. "I'll pay for your ticket. Just bring your homework. I don't want to do Thanksgiving without you."

"Hello to you too. I'm doing well, thanks for asking," she answered.

"I'm good, you're good. Now you need to come home for Thanksgiving."

"I can't. And what you meant to say is you don't want to do Thanksgiving alone with Mom."

"Isn't that what I just said?" I asked.

"No. You said 'I don't want to do Thanksgiving without you' end quote. A subtle but important difference. Details matter—in contracts and in life." She was quoting one of my dad's favorite legal sayings. I rolled my eyes but smiled.

There was a reason Thanksgiving was my least favorite holiday; our dad had died the day after Thanksgiving, and Ava fell apart shortly afterward. I'd met the funeral director and planned the funeral without Ava since my dad's brother, Keith, lived overseas and Ava didn't have any close family.

The funeral director had enlisted his wife to help me, and she ended up holding and comforting me while I sobbed uncontrollably the morning of the funeral. I sent them a Christmas card every year.

I huffed. "Okay, I should have said I don't want to do Thanksgiving at all, *especially* not with Ava. And I miss you and want to see you."

"I miss you too, Har. Sometimes I get mopey and a little lonely too. No one knows me here, or my dark side."

"Your dark side being your creepy love of horror and slasher films?"

Olivia laughed. "My roommates know all about that. A few of us aren't wimpy babies, and we have a scary movie night."

"I honestly can't think of anything I'd rather do less."

"At least I don't watch weird, brain-warping indie movies. How's Mom doing, anyway?"

I thought about it. "She's golfing a lot and still does her meditation golf videos. Addiction-wise I think she's hanging in there."

"Have you seen any signs she's using again?" she asked.

Olivia and I learned long ago to be completely honest with each other when it came to our mother. Ava tried to triangulate and gaslight us after Dad died, but we'd quickly learned to work together since we didn't want to end up in foster care or with a dead mother.

"She's drinking alcohol again. It seems minor, but it worries me."

"What about you two?"

I blew out a breath. "She's *still* pissed about Gary, and she's edgier lately. She lashed out at me in front of everyone when I took her to a friend's birthday brunch. Luckily, Grace and Sheila were there."

And Damien, but I didn't say that out loud. I wondered what he was doing for Thanksgiving. I explained to Olivia what had happened at the restaurant.

She groaned. "Holy shit. I'm sorry she did that to you. I wonder what triggered it?"

I hummed. "I don't know. Maybe she's tired of us watching out for her."

"Are you still watching over her accounts and paying her bills?"

"She's paying her bills now. I still check on her accounts and balance them, just not as often. But I'm tired, and I don't know how much longer I can do this." A tear slid down my cheek, and I wiped it away, annoyed at myself.

Olivia sniffed. "I know, Har. I'm almost done here, then I'll come and help."

If I were a bigger person, I'd tell her not to worry about us and go live her life. I settled for a half-answer. "We'll be fine, Ollie. I'm just being whiny."

"I can take over the financial part though. Mom and I can FaceTime, and I can manage her accounts online. Let me do that at least."

So I agreed to transfer that burden to Olivia. We'd been watching Ava's accounts since we found out she'd maxed out her credit cards and gone through her savings less than a year after my dad died. Luckily, most of their assets had been tied up in retirement accounts and their home.

I'd silently cried myself to sleep so many times during those high school years as I tried to keep what was left of my family together. Thinking about the past made me feel bruised and guilty.

Early Thanksgiving morning, I took Gary on a hike at the Mission Creek Preserve. The Preserve allowed dogs, and it was one of the more interesting hikes in the area with the remains of several old stone cottages left over from an old dude ranch in the 1920s. I also needed to clear my head and recalibrate before Thanksgiving dinner.

As we hiked, I wondered again who Damien was spending Thanksgiving with, and I thought about the last time I'd seen him at the gym.

After I got home and had just finished getting ready for the day, Ava came over. I noticed she hadn't showered or gotten ready yet. She rarely left her house without going through a long makeup and hair routine, and she usually always looked stylish and well put together. This had probably helped her camouflage her addiction when we were growing up.

My stomach clenched, and I prepared myself for either a relapse or a confrontation of some kind.

"What's up?"

She looked at me, then down at Gary. "May I come in?"

I motioned her inside. "Sure. Have you had coffee yet? I can make some."

She stared at me. "Thank you. That would be nice."

We hadn't talked much since Jonathan's birthday brunch. I walked over to the kitchen area and started making coffee. She followed me over and sat down on a stool at the bar. She had something to say, so I stayed quiet and let her start the conversation.

"Olivia just called me a few minutes ago. I think she forgets sometimes she's three hours ahead."

I glanced over at the clock and noticed it was just after ten. I'd been up for at least three hours. "How's she doing?"

"Fine. But she told me you two decided she'd take over my accounting."

"We did. She's the one who suggested it. She said she could FaceTime you and do everything else over the Internet."

Ava's lips tightened, and she clasped her hands in front of her. "You should have talked to me first." She was upset, but she was trying to be civil and keep her composure. That was something new.

I looked at her. "You're right. We should have."

"You... you think I'm right?"

"Yeah. I do. You've been stable for over a year now, and we should've let you know. Let me get Olivia on the phone." I pulled my phone out of my back pocket and rang Olivia. Luckily, she picked up on the second ring. "Hey, Har. Is everything okay?"

"Yes, it's fine. Ava's over here and said she talked to you this morning. She also said that we should have talked to her about having you help with her accounting. I told her she was right. I'm going to put you on speakerphone, okay?"

"Yes, that's fine."

I pressed the speaker button. "Can you hear us?"

"I can hear you. Hi, Mom."

"Hi, honey. I didn't mean to cause problems, but I thought Harley should have talked to me first," Ava answered.

"Actually, *I* should have talked to you first, not Harley. It was my idea," Olivia told her.

I poured two cups of coffee and pushed one over to Ava.

Ava picked her cup up. "Oh. Well, I think I'd prefer to keep things the way they are."

"Mom, Harley has enough on her plate right now. Her practice is busy, and honestly, you can be a bit of a handful."

Ava's shoulders tightened, and she scoffed. "That's not true. Everything's been fine lately."

"I heard about how you behaved at her friend's Sunday brunch the other day."

Ava glanced at me with a hurt look. "She shouldn't have told you."

"*You* should have told me. Or better yet, not acted that way," Olivia retorted.

Ava's hand tightened around her coffee mug. She didn't like having her favorite daughter call her out.

I tried to reason with her. "Ava, Olivia's more qualified than I am to help you with your finances. She's getting a degree in accounting, for God's sake. And you two work together better than we do. I'm sorry you feel like we didn't consult you. As Dad would have said, it's not a material breach. We should have, we didn't, but it's not significant. So let's move on."

"Harley, I don't want to 'move on,' and I don't see why you can't keep doing it."

Olivia cut in. "She's doing more than enough. She's burned out and needs a break."

Ava seemed to deflate. "Okay. If that's what you think is best."

Olivia cleared her throat. "Now tell me what you're both bringing to Thanksgiving dinner so I can be sad that I'm here stuck with a frozen turkey pot pie."

A few minutes later, Ava went home to get ready. She seemed to have calmed down, but I could tell she was still mad.

The Thanksgiving meal was delicious, and we ate out on Sheila and Grace's beautiful patio overlooking the tropical pool area. While we ate, Grace told us about her golf round from hell.

"They paired me with three older men because the course was crowded this morning," Grace told us. "It wouldn't have been a big deal, but they all groaned out loud when the shop assistant told them I'd be playing with them. In front of me."

I shook my head. "What jackasses. Did it get any better?"

Grace grimaced. "Hell no, it got worse. They were terrible golfers, and they brought their own booze and 'pre-gamed' until the beverage cart came around. That's what they called it. They were piss drunk by the end of the round."

I grabbed the chocolate pie and lemon bars I'd brought for dessert, and we talked some more about our best and worst golf days.

We were cleaning up, and Grace asked me if I wanted any leftover turkey scraps for Gary. Ava tensed. She probably wasn't happy Grace had asked me about the leftovers instead of her. I ignored Ava.

"That would be nice, thanks."

Ava fumed as we finished cleaning up, but she held her tongue until we'd said goodbye and walked out of their house.

We were less than fifty feet from their front door when Ava started in. "You stole my dog," she said in a hurt voice.

I sighed long and loud. "Let's not kid ourselves. We're his humans, and he puts up with us in exchange for kibble and walks."

She ignored my attempt to deflect an argument. "You even named him."

"You called him doggie for two months," I retorted.

"I was trying to decide! I think you did it on purpose just to get under my skin."

I looked down at her. "That's not true. He's a dog, Ava. He likes walks, food, and the dog park. And people spending time with him. It was inevitable he'd prefer me."

"What are you saying? I took him for walks." Ava looked affronted.

"Yeah, in your flip-flops. For maybe five minutes so you wouldn't be late for your morning tee time."

"So? He had a big yard with lots of room to run."

"I'm sick of this conversation, and this is the last time I'm having it with you. When you left for two months last summer—and the summer before that—to get out of the heat, you didn't give Gary one single thought."

"That's because I knew he'd be with you."

"Exactly. You knew I'd take care of him. When you first got him, I found his water bowl bone dry on more than one occasion. And you forgot to feed him sometimes."

"That only happened a few times," she said more softly.

"I shudder to think what would have happened to him if I hadn't been around. So yes, he prefers me. He's my dog now. I'm claiming him through adverse possession—look it up. And you need to stop whining and guilt-tripping."

"I can't talk to you when you get like this." She started walking toward her house.

I stared at her back. "Yeah, you never did like hearing the hard, cold truth."

She stopped dead for a second, then kept walking.

I didn't know how much longer I could do this with her. We'd had the same argument about Gary so many times, and it frustrated me that I hadn't controlled my temper better.

Before my dad died, I hadn't thought much about Ava and her behavior. She'd haphazardly run the household and helped my dad a little at his firm sometimes. But other times she'd lain in bed all day or been so out of it that I knew better than to try and have a conversation with her. I had vague memories of her taking Olivia and me to the park or the library. But those times were few and far between.

My parents never talked to us about it, but when I looked back Ava had likely been abusing opioids for years. My dad had just buffered us from the worst of it.

Chapter 13

On Saturday, I brought Gary to the volleyball match and arrived early so I could talk with Damien about Shanda's case. His team was playing one of the best teams on the roster right before my team's match.

Gary and I sat on the grass and watched. They'd been playing for a while, and everyone was nice and sweaty. I became mesmerized by Damien's tan, muscular body. It looked like he was having a good time, but he was also laser focused.

Zeke was just as handsome, and he didn't get under my skin the way Damien did. But Damien was the one who made my heart jump and my stomach flutter.

Damien and Zeke played well together. If their back row gave them a decent bump, they had a nice system at the net, rotating who would set and who would hit. Finally, Zeke drilled the winning point into the opposing team's back row between two players.

"Goddamn it, you morons! How many of those have you missed today?" A player from the other team yelled at his two teammates.

One of the players froze and looked stricken. The female player scowled at the jerk and fired back. "I didn't see you block anything from where you were standing, Ray. You seemed pretty flatfooted today."

Ray, the one who'd called his teammates morons, let out an ugly laugh. "Corey, you and Steve are the fat, flatfooted ones."

Corey was medium height and build, and I thought she'd been a solid player. I would have been happy to have her on my team. The woman looked like she wanted to punch Ray, and I couldn't blame her. The rest of their team stood around awkwardly, and a couple of them walked away from the escalating confrontation.

Ray backed up a few steps, and before I knew it he was on top of Gary and me. He tripped over Gary and went down hard on his ass.

Gary yelped and tried to scoot away. I quickly let go of his leash so he could move more freely, and we both scooted back from where Ray lay sprawled on the ground.

He got up and started in on me. "Get out of my way, and keep your dog on a leash," he sneered.

I stood up and grabbed Gary's leash again. "You're the one who backed into us. Do you always treat your teammates that way?"

Corey came over and stood next to me. She looked like she wanted to go WWE on Ray.

I glanced over at her. "I know you want to nut-punch him for being such an asshole, but he's not worth an assault charge."

"It still might be worth it," she said flatly.

I smiled despite the tension. "It just might be. He's a dick."

The other player Ray had yelled at turned to Corey. "Let's go. I don't plan to come back next week. Or ever."

I looked at them. "I think you guys should file a complaint with the parks and rec department and have Ray banned for the season."

"Who the fuck are you? Mind your own business, you nosy bitch." Ray puffed up his chest and gave me a death glare.

I gave him my best resting bitch face. "The rules are clear that while general good-natured ribbing is tolerated, mean, belittling, cruel, biased, and racist comments are not." I didn't know exactly what the rules said, but it sounded good.

The team captain on Ray's team finally spoke up. "She's right, Ray. You were a jerk to Sherrie and Georgie last year too and ran them off. I can't find any more decent volleyball players. So we'd like *you* not to come back."

Ray's face got red, and he started clenching and unclenching his fists. I watched in fascination. Someone took hold of my arm and gently pulled me out of the middle of the team's argument.

When I looked up, Damien stared down at me with laughter in his eyes. "Hey, Legs."

"Hi, Dimples." I looked down and noticed he was petting Gary. "What're you doing?"

"Making sure you don't get hurt."

Zeke walked up and gave me a squeeze around my shoulders. "You're always in the middle of the drama, Harley. Why is that? I like the braids by the way."

I couldn't deny it. "Hi, Zeke. I don't want to be, it just happens. You two looked pretty good out there."

"Thanks. That's a compliment coming from you," Zeke said.

"You're a little slow getting up though, and your back row needs work."

"There's the Harley I know and love." Zeke chuckled and gave me another squeeze. He was a big guy, and his arm felt like an enormous tree trunk wrapped around my shoulders. It made me want to squeeze his bicep.

Damien carefully pulled me closer to him, dislodging Zeke's arm. Zeke gave him a shit-eating grin, but he stepped back.

I started stretching while we talked about the Ray incident and eavesdropped on the other team discussing their drama. Damien and Zeke watched me stretch, and I absently pulled my leg up to my shoulder and stretched out my hamstrings. Then I stretched the other one.

I sat on the grass and continued to stretch. The men had gone quiet, and I glanced up to see both of them staring at me.

"How flexible are you?" Zeke asked.

I shrugged. "Pretty flexible."

"Can you do a backbend and the splits?" he pressed.

"Yeah. Can't most people?" I asked.

Zeke looked at me with a funny grin. "You never disappoint me, Har." Then he shook his head at Damien. "Don't fuck it up, asshole. I gotta go, I have shit to do today."

Zeke walked off, and I turned to Damien. "Hey, I came early because I wanted to know if there are any updates about Shanda's case." I held up my hands. "I know the pay is lousy, and it's probably not a priority case for you, but I'm worried about her."

He seemed to shake himself out of whatever he was thinking. "You're right, the pay *is* shitty. But I spent half of Thanksgiving checking out her social media, and I've got a few leads. With the holiday weekend, it's been harder to get a hold of people."

I felt both relief that Damien was taking the case seriously, and frustration that we still hadn't found Shanda.

"Thank you. I owe you."

"I'll trade you a favor," he replied.

I eyed him. "What favor?"

He shrugged. "I don't know yet."

My eyebrows went up, and I folded my arms.

He grinned. "Relax. I'm talking about *work* favors. Sometimes I need help with surveillance or a witness to come with me on a job."

"Hmm, that sounds interesting."

He smiled wryly. "It's not. Surveillance is boring as hell. The favor won't be anything bad, I promise. Your legal background might be useful."

"Of course. I can do that."

"Okay, it's a deal. Your match is starting. When do you want to meet?"

"Is today too soon?" I was getting a little panicked about Shanda.

"Sounds good. How about one o'clock at my office?"

Some of my tension eased. "That would be perfect. Thank you." I started walking backward toward my team, with Gary next to me. "I'll grab some lunch and bring it with me."

He nodded, then folded his arms and watched me walk away.

When I reached my team, Jaime and Tiana smirked at me, and Kevin narrowed his eyes and stared back at Damien.

"What?" I asked. Gary nudged Frankie's hand for a pet.

Tiana pointed at Damien. "That man is hot."

"He's also the one she hit in the face with a volleyball last season," Jaime added helpfully. Jaime was a troublemaker.

Tiana hadn't been at that match, but she'd heard all about it. "Hmm. I'd hit that all right, just not with a volleyball."

Jaime laughed and gave Tiana an underhanded fist bump.

"Lord, help me," I muttered.

Tiana poked her finger at me and then at Damien. "The Lord helps those who help themselves. And I say you should help yourself to some of that."

Chapter 14

We won our volleyball match that morning, mostly because the other team was either still a little drunk or hung over from a bachelor party they'd attended the night before. An autobody shop sponsored the team, and the owner's son was getting married on Sunday.

Most of them bitched and groaned through the match, and one even threw up toward the end of the third set.

Jaime and I watched the poor guy retch.

He wrinkled his nose. "That right there makes me glad I gave up drinking."

After the match, I went home and got cleaned up then assembled a few turkey and avocado sandwiches to take to Damien's office for lunch. I changed my outfits a few times and finally got irritated at myself and just picked something.

When I walked in, Damien stood behind the front counter talking on his cell phone. There wasn't a receptionist today, probably because it was a Saturday. I set the lunch cooler and my laptop on the coffee table and wandered around, then stopped to look at Laurel's photographs again.

Damien got off the phone and walked over. "Hey." He'd cleaned up since the volleyball match. I sniffed him discreetly. He smelled like aftershave and something faintly spicy, and his hair was a bit messy as usual. I mentally reminded myself to keep this professional and friendly.

I pointed at Laurel's photographs. "Laurel and I are going camping in a few weeks with Martina when my sister gets in town. Laurel said she planned to spend some time on the hike taking photographs."

He looked down at me. "I know. She invited us to go along."

"Huh. I didn't know that."

"Do you care if Sebastian goes?"

I shrugged. "No. He's not much of a talker."

He slowly grinned at me. "Do you care if *I* go?"

I hesitated, not because I didn't want him to go but because I liked the idea too much. I shrugged again and smiled back at him. "No. But if you can't keep up or whine, we'll leave you behind. You've been warned."

"So you're more a *Lord of the Flies* hiker than a glamper, huh? That doesn't surprise me."

"It's not that extreme. But no one wants to hike with a whiney complainer."

"Fair enough." He nodded toward the cooler. "What'd you bring for lunch? I expected burgers and fries from a drive-thru."

I wrinkled my nose. "Only if I want to be bloated for the rest of the day. Turkey and avocado sandwiches and fruit. I forgot to ask if you're vegan or vegetarian."

"I'm not, and that sounds good. Thanks."

He grabbed the cooler, and we headed back to the office area. He led me into a good-sized conference room with a sleek modern table and plush chairs.

"We can spread out here," he said and set the cooler down.

I started methodically unpacking it and he grabbed some drinks and plates from the breakroom. I noticed he had nice hands and a quick, efficient way about him. Then I reminded myself again to keep my thoughts contained.

He'd brushed off the hostess at the restaurant on Jonathan's birthday, and she'd been beautiful and perfectly made-up. I was not beautiful, and I needed his help.

We spent the next two hours eating lunch and going through the case, which included Shanda's social media accounts, her subpar home life, and her current situation. Damien studied the only photo I had of Shanda.

"She looks so young."

"She *is* young. She's barely eighteen, and Jason is thirty-two. He has just enough good looks and fake charm to fool young women like her into falling for him."

I thought about my last conversation with Shanda. "I already told you she warned me about him. She said he knows bad people."

Damien looked down at Shanda's photo again and thought for a moment. "Didn't you say she has some kind of license?"

"Yeah. Her stepdad called it a CBD license." I snickered. "But Shanda's mom clarified it's a CNA license. They have a program at her high school."

He raised an eyebrow. "That's not bad for an eighteen-year-old with a shitty home life. Did her mother say whether she planned to use it to get a job?"

"No. She didn't seem concerned about Shanda being gone either. And she knows her husband is using, but she still leaves the two-year-old alone with him for hours."

He shook his head in disgust then leaned back and studied me. "Does your office complex have security cameras or an alarm system?"

I absently rubbed my cheek. "I don't think so. We're in the back of a two-story complex on North Palm Canyon Drive. We didn't put any in, and I haven't noticed any cameras. Sariah does mostly real estate law, and Yun is a commercial contracts attorney. Security didn't cross our minds."

He shook his head. "I don't see those two having clients or business associates who'd be a potential danger."

"I don't either."

"But *you* do criminal defense work. I'm sure you know sometimes attorneys become targets."

I sighed because I knew where he was going. "What're you suggesting?"

"You need cameras and some type of security system. At home and at your work."

It sounded involved and expensive. "Damien, I really don't think it's necessary. There's never been a problem before."

"Humor me, Legs. It would be great if you never needed it. I have time tomorrow." He paused as if weighing his words. "Shanda's stepfather probably told Jason you're looking for Shanda. I'm sure Jason's looking for her too. And it's probable he's watching you to see if you find her."

"I doubt he's that organized."

Damien laid his hand on my forearm. "Harley, if Dickie's right about Jason being a major dealer now and Shanda's right about him being unhinged, we need to do this."

Lunch suddenly felt heavy in my stomach. "Okay. You're right. An ounce of prevention and all that. I'll pay you. Just send me the bill." I cringed inside a little.

"How about you pay my cost for the equipment and owe me another favor for the installation?"

I smiled. "Deal. And thank you."

He looked at my mouth for a few seconds, then slowly grinned.

On Sunday, noon came and went. When I didn't hear from Damien, I assumed he'd either forgotten or gotten sidetracked. But when my doorbell rang around three and I looked through the peephole, he was standing on my porch checking out my neighborhood.

He wore aviator glasses, and his hands rested on his hips. I swallowed a little and took a deep breath. A fit, muscular body was on my short list of favorite things. Damien definitely had one. And then there was the dimple.

Gary looked up at me, probably wondering why I was just standing there staring through the peephole. "What? I can look," I murmured.

Stepping back, I opened the door. "Hey. I didn't know if you still planned to come today." My short blue swimsuit coverup was opaque, but it hung off one shoulder, showing my bikini strap underneath.

Damien eyed me. "One of our security systems at a home in Big Horn went down this morning. Turns out the owner's daughter didn't want her dad spying on her and her friends all weekend, so she took it offline."

I swung the door wide and motioned for him to come in. "Did you get it working again?"

He walked past me into the little entryway and looked around my living space. He set down his toolbox and backpack, then bent down and scratched Gary behind his ears. Gary leaned into his leg, then came back to my side.

My house was small, but cozy. A soft comfortable oatmeal-colored couch took up a good portion of the living room and faced a decent-sized TV. A small potted olive tree sat in the sunniest corner of the room, and a couple of framed photos stood on the entryway table.

I walked over and took a seat on the couch, and Damien followed me over.

He rubbed his face. "I ended up playing referee between my client and his daughter."

I winced. "What happened?"

"They finally agreed to keep the exterior cameras and security system on, but turned off the cameras inside the house and backyard. It was tense for a few minutes though."

"I hate getting in the middle of family issues like that. You should charge hazard pay."

He looked at my muted desert landscape painting and the two mid-century modern architectural prints on my wall. A few work periodicals and a half-finished novel sat on my vintage wood and glass coffee table.

"I like your house. It suits you. Did I interrupt anything?" He looked at my hair twisted in a messy knot on top of my head, and my swimsuit and coverup.

"No. I was just sitting outside with Gary, finishing up some work. Nothing important."

"How long have you had Gary?"

Gary lifted his face off my lap when he heard his name.

"A couple of years." I grimaced. "He's technically Ava's dog, but he prefers me. When Ava first got him, she'd forget to feed and water him sometimes. So I unilaterally re-homed him."

He smirked. "Huh. And your mom lives next door?" He nodded toward her house.

"Yeah. She's probably golfing today."

"I get the impression you two aren't very close. So why do you live next door to her?"

I looked away and thought about how to answer. Damien was becoming my friend, and he'd come to my aid at Jonathan's birthday lunch. So I decided to trust him a little.

"Because she needs family around to help keep her on track. I can pick up on the warning signs better if I see her a few times a week. She's a recovering opioid addict."

Damien didn't flinch or frown. "Is that the 'illness' she referred to the other day?"

"Yes. I guess it is an illness in a way."

He nodded. "I'm sorry. She also said your dad and fiancé died. What happened?"

I studied him. "My dad had a heart attack. It was sudden. I was a sophomore in high school at the time."

"I'm sorry. And your fiancé?"

It had taken a long time to stop wearing my engagement ring. The sharp pain of losing Ryan had ebbed over the years, but I wondered if I could even love someone like that again.

"He died in a car wreck when I was a junior in college." Damien waited for me to expound, but there wasn't much more to say. "Don't feel sorry for me. I've had a good life. When Laurel told me about how her father treats her and her little brothers, I couldn't fathom a dad treating his daughter like that. So I feel lucky all in all."

He watched me. "That's one way to look at it."

"What about your family?" I asked, obviously changing the subject.

"My parents are divorced, but they're both stable. They're good people, and my childhood could have been a lot worse."

"You're right. It could've been." When I started working in the juvenile court, I got involved with some severely dysfunctional families. It'd helped me to be more grateful for my own family, warts and all.

He rubbed Gary's belly absently. "I have a younger brother. He's a building contractor here in town, and we try to get together a couple of times a week."

"You're lucky to have him close by. You know about my younger sister, Olivia. She's finishing up her accounting degree in North Carolina. I had a little brother too, and his name was Theo.

But he died when he was eleven months old. They think it was SIDS."

I absently ran my finger over the small scar on my cheek. I'd always wondered if Ava's addiction had somehow contributed to Theo's death.

Olivia had only been seven years old when Theo was born, and she didn't have many memories of him. But I remembered him well. He had soft, curly blond hair and big cheeks that none of us could resist.

He loved me almost as much as he loved my dad, and he'd sit in my arms and look up at me with his big, round baby eyes and just stare at me while I fed him a bottle. When he died, we were devastated.

Damien reached over and squeezed my hand, bringing me back to the present. "I'm sorry about your brother too. Is your sister going to move here when she graduates?"

I shrugged. "Probably. She talks about it. And we're close, so it would be nice. I feel lucky, except maybe when it comes to the men in my life."

He straightened. "Men in your life?"

"Yeah. My dad, my fiancé, and my little brother. I'm like a death harbinger or something. If I love someone, they tend to die." I looked away, embarrassed. I'd never admitted that to anyone before and hadn't meant to share.

Damien studied me. "Zeke was in the service."

I nodded. "Laurel told me."

"You might want to talk to Zeke about survivor's guilt sometime." There were shadows in Damien's eyes too, and I wondered what put them there.

"Maybe. Putting a label on our heartbreak doesn't lessen it though." Suddenly, I felt too vulnerable and stood up. "Thank you for coming over on a Sunday. Let me go change and we can get started."

I sat on my bed for a moment. Talking with Damien had dredged up feelings and memories I usually kept buried, and I needed a moment to tuck them away again.

We went over to my office building first, and Damien installed two cameras there. When we first walked in, I saw him looking around at the reception area that had a couple of antique book-shelves interspersed with legal books and curiosities, a handwoven rug, and leather armchairs in the waiting area.

Our sign hung behind the reception desk. My office was a lit-tle more spartan, but Yun had found a striking orange blossom painting, and I'd bought a beautiful albeit used desk and credenza set at an estate sale.

Damien gazed around. "I like your office."

I smiled. "Thanks, I liked yours too. It has a nice feel to it."

He flew through the installation and set-up process and helped me position the cameras. Then we headed back to my house and installed two more cameras there. It was getting dark, so we de-cided to install the security system another day.

I turned to Damien as we were finishing up. "I have chicken kabobs marinating, naan bread, and zucchini I plan to grill for dinner. I have enough for two if you're hungry."

He glanced down at me. His arms were raised above his head, and he was screwing in the camera mount. His biceps and abs were stretched out on full display.

Damien grinned when he caught me looking. "You sure?"

I pulled my eyes off his torso, swallowing a little. "Yes. Consider it part of my payback. No worries if you have things to do."

He climbed off the stepladder. "That sounds good. Do you have kabobs marinating already? And you grill? I'm impressed."

"Why? You don't plan ahead, or you don't own a grill?" I asked.

He shrugged. "I own a grill because I'm a normal red-blooded male. But I rarely plan ahead enough to use it."

"Grilling is fast, the food tastes great, and clean-up is easy. The perfect combination. You just have to go to the grocery store occasionally."

"If you say so."

I grinned. "I do. And so do the millions of other red-blooded *females* who own grills. I'm a mediocre cook though."

We walked out to my back patio, and he checked out my newer ocean-blue Weber grill. It matched the cushions on my patio loungers. I turned on the propane tank and lit the burners, then rubbed the already clean grate with a wire brush. He watched me go through the process.

"Huh. You do know how to grill."

I raised my eyebrow and pointed the wire brush at him. "Don't be a chauvinist."

He chuckled and pulled on a piece of my hair that had slipped out of my topknot. "I'm just yanking your chain."

I reached around him and grabbed the little remote on the side table, then turned on the outdoor café lights.

He looked around. "This is a nice spot."

Damien wandered over and took in my little spool and backyard area. Tall hedges grew around the perimeter, and the small potted lemon and orange trees gave off a citrusy smell. The space had a vintage Palm Springs poolside feel to it.

"Thanks, I think so too. It's a nice place to recharge." It felt a little strange having someone besides my family share my favorite spot. "Where do you live?" I asked.

"In south Palm Springs in the bench area. Luckily I bought the house not too long after I moved here. I have a spa and a separate pool, but it's a pain in the ass to heat in the winter."

I smiled. "The one advantage of my little spool is it does heat quickly. And it has nice jets."

He squatted down and felt the water. "You were heating it when I came over, weren't you?"

"Yes. But I can use it tomorrow."

Damien stood up. "You should get in after we eat."

"You're welcome to soak after dinner with me if you'd like. But I don't have any men's swimsuits." I extended the invitation before I realized what I'd done, and I wasn't sure if I wanted him to say yes or no.

He grinned. "I'd love to. I have shorts in my workout bag in my truck if you're not comfortable with me going commando."

I nodded vigorously. "That would probably be better."

He grinned. "For now."

My stomach fluttered, and I cleared my throat. "Would you like a beer or some wine? I'm going to start grilling."

"Beer for me. I'll help you." He put his hand on the small of my back as we walked inside, and I shivered at the contact.

We puttered around fixing dinner together and talking. He set up my little portable speaker and put on a mellow jazz playlist from his phone. I brought out a cold bottle of beer for him and a glass of wine for me, and we sipped while we grilled. Then we ate on the patio.

"Thanks, Legs. This chicken is damn good, and I've never grilled zucchini before. What'd you sprinkle on it?"

"Chile lime seasoning. It's not too spicy, and it has a nice flavor."

"Do you grill out here often?" he asked.

"Yeah."

He looked at me intently and took a pull of his beer. "By yourself?"

"Yes. Sometimes Olivia's in town, or I have Ava over. And occasionally Grace and Sheila."

"No men, or a boyfriend?"

I looked over at him and put my wine glass down carefully. "No. I guess you already know that, thanks to Ava."

Gary nudged me right then and reminded me about his dinner. I jumped up to feed him, grateful for the interruption. He ate, then came back out and laid down by my feet.

We cleaned up, and I grabbed a couple of towels and showed Damien where the guest bathroom was. I changed back into my swimsuit, and when I walked out to the backyard, Damien was standing there in his workout shorts with his towel in his hand.

He had defined abdominals and a firm, tight ass. I swallowed again and hoped I could keep my eyes to myself.

Damien turned to me and slowly grinned. "Nice suit, Legs. You look like a 1950s pinup model." His eyes swept me up and down.

I had on a green bikini with boyshort bottoms. I shifted restlessly. "Thanks." I led the way out to the spool, feeling his eyes bore into my backside the entire way.

Damien groaned when the jets hit his back. "Holy shit, you weren't kidding. Your jets have great pressure."

I positioned myself so one hit me just right then leaned back with a soft sigh. "When I have a particularly rough day, which is usually after juvenile drug court, I'll come out here in the evening with a margarita to decompress."

The night was cool, and a little steam wafted up from the spool and swirled around us. It felt intimate and cozy. Damien asked me about juvenile drug court, and we talked about his work. Before I knew it, we'd been in the spool for over an hour.

When we finally got out, and he got ready to leave, I walked him to the door.

"Thank you again for your help with Shanda's case, and the security equipment and installation. Maybe Ava will quit nagging me about being a criminal defense attorney now."

Damien shook his head. "I doubt it, but you should be a little safer. I'll call you this week sometime to finish up. Thanks for dinner, and the soak."

It had been a good night, and I felt less lonely when I went to bed that night. I also dreamed about hard, wet abs and gray eyes.

Chapter 15

By the time juvenile drug court wrapped up on Tuesday afternoon, my left eye was twitching. I also wanted to kick Roland in his ass. He was my biggest repeat offender, and he'd really outdone himself this time.

Christian, the juvenile prosecutor, let us know about Roland's birthday party over the weekend when we got to our staffing meeting. Roland and a few of his friends had celebrated his sixteenth birthday in style.

They'd used a parent's credit card to rent a motel room, and they'd gotten a hold of a few kegs of beer and a couple of bags of edibles. Then one of his friends got the bright idea to hire escorts.

Christian, the prosecutor, reviewed the probable cause statement out loud during the drug court staffing meeting while pinching the bridge of his nose. When he finished, he tossed the report down on the table in front of him.

"I couldn't make this shit up if I tried. Honestly, I'd probably be laughing my ass off right now, if I weren't so pissed at the little shit."

Judge Perez's lips twitched. "I can tell you're mad because you've sworn three or four times in the last two sentences." He looked over at me. "The charges are pending, so we can't fully address it today."

Christian shook his head. "I have no idea how they figured out how to hire escorts."

I shrugged. "They're teenagers. Most of them know how to navigate the internet better than any of us do."

"I heard one escort knew right away the boys were underage, and she's the one who called in an anonymous tip," Wendy added.

My week was already full of new clients. Thanksgiving weekend had been eventful for a lot of people.

Judge Perez turned to me. "What do you want to do today?"

"There's nothing I *can* do. I doubt my client's been served the Petition, and I haven't seen the police report. I need to talk to him about the charges and get his side of the story."

He nodded. "We'll have to table it for today, and just let him know we're aware of the alleged incident."

Pauley, the drug court coordinator, leaned forward and smacked his hand on the table. "He needs to be removed from his mother's care since she obviously can't handle him. And he needs to spend at least a week in jail."

I was not in the mood to deal with Pauley's bullshit. "He has a presumption of innocence, Pauley. And we've talked about how incarcerating minors does not deter behavior so many times I'm not going to insult everyone by spouting it off again."

"Thank you for sparing us," Christian muttered.

Wendy scooted forward. "Pauley, DCFS can't remove every unruly teenager from his or her parents' care. We'd be overrun."

We finally moved on to the other drug court participants.

Wendy looked down at the next name on the list. "Darla's dad reported to me yesterday that while Darla hates mowing lawns and trimming bushes, she likes having money."

I smirked. "Don't we all."

"He told me that after she stopped bitching so much, she's turned into a decent worker," Wendy continued.

Judge Perez nodded. "And no new incidents or issues. Pauley's treatment team indicates she's been testing clean and appears to be adequately engaged in treatment."

He looked up over his reading glasses at Pauley who was shaking his head.

Judge Perez waylaid Pauley. "I'll take adequate any day. Perfection isn't the standard." That was one of his signature sayings, and I'd always agreed with him. Hell, none of us were perfect.

We continued through the rest of the participants, then the bailiff brought my clients and their parents into the courtroom, and we started the drug court hearing. It was shaping up to be a tequila Tuesday, and a homemade margarita was calling my name.

After drug court and a long tense conversation with Roland, I walked out of the courthouse feeling tired and annoyed. My cell phone vibrated, and I pulled it out to see a text from Damien.

Damien: Do you want to finish the installation tonight?

I expected the usual flash of irritation when someone interrupted my quiet evening. Instead, anticipation zinged through me. That instinctive reaction probably wasn't good for my heart, but I didn't care right then. It had been a lousy day.

Me: Yes. 6ish okay? And do you want to grill again?

Damien: 6 is good. Yes, to grilling. I'll bring drinks and dessert.

I stopped by the store to grab a couple of pork chops and some salad ingredients on my way home. We'd decided on a wireless security system for my house, and Damien said it would be easy to install.

Gary met me at the door, and I put my groceries away, changed my clothes, and took him for a walk.

Damien knocked on the door not long after we got back. He had a six-pack of beer, a bottle of wine, and a large turtle brownie from my favorite bakery.

I smiled up at him. "Hey. How was your day?"

He tucked the wine under his arm and gave Gary a rub when he stepped inside. "We installed two security systems, caught one cheating spouse, and found the person stealing from a cannabis dispensary in Indio. All in all, it was a good day."

I held up my hand. "Let me guess. The thief was an employee, and you caught it on camera. Probably a camera your company installed."

"Exactly." He sounded like a proud parent. We walked into the kitchen area, and he perched on a stool at my kitchen bar. "I also found a few leads on Shanda."

I stopped short. "You did? What'd you find out? Tell me!"

He grinned and shook his head at my impatience. "I tracked down a couple of her friends through her social media. They said they hadn't seen her but would put the word out for me."

"Okay, that's good. Anything else?"

"I spoke with a couple of her high school instructors, and her CNA instructor specifically. She could work in a nursing home or an assisted living center with her certificate, and they're always looking for people. The pay is probably shit, but it might be better than a fast-food restaurant."

I bit my lip. "But where has she been living?"

"No one knows. And as you're aware, if she misses her next court date, the judge will likely issue a bench warrant against her."

Shanda worried me, and I didn't know how to help her.

He leaned over and grabbed my hand. "There's nothing else we can do tonight. Let's install your system." Damien picked up his toolbox and the security system still in its packaging and started pulling it out.

I sighed, a little deflated. "I'm going to make margaritas to go with the beer and wine. It was a rough day in juvenile drug court. Do you want one?"

He eyed me. "What flavor?"

"What *flavor*? The only flavor worth making. Lime of course."

"Laurel and Martina prefer the fruitier versions. Like mango, strawberry, or peach."

"No, no, and *peach*?" I made a face. "I need to talk to Laurel. Traditional, old-school margaritas are the best." I ticked off the ingredients on my fingers. "Lime juice, triple sec, silver tequila—or occasionally mezcal. And Grand Marnier if I'm celebrating. That's it. The end."

He grinned. "Sounds good."

"Is on the rocks with a little salt on the rim okay?" I asked as I walked to the fridge.

"Perfect. Thanks."

While I made margaritas, Damien installed the main panel close to the front door. Then he went through the house installing sensors on all the openings.

I showed him my second bedroom, which was set up as an office with a double bed, and then my bedroom so he could install sensors on my patio door in there.

My bed was covered with a fluffy white waffle duvet and soft throw pillows. A small lemon Cyprus tree stood in the corner.

It was strange seeing Damien in my room as he gazed around and took it in. There hadn't been a man here since my furniture had been delivered a few years ago.

He turned to me and his lip quirked in a smile. "Nice bedroom, Legs."

Those three words sent my heart rate skyrocketing. "Thanks. I'll, uh, leave you to it."

I went outside and fired up the grill, then made dinner and slowly got myself under control. By the time he was done installing the sensors, the pork chops were done.

I motioned to Damien. "Dinner's ready. And again, thank you."

"My pleasure. And it smells delicious."

He grabbed my little wireless speaker, this time putting on some vapor soul music. We gathered the plates and drinks and walked out to the back patio. While we ate and sipped margaritas, I told him about drug court that day, and Roland's birthday weekend.

He laughed and shook his head. "That's a birthday he'll never forget. And they hired escorts? The kid has some balls."

"Yeah, it's funny if you're not the little shit's parent. Or his public defender, or drug court judge."

"I'm not his parent or his public defender, so I *can* laugh. And they were busted by an escort." He chuckled again and took a bite of pork chop.

I shook my head. "I'm sure the police officers who responded got a good laugh out of it too."

"This is delicious. Where'd you learn to cook like this?"

"My dad and I used to grill together a lot. I like grilling and puttering around in the kitchen. It's therapeutic." I jerked my shoulder.

"My therapy is playing or watching sports and working out. Are you going to the gym tomorrow?"

"No. I usually go on Mondays and Thursdays. Then I try to take Gary out for a run or a hike over the weekend. What days do you go?"

"Either Monday or Tuesday, depending on how busy Mondays are. Then Thursday and Saturday mornings. Sebastian's been missing a lot of Saturday mornings recently though."

I smirked. "Gee, I wonder why?"

"Yeah, I'd miss a few Saturday mornings if I were him too."

His comment sent an unexpected spear of jealousy through me. I didn't like it and tried to push it away.

"Ditto," I said casually.

He narrowed his eyes.

I cleared my throat. "My practice is busy, so I'm trying to get an earlier start in the mornings."

He stood up with his empty plate. "Sounds good. I'll race you on the treadmill on Thursday."

"Just don't hog the thigh master machines and we'll be fine."

Chapter 16

In retrospect, I should have gone to check on Frankie when she didn't show up for the last volleyball match or for drug court that Thursday. At our practice at the beginning of the season, I should have taken her tired eyes and weight loss more seriously and been less distracted with other things. But the clarity of hindsight can be cruel sometimes.

On Thursday morning I went to the gym. It was a beautiful morning and Kurt, the owner, had opened an overhead sliding door built into the exterior wall of the gym to let in the air and sun.

Kurt's golden retriever, Jack, got up and walked over to me, his tail wagging.

"Hi, guys. How's my good boy, huh?" I'd grabbed one of Gary's dog treats on the way out of the house, and I pulled it out of my pocket. "Can I give him a treat?"

Kurt smiled. "Yeah. But you're already his favorite member. You don't have to bring him treats too."

I squatted down and gave Jack the treat and a good scratch behind his ears. "I'm also his favorite because I give the best big boy pets. Don't I, you handsome guy?"

Jack gave a happy whine. I heard someone clear his throat behind me, and I glanced back.

Damien grinned down at me. "You give the best big boy pets, huh? Good to know."

I shook my head and straightened up. A man stood beside Damien, and by his build and facial structure, I could tell it was his brother.

"Don't finish that thought, Dimples. Or I'll put another ball in your face."

The man beside Damien went from grinning to laughing. "Wouldn't that usually be the other way around? And wouldn't it be two balls?"

I didn't look at his brother but kept staring at Damien. "He's your brother, isn't he? I can tell because he's got the same smart-ass mouth and smirky grin."

Damien grinned, and it was the exact grin I'd just been talking about.

He motioned to his brother. "This is Brock. Brock, this is Harley."

I finally looked at Brock. He wore a tight black t-shirt with a worn BA Construction logo across the front. He held out his hand, and I slowly reached out and shook it.

My eyes widened. "Oh Lord, you've also got a dimple."

Damien leaned over and murmured in my ear. "He's a troublemaker, Legs. Do us both a favor and don't start calling him Dimples too."

"We have history, and you earned that nickname. Don't worry." I patted Damien's chest.

Brock studied me. "Are you two colleagues, friends, a thing? What?"

I stayed silent. Brock was Damien's brother, so he could deal with him.

Damien glanced at Brock. "As far as you're concerned, all the above."

I raised my eyebrows but didn't contradict Damien. Maybe Brock was a player and Damien felt protective of me. Or maybe because we were working together, Damien didn't want things to get awkward.

Brock let out an exaggerated sigh. "Okay, then." He pointed a finger at me. "Let me know if anything changes."

I blinked in surprise. Brock was about the same height as Damien, a little leaner, and he had light brown hair instead of dark blond. He also had the same angular face and sharp jawline. They were both extremely good-looking. There must have been some good genes in that family.

Damien growled and Brock laughed. Whatever. I was an ass to my sister sometimes too.

I tilted my head toward the treadmills. "Let's go get our sweat on."

Damien and I ended up trying to race on the treadmills, then we lifted weights, and I did some strength training while they bench pressed and ribbed each other. It was one of the more enjoyable workouts I'd had in a while.

By the end of the day, my happy workout buzz was long gone. Just like juvenile drug court earlier in the week, felony adult drug court didn't go well. I understood the stresses and triggers of the holiday season for people in recovery. But we were barely into December and almost half my adult drug court clients had relapsed or missed a urinalysis test, also known as a UA. By the end of the day, I just wanted to go home, lounge on my couch with Gary, and watch a mindless movie with a big glass of wine.

Kevin and Josh from my volleyball team were still doing well, thank God, but Frankie hadn't shown up for drug court. She'd also missed her treatment sessions and UAs since late last week. I was afraid she'd relapsed or was actively using again.

When I walked out of the courthouse that afternoon, I called Frankie. She didn't answer, so I called her mother. She didn't answer either, so I left a voice message.

Then I texted Jaime and Tiana and asked if they'd heard or knew anything about her. I felt guilty for reaching out to them, but they had better contacts than I did.

On Friday, Laurel brought Martina with her to our Friday potluck luncheon with my law partners. Martina brought tres leches cake, a bottle of tequila, and a lime as her contribution. Sariah scrounged around in the community breakroom and found little packets of salt.

It seemed like I wasn't the only one who'd had a rough week, and after a couple of shots, we were all good and buzzed.

"So, you're Sebastian's cousin?" I asked Martina with one eye closed. Laurel had just mentioned that fact, and I was having a hard time processing it.

"Uh-huh," she drawled out.

I stared at her some more, then shook my head. "I can't picture it. You're nice, and funny, and friendly." And crazy, but I wasn't buzzed enough to say that out loud.

Laurel laughed. "I said basically the same thing when Sebastian told me."

"What's the deal with you and Damien?" Martina asked.

"What? Why do you ask? Nothing."

Yun and Sariah both perked up.

"Who's Damien?" Sariah asked.

I dug into my cake. "No one."

Yun slapped the table. "Harley hasn't dated one guy since she moved to Palm Springs. Not one." She stuck her index finger in my face.

Laurel grinned and put her elbows on the table. "Do you know how they met?"

I leaned back and looked up at the ceiling. "Oh, God. Here we go."

For the next fifteen minutes, Martina and Laurel told Yun and Sariah about how Damien and I first met, how hot he was, and how cute we'd be together. I wanted to bang my head against the conference table. Luckily Sariah's husband stopped by, and the party broke up.

I knew it was a brief reprieve because Laurel and Martina had invited me over for dinner that night so we could plan our camping trip. After metabolizing the tequila shots by taking Gary on a long walk and drinking lots of water, I got cleaned up for the evening and made crispy broccolini with bacon bits as my contribution to dinner. I felt tired and a little sluggish, but I'd done it to myself by drinking in the middle of the day.

When I got to Laurel's house, Damien's white Ford Raptor was parked outside along with a couple of other vehicles. When I rang the doorbell, a kid around four or five years old answered the door. He wore a red cape, and nothing else.

"Well, hello. What kind of superhero are you supposed to be?" I asked.

Laurel rushed into the foyer. "Lennie, you still have to wear pants, even if you have a cape on." She sounded exasperated, like she'd told him this a thousand times.

Another boy, who looked a lot like Lennie except with straight hair, ran into the foyer. He had on a kickass cowboy hat. "Yeah, Lennie. We can still see your winky, remember?" he yelled. "Mom said if we can see your winky, you don't got enough clothes on."

"But I don't like the way clothes feel on my winky," Lennie whined. He looked up at me, silently pleading for support.

"Hey, Lennie, I'm Harley. I don't have a winky, but I've heard some guys don't like to cover theirs either."

His brother walked up and stood next to Lennie. "I'm Willie." He put his hand on my leg and looked up at me with innocent blue eyes. "Have *you* seen a lot of winkies?"

I tried to suck in my startled laugh and choked a little. His name made our discussion about winkies that much more unfortunate.

I looked at Laurel for help, but she just held up her hands. I noticed Damien standing in the foyer entryway leaning against the wall. He was also trying not to laugh. I shot them both a dirty look.

Clearing my throat, I looked down at the twins. "No, Willie, I haven't. People's private places are important and... private." Okay, that was lame. "And should be treated respectfully."

"Yeah, Laurel told us about our private squares. It's a private circle though," Lennie answered, gesturing in a circle around his waist area.

"Nuh-uh, they're private triangles," Willie contradicted loudly.

I stared at Laurel. The conversation had gotten completely away from me. Damien was still struggling not to laugh. He was no help and this was a serious conversation, so I ignored him. I set my bags down on the entryway table to use my hands.

"You can call it your private circle or triangle, but the rhyme doesn't work as well. 'Stop, don't touch me there. That is my private *square*' is easier to remember. And if you ever need to say it to anyone, you should shout it."

Lennie gazed up at me. "Willie's loud, he can do that."

"You can too, Lennie. Like this." I put my hands up in a dramatic gesture. "Stop, don't touch me there. That is my private square!" I shouted and gestured to my private square.

Damien covered his mouth and was turning a little red from trying not to laugh. Damn him. Martina, Sebastian, and Zeke came in from the kitchen to see what was going on.

Martina looked around. "What're you guys doing in here? It sounds way more exciting than what's going on in the kitchen."

Laurel motioned to the twins. "Harley's talking with the boys about what to do if anyone ever touches them somewhere that makes them feel uncomfortable."

"Ah," Martina drawled out. "That's pretty important to know."

I nodded. "It kind of came up in our conversation. I'm not exactly sure how that happened, but it *is* important. Remember, the louder the better."

They stared up at me and nodded.

Laurel finally stepped in. "Your mom will be here any minute, so go get your stuff. And Lennie, put your pants back on."

"Bye, Harley." Lennie patted my leg, and they took off running.

"Bye!" I called after them.

Sebastian shook his head in disgust. "It took three or four months for Lennie to purposefully stop fucking up my name. And it takes you five minutes."

I picked up my bags and shrugged. "They look at me a little differently, I think. And *I'm* not trying to get into Laurel's private square."

Martina laughed and Laurel blushed beet red.

Zeke grinned. "Laurel, you're going to tell us exactly what we missed. Because that last part was funny."

She nodded. "When Boo and Lennie leave, I'll fill you in."

"I can hardly wait," I said unenthusiastically.

Then Damien started laughing too and walked over to wrap his arm around my neck. "Legs, that wasn't just funny, that was fucking hilarious."

When the boys left, we took our dinner outside to enjoy Laurel's beautiful back patio. It was one of the most inviting backyards I'd ever seen. The soft lighting climbing up the tall palm trees gave the area a soft, warm glow. The big loungers with black and white striped cushions and the assortment of pool toys made me think they spent a lot of time out here.

Laurel looked at me. "Harley, you said your sister gets in town next Thursday. So I propose we go that Friday or Saturday night."

Damien raised his hand. "Zeke, Harley, and I have rec volleyball on Saturday mornings. So Saturday around noon would work better."

Laurel nodded. "Then we'll go next Saturday."

"Joshua Tree would be a good choice. Or we can go to the San Jacinto wilderness area. It'll be cold in mid-December though," Damien said.

I sipped my wine and nodded. "Olivia and I are happy to go anywhere, but she's never been to Joshua Tree, so that might be good for her first time."

"I can get the permit," Zeke volunteered.

Leaning back, I could feel Damien's arm draped across the back of my chair. I cleared my throat. "One of these days I'd like to go to Zion National Park or maybe the Grand Canyon. Or even Moab."

Damien had mentioned he and Zeke liked to mountain bike.

Zeke grinned enthusiastically. "I'd take a week off for a trip like that."

"Getting back to *this* trip," Martina interrupted. "If all goes well, and no one wants to kill each other by the end, I'd love to do something like that."

Sebastian smiled. "Yeah, we used to take some fun road trips with our cousin, Matías."

Martina gave Sebastian a disgusted look. "I still haven't forgotten when you and Matías left me at the hotel room in Venice Beach while you took off with those two big-boobed college girls on spring break."

Sebastian winced. "I know you haven't forgotten. You still bring it up, and it's been eight or nine years."

Laurel patted his chest. "He's trying to do better."

Sebastian gathered Laurel in his arms and kissed the side of her neck. "*Cielo*, I have done better. I've got you."

I smiled at them, but my heart still ached a little for what I'd lost years ago.

Chapter 17

We were scheduled to play Damien and Zeke's team at ten that morning. It was our first match of the season against them, and I wanted to win so badly I could taste it. I sent out a text to my team an hour before the game, telling them if we won I'd take them all to Norma Jean's Café for breakfast afterward. If bribery got us the win, I was perfectly fine with that.

I thought my braids looked especially intimidating, and I was mentally ready. I'd eaten my go-to pregame breakfast of wheat toast and a fruit smoothie, and on the way to the park, my pump-up playlist was blaring. I'd also turned off my phone to cut down on any distractions before the match.

At the park, when I pulled into the parking lot, I noticed most of my team was already there. They were huddled together talking. As I walked across the lawn, I noticed Kevin look up and spot me. He spoke to Jaime and pointed at me.

Jaime's face was somber, and I realized with a jolt he'd never looked at me without a smile, a smirk, or even a cocky wink before.

Looking back, somewhere in my subconsciousness I must have known something was wrong. Jaime gazed down at the ground for a moment, almost like he was praying or gathering courage, and then started walking toward me.

I noticed out of the corner of my eye Damien watching on the other side of the net. Jaime finally stood in front of me, blocking my path.

"Harley…" He stopped, then took hold of both my arms.

The look on his face frightened me. "Jaime, what's wrong?"

"You texted me about Frankie. *Dios*, there's no easy way to tell you this." He closed his eyes.

I dropped my bag and water bottle then grabbed the front of his shirt. "Jaime, what happened?" I whispered.

He looked at me and laid it out. "She overdosed on Thursday night. Her mom found her in the bathroom. They think she took a dose similar to what she'd been taking before she got clean." Jaime swallowed. "She's gone."

I shook my head and let go of him, then stepped back. I absently noticed my hands shaking.

"No," I said softly.

"Yes. Harley. She's gone."

I slowly folded over and clutched my stomach.

"No. No!" My team came over and stood around me.

I looked up at their faces, hoping this was some sick, fucking joke. Tiana had tears running down her face, and Josh appeared to be in shock. Kevin was clenching his jaw and looked like he wanted to punch someone.

Tiana pulled me up, then put her arms around me. "Honey, it's gonna be okay. She was struggling. Every day was a struggle for that girl." She wrapped her arms around me and whispered in my ear. "She's finally at peace, Harley. She's free."

"Why, Tiana? Why? She was amazing and sweet. And kind. She didn't have a mean bone in her body." We were both crying. "Why?" I softly wailed.

Tiana let go of me, and I felt strong arms wrap around my torso. Josh hugged Tiana while she cried.

"I've got her." Somewhere in my mind I registered it was Damien who held me.

Jaime stepped forward. "I need to get her out of here. She's taking it hard."

Damien eyed him. "She's mine, Jaime. I've got her. Can you help Zeke get her Sequoia back to her house? She's in no shape to drive."

I watched through a haze of tears and pain as Jaime studied Damien, then finally nodded. "Yeah, man. Whatever she needs."

Everything seemed to be hazy, and I couldn't process what people were saying. I was probably going into shock.

Johanna, one of the women from Damien's team, stepped up and wordlessly handed Tiana and me a wad of tissues. Jaime put his arm around Tiana and walked her over to a nearby bench.

"Thank you, Johanna," I whispered. She seemed startled I knew her name. My face crumpled again, and more tears escaped. I turned into Damien's arms and buried my face in his neck.

"Come on, sweetheart. I'm taking you home with me." He turned me toward his truck, and I followed him blindly, feeling numb with shock and grief. Frankie had been different. She'd been innocent and kind, and she'd gotten under my skin and through my defenses.

Damien unlocked his truck and helped me into the passenger seat. Zeke followed us over and squatted down next to me. "I'm sorry as hell, Harley. She seemed like a good person."

"Thanks, Zeke. She was."

"I have your bag and your water bottle here. If you trust me, I'll drive your Sequoia home and Jaime will bring me back here to pick up my truck."

I nodded and looked at my bag for a second. My brain was sluggish, but I focused and slowly dug inside to find my keys.

"Thank you. Will you check on Gary while you're there? I'm sure he's fine…" I didn't finish.

Damien spoke up. "She's got a security system you'll need to disarm. I'll text you the code."

Zeke looked at Damien. "Did you install it?"

"Yeah."

"Good." Zeke stood up. "I'll talk to you later. Hang in there, honey."

When Damien got in, he turned to me. "I'm taking you to my place, Legs."

I nodded and turned my head away to stare out the passenger window as tears slowly leaked out. I watched the landscape go by and thought about Frankie. Damien finally reached over and squeezed my hand. I squeezed his back, then held on tight the rest of the way.

When we pulled up, I saw a white mid-century ranch house with a small accessory rental tucked to the side. I didn't take in many details beyond that.

Damien came around and opened the truck door for me. I slid out and he reached in and grabbed my bag, then led me into the house. He set my bag down in his living room and gathered me in his arms. I cried for a few more minutes, then pulled away and looked up at him.

"Thank you for taking care of me. You don't need to babysit me though, I'm sure you have things to do. I'll be all right, it just hit me hard."

"I want to, sweetheart."

Looking down at his jersey, I noticed the wet spots on it from crying on him. "Frankie was technically just my drug court client and teammate. But…" I swallowed.

"I know. You spiked a ball in my face when I insulted her last season, remember?"

Smiling a little through my tears, I nodded. "Yeah, I remember."

"Let's go outside to the backyard. It's not as homey as yours, but it's a nice spot."

"Okay."

We walked outside, and he led me over to an outdoor sofa and moved some pillows. He pulled me down next to him, and I curled my legs up then leaned against his shoulder. The sofa rocked, and Damien slowly pushed it back and forth when we'd settled.

"Talk to me," he said after a few minutes. "Tell me about Frankie and your other teammates. And why you do public defense and drug court work."

So I did. I told him about Frankie and how she seemed to be progressing in her treatment and recovery—until she wasn't. How kind and soft-hearted she was, and how everyone seemed to love her. I told him about the constant highs and lows of drug court.

Then Damien talked about his time on the police force and why he'd decided to quit and go into private practice.

He shook his head. "It was frustrating. I did it for seven years and made detective while I was there, but I was already burned out. Then I got pushed over the edge. I had a girlfriend until just before I quit too."

While we talked, I slowly undid my braids and let my hair down. Damien watched, then he wrapped his arm around me and ran his hand through my hair and down my neck. It felt like heaven.

"What happened with your girlfriend? Was it serious?"

He glanced away and I could tell he didn't like talking about her. "Yeah, it was serious. And she's another reason I quit."

"What did she have to do with you quitting?"

"Not a lot. But when we first started seeing each other, she swore she could handle me being on the force."

"I can hear a 'but' coming."

He smiled faintly. "*But* the hours were long, and I probably wasn't great company after a stressful shift. She finally told me I either needed to quit and go find another career, or she'd leave and go back to Los Angeles."

"I'm confused. You aren't on the force anymore, but your girlfriend isn't around from what I can tell. What happened?"

"I'm not a big fan of ultimatums; that's not how relationships should work. So I broke it off, and then I quit the force not long after that."

I shook my head. "I agree about ultimatums, but I bet that stung a little."

"There were other issues. My friends also didn't like her. That was probably the biggest red flag. She was angry when she found out I'd quit." He shrugged. "But by then I didn't give a fuck."

"If you didn't quit because of her, why did you?" I asked.

"I was frustrated, and the pay was shit. We'd go to the same houses in the same neighborhoods three or four times a month. And nothing would change. We were always arresting the same people for the same charges, and nothing seemed to get better. It felt like *Groundhog Day* sometimes."

Patting his knee, I nodded. "I get it. I struggle with the same thing."

He studied the skyline. "There was one perpetrator who kept beating the shit out of his wife and two little kids. But his wife would never press charges. This happened maybe five or six times."

"Oh, God. I hate it when little kids are involved."

Damien nodded. "I got to know those kids from going over to their house so much. The little girl would run up and grab my pinkie finger then pull me over to her mom, like she expected me to fix whatever was broken."

"What happened?" I asked, dreading the answer but needing to know.

He sighed heavily and ran his fingers through his hair. "I was called out to a homicide case involving a little three-year-old. It was her. He'd beaten her to death for crying too much." I suddenly knew where the shadows in his eyes came from.

I squeezed his hand and laid my head on his shoulder. "I'm so sorry."

He squeezed my hand back. We sat in silence for a few minutes.

Damien leaned back. "Zeke was coming back from a deployment, and he planned to leave the military. We've been best friends since middle school."

"You two seem to know each other pretty well."

He nodded. "He wanted to start a business that complemented our backgrounds, and Sebastian was good with security systems and low-tech voltage."

"It sounds like a good arrangement."

"Yeah, it has been, and we're all doing well." He reached out to take a lock of my hair between his fingers. "What about you? Are you happy with your work?"

I didn't have to think about it. "Yes, and my two office mates are as well. There's a lot to be said for being your own boss."

The soft tug on my hair from him playing with it felt soothing. A breeze kicked up, and I could smell the sage in his yard. I felt a little more grounded since hearing about Frankie's death.

"When I have clients who relapse or re-offend. Or die..." I swallowed. "It's hard, I need to keep a better emotional distance. Jaime says I'm shit at it."

His lips tipped up. "He's right, you are."

"I'm offended," I said in mock anger.

He smiled, then put his arm around me. "That's one of the things I admire about you. You remind me of Don Quixote, fighting against windmills. Except you're a hot, blond female. But you're both tall."

"Don Quixote, huh? Wasn't he delusional and crazy? Thanks."

He winked and kept playing with my hair.

I sighed and rested my head against his shoulder. "After my dad died, I felt so overwhelmed and alone." I turned to look at him. "Maybe I want other people who feel isolated and alone to know someone understands and cares, and they aren't alone. Does that make sense?"

"Yeah." He softly kissed the top of my head.

We talked for another half hour, then we sat in silence until I drifted off, the warmth of Damien's body along my side lulling me to sleep. When I woke up a little while later, my head lay in his lap, and he absently stroked my shoulder. It felt so good, I couldn't find it in me to be embarrassed.

He looked down at me when he felt me stir. "Hey."

"Hey, yourself." I sat up and stretched, then sat back and examined his backyard. There were several long thin palm trees around the perimeter and a fence with tall Mexican fence post cactus running along the sides. A trimmed Ficus hedge along the backyard gave the yard privacy, and created a quiet, soothing space.

"This is wonderful. And your mountain views are stunning."

Damien smiled. "Thanks. That was one of the reasons I bought it."

I glanced at him. "You'd make a great therapist if you ever want to quit your day job. Thank you."

He squeezed my hand. "I'll take that under advisement. And you're welcome. You ready for lunch? I enjoyed our grilled dinners at your house so much I stocked up on a few groceries."

"Really?"

He nodded. "I have chicken breasts, asparagus, and a loaf of sourdough bread, if that sounds good to you." He stood up.

"That sounds wonderful. I didn't know crying could make me so hungry."

Damien walked over and started his grill, then we prepared a late lunch together in his sleek modern kitchen. We ate out on his back patio in comfortable silence.

Before Damien took me home, I called the adult drug court treatment supervisor and let her know what had happened. Stacey was upset but also stoic.

She sighed. "The reality in this line of work is you're going to lose clients sometimes."

"This hasn't been my first death, but this one hit hard," I admitted.

She exhaled slowly. "I know. Frankie was one of those special ones. I think all of us who work in drug court usually suffer from some kind of ancillary trauma or second-hand PTSD."

I sat on a barstool in Damien's kitchen. "The attorney I replaced mentioned it was starting to get to him."

"It's a real thing. I hope you have people around who can help you. Take care of yourself."

Damien stood at his counter, looking through his emails while he waited for me. "Thanks. I do." At least for today, anyway.

"I don't know if this makes it better or worse, but Frankie considered you one of her greatest mentors and friends. She talked about you and your volleyball program in a group treatment session one time."

A lump formed in my throat, and it took me a minute to respond. "That means a lot."

I felt a little more human again by the time Damien took me home. He seemed to sense I didn't want to be alone with my thoughts, so we walked Gary to the dog park together, then made plans to watch a movie and order pizza.

At the dog park, Damien got a call. He looked down at the number and winced.

"It'll just be a minute." He put the phone to his ear. "Hello, Sadie." He turned to walk further away.

Before he turned, I smiled at him. My smile felt completely fake. I watched Gary sniff around and pee, and I glanced over periodically at Damien, who was on the phone for over twenty minutes.

Another dog owner came over to talk with me. Roberto's dog was a little border collie mix named Lyla, and Gary and Lyla sniffed each other to say hello. Roberto sometimes came to the park with his boyfriend, but today he was alone.

He was in his late thirties and sold real estate. Roberto was handsome and friendly, and I think he'd even picked up a client or two at the dog park because of his good nature. We stood and talked about our dogs for a few minutes while Damien finished his phone call.

Roberto put Lyla back on her leash, and I said goodbye to him as Damien walked back over.

"Who was that?" he asked.

"Roberto. He's here a lot with his dog. I think Gary considers Lyla his girlfriend."

"Hmm." He stared at Roberto walking away.

I turned to him. "Do you need to get going? It's no problem if something came up. I've taken up enough of your day."

He studied me. "Are you trying to get rid of me, Legs?"

"No, but I don't want you to feel obligated. I know you prob- ably have other things to do on a Saturday night." I nodded at the phone in his hand.

He shook his head and grinned. "No. Pizza and a movie with you tonight sounds fucking great."

If he was okay with spending a Saturday night with me, then I was more than happy to hang out with him. We walked back to my house and ordered pizza, then scrolled through the movie selections.

We finally agreed on the first episode of *The Last of Us*. It seemed like a safe choice.

"It's kind of a tragedy that you've never seen it before," I told him.

"Did the video game or the movie come first?"

"I think the videogame. Which is odd, I know. But Pedro Pascal and Bella Ramsey are great in it. And the third episode of the first season is... I have no words."

He stared at me. "You're kind of a movie nerd, aren't you?"

"Yep. Except for horror movies, and my sister loves them. But I like being entertained, not traumatized."

"Fair enough. Okay, let's see what all the fuss is about."

We ended up watching three episodes, and we only quit because I was yawning almost nonstop by the time the third episode was over.

"You were right, that was great," he admitted. "It's not very happy though, is it?"

I laughed. "No."

At the door, he held my cheek. "Are you going to be okay?"

I nodded and gave him a tight hug. "It's been years since anyone took care of me the way you did today. So thank you." I felt awkward, but I wanted him to know.

He brushed my unruly hair behind my ear. "It was my pleasure. Get some sleep."

I nodded, and he leaned down and kissed my forehead.

"Sweet dreams." Then he turned and walked out.

Damien texted me on Sunday in the early afternoon. I'd woken up that morning and knew I needed to get out and get some fresh air. So I packed some hiking gear, food and water, and took Gary to Fern Valley to find a hike and some solitude.

Damien: How r u feeling today?

Me: Better. Thanks for yesterday. Owe u one.

Damien: No, you don't. What r u doing today? I'm catching up on a few things.

I wondered if he was catching up with Sadie, whoever she was. Then I felt bad for being jealous and snarky.

Me: Hiking with Gary—a little outdoor therapy.

Damien: Be safe, enjoy the day.

Me: U too.

After stopping by the ranger station in Idyllwild to pick up my day pass, I'd grabbed a quick lunch at a little café in town. It was a lot colder in the higher elevation, and I was glad to have my favorite Cotopaxi down jacket on. The cheery striped blue and green colors always made me happy.

I'd also brought microspikes for my hiking boots, and we hiked a portion of the Devil's Slide Trail. Gary was ecstatic to get off his leash for most of the hike.

Gary frolicked in the snow, and the dark pines against the blue skies and white snow reminded me how lucky I was just to be here to enjoy the day. A few miles in, I decided to turn around.

I hadn't planned to make it to the summit, and the trail was icy in spots. But it was a beautiful, crisp day, and I only passed two other people.

Frankie would miss out on so much life. But Tiana was right. Frankie was free and she wasn't suffering anymore. A few tears slipped out as I gazed out at the pine trees and skyline and thought about Frankie. Life was fleeting, and maybe it was time for me to start fully living mine.

Chapter 18

On Monday morning, I sat at the side of my bed thinking about Frankie's death. Gary stirred from his dog bed in the corner. He was tired from our long hike yesterday, but he walked over and put his head in my lap.

I finally roused myself and fed Gary, then started coffee. It had been a rough weekend, but Damien had been my silver lining. Depression and sadness dogged me throughout the day. When I got home that evening the house felt lonely, so I was happy to get Damien's text.

Damien: I need to call in a favor tonight if you have time. Can I swing by in a few?

His text sent a zing of anticipation down my spine.

Me: Sure, come anytime. Just walked in.

He rang the doorbell half an hour later. I'd changed out of the cutoff sweat bottoms and t-shirt I'd thrown on when I got home, and put on a pair of my favorite jeans and a soft sweater.

Damien glanced down at my bare feet, and his lip tipped up. "Hi, Legs." His eyes looked tired. "I had a shit day today."

"That's a Monday for you. Are you okay?"

"No, but I will be." He put his hands on my shoulders. "How was your day?"

"I've had better too."

He gazed at me. "I want a hug, sweetheart."

"Okay." It was a dumb response, but I didn't know what else to say. I also wanted a hug, and him calling me sweetheart had short-circuited my brain and made my heart skip a few beats. He pulled me in, and I wrapped my arms around him.

Resting his chin on my head, he pulled me in closer. "You feel good, and you smell even better."

I laid my cheek on his shoulder. "So do you."

He smelled faintly of some spicy masculine soap, mixed with his own male scent.

Damien leaned down and sniffed my neck. Goosebumps erupted along my skin. His back felt muscular and solid under my open palms, and my breasts brushed against his hard chest. I hadn't realized how good a hug could feel.

He slowly stepped back. "Thanks. I feel better."

I smiled. "So do I. Would you like some of the beer or wine you brought over the other night? I also have tequila, but it wasn't juvenile drug court today, and I try to save it for emergencies."

He chuckled. "I'll have a beer. Thanks."

I popped the cap off a cold beer bottle and slid it over to him.

Then I poured myself a glass of wine and leaned against the counter. "Tell me about your day."

He ran a hand through his hair. "One of my biggest clients was burglarized early Sunday morning."

"Oh, no. What happened?"

He sighed. "The thief shut the security system off with a valid code, then robbed the house."

"Did you tell him that?"

"Yeah. He got scary quiet. His safe was also robbed, but we didn't install that."

"Did he try to blame you guys?" I asked.

"No. I think he might have a couple of ideas, but he didn't share them. Someone with a code shut off the system and most of the cameras."

I paused. "*Most* of the cameras?"

He nodded and took a swig of his beer. "Yeah. Zeke's not very trusting and doesn't like to depend on one system. So we sometimes set up a few simple hidden motion sensor cameras."

"How does that work?"

"They record, but the recordings have to be retrieved."

"Do your clients know about the additional cameras?" I asked.

Damien nodded. "Yes. But most of them forget."

"What can I help you with tonight?"

He took another sip of beer. "I need you to be a witness and a buffer when I go over to my client's house and play what we found on one of the cameras."

I nodded. "I'm happy to go with you, but why aren't you taking Sebastian or Zeke?"

"Zeke is out of town doing some work in Riverside, and Sebastian doesn't have the patience for this kind of thing. He's more apt to make the situation worse."

That was probably true. Sebastian wasn't very talkative or particularly friendly. I guess it wasn't surprising he and I got along.

His client's house was located in one of the most exclusive gated golf communities in the La Quinta and Palm Desert area. The residence was a sprawling, white modern structure with a massive, manicured yard and a swimming pool. The garage alone was probably three times the size of my house.

"Who's your client?" I finally asked.

"A retired professional hockey player, but his primary home is in Canada. He has a stake in the new Seattle team that's starting up next season, and they have a feeder team in Palm Springs now. We should go catch one of their games."

"I'd go with you. Martina and I talked about it the other day. Hockey is a great sport; they can get away with *so* much shit. This is Connor McCoy's house, isn't it?"

"Yeah. But he's not in town much," Damien answered.

"Martina told me she knows his local assistant. The woman recently quit, and she said Connor's brother is Lucifer reincarnated."

We walked up to the enormous front door and Damien pressed the doorbell. He had his laptop with him. A large tasteful Christmas wreath hung on the front door, and I could see a glimpse of a massive, professionally decorated Christmas tree through the side panel next to the front door.

It reminded me I hadn't decorated for Christmas yet, and Olivia was coming in a few days. A sibilant chime rang through the house, and a moment later a fit, middle-aged man with laugh lines around his eyes opened the door.

He seemed relieved to see us. "Hello, Damien. Come in."

"Javier, this is Harley. She's working with me tonight. Harley, Javier is Connor's property manager and landscaper. He lives on the property in the smaller home."

Javier didn't waste time. "Connor's brother is blaming the break-in on Isa. There's no proof because she'd never do this. Her biggest faults are she's got a sharp tongue and has poor taste in music."

"Who's Isa?" I asked.

"My daughter, Isabella. She's been going to school in Seattle, and she comes to visit me sometimes. But she's living here now."

Javier led us down the hall to an open living room with enormous floor-to-ceiling glass doors looking out into a lush courtyard with a pool and spa. The beige linen couch could seat maybe twenty people, and the tasteful paintings hanging on the walls looked like they came from an art gallery.

A tall, broad-shouldered man dressed in expensive, casual clothes had his back to the room. He stood with his arms folded looking out at the courtyard. He turned when he heard us walk in. He was probably in his mid to late thirties. He'd broken his nose at some point, and had a scar running across his cheekbone that looked like a skate blade had gotten him.

I absently rubbed the small scar on my own cheekbone. I'd heard about Conner McCoy from a couple of news articles when he'd bought into the new hockey team in Seattle, and also from Martina.

A man lounged on the couch in a relaxed pose. He smirked at us when we walked in, and I assumed he was Noah. His arms were stretched out on the back of the couch, and he'd propped a foot up on the coffee table. He was smaller than Connor and handsome in a vague way.

A small, gorgeous younger woman in her early to mid-twenties sat up straight on the other end of the couch. Her hands rested on her thighs. She was tan and had dark brown hair and startling light brown eyes.

I knew she was Javier's daughter from her unique eye color. Javier sat down next to her.

Connor came forward, and Damien nodded toward me. "This is Harley. She's working with me tonight."

Over the next few minutes, Noah spewed utter bullshit about Isabella using a code to get onto the estate, and somehow breaking into Connor's home and stealing his valuables.

I stood slightly behind Damien, and I saw Isa glance at Connor with disappointment and vague disgust. She didn't give Noah a second glance.

Javier finally had enough. "That means you heard Connor's code too, since you were there," Isabella didn't try to defend herself.

I watched Connor's face and saw sadness and anger creep in when he seemed to realize what his brother had done. I suddenly felt a little sorry for Connor. My sister, Olivia, was my best friend. That kind of betrayal would hurt.

Damien finally ended the discussion. "This will be easy to clear up. There are two backup security cameras in place in case the main system goes down."

Noah froze. And then he started panicking.

Isa turned to Javier and stood up. "We don't need to stay for this. Are you ready to go?"

I watched Javier to see what he'd do. He looked sad when he turned to Connor. "Tomorrow morning I'll be putting in my official notice." Then he glanced at Damien. "Tell Zeke thank you, for being a cynical bastard." Then they walked out the front door together. Seeing them made me miss my own dad.

Connor watched them for a moment, then turned to us. "I'll be right back."

He strode out the door and caught up with them. It looked like Isa was giving him hell. Noah was a lot less relaxed than when we'd first walked in. He leaned forward, and his leg bounced up and down.

Connor walked back in a few minutes later and turned to Damien. "Do you have access to previous footage before this weekend?"

"Are you really going to listen to her?" Noah cut in. "She's a lying little cunt." Both Connor and Damien glared at him.

Damien nodded. "Yes, I can get you footage. If you can narrow down what you're looking for, that will help."

"The times Noah has been here when I haven't. Now let me see the video from Saturday."

Damien didn't waste any time. He played a few video clips showing Noah carrying several bags out of Connor's house to the trunk of one of the five or six cars in the garage. It looked like Noah was whistling in one of the video clips.

Noah sat on the sofa with his head in his hands. "I can explain."

Everyone ignored him.

"Are you going to involve the police?" Damien asked.

For the first time, Connor faltered. "I don't know. What do you think?"

Damien looked at me. "Harley's a criminal defense attorney. She's not here acting as anyone's attorney or giving legal advice. But she may have some objective insight."

Connor straightened and finally turned to me. "What would you do if you were me?"

I didn't even hesitate. "I'd call the police and report it. I'd also tell Noah if he doesn't go into rehab and make some meaningful changes in his life, you're going to cut him out. Then I'd follow through."

Connor studied me. "Why do you say he needs to go into rehab?"

"Because I've lived with an addict most of my life. Trust me, I know drug addiction behavior when I see it."

Noah glared at me. "I'm not an addict, you stupid bitch. You don't know what the fuck you're talking about."

I ignored him. "I have a friend who knows your former assistant. She quit because of your brother."

Noah lunged off the couch and started toward me. "That's not why she quit—"

Damien stepped in front of him and shoved him back a little. "Don't get near her."

Connor grabbed Noah's arm and pulled him back.

I looked at Connor. "Do you want to know what else I think, or have you had enough for tonight?"

He studied me. "Tell me."

"Okay. I wouldn't be surprised if he treated Isabella and Javier the same way. And people rarely steal from family members unless they have an addiction they're feeding. Isabella also knows about him, and she seems pretty levelheaded to me."

"You'd call the police on your own family?" Connor asked.

"Hell yes, in a heartbeat. I also think you're enabling him and making it worse by letting him get away with his behavior."

Connor studied me for a moment, then he turned to Damien. "I didn't know you fuckers gave family counseling sessions along with your security services."

Damien raised an eyebrow. "I'd assess Noah as your biggest threat, and I think Harley's advice is dead on."

Connor nodded, his face going hard as he turned to Noah. "Your free ride is over, Noah. Damien, will you call the police and stay here to help make the report?"

Noah started bawling.

Chapter 19

We left Connor's house around nine, and on the way home I noticed I'd missed a call from Frankie's mom. She'd left a voice message.

When I finished listening to her message, Damien reached over and took my hand.

"You okay?" he asked.

"Frankie's mom let me know about a small service they're having for her tomorrow evening in Desert Hot Springs."

The cab of his truck was dark, and I hoped he couldn't see I was a little teary-eyed.

"Are you going?"

"Yes."

He squeezed my hand. "Okay. I'll go with you. What time?"

"You don't need to do that. Really. I've already monopolized enough of your time."

"No, you haven't. You came with me tonight and made it much better. I'd like to go with you."

He was right. Being with him made things better. "Okay. Thank you. It's at six at the Rosewood Mortuary. And if you have time, I'll take you to the best Mexican food restaurant in Desert Hot Springs for dinner afterward."

He grinned at me, and I could see the flash of his beautiful white smile in the dark cab of the truck. "It's a deal."

When he pulled up to my house, he cut off his engine and then turned to me.

"Do you want to come in?" I asked.

He nodded. "I do, but we both have work tomorrow."

"It's okay. I have leftover grilled chicken, and we can throw together some chicken quesadillas. I'm starving."

"That sounds good. I'm hungry too."

We made chicken quesadillas, and a tossed salad together. Whenever I grilled chicken, I always grilled a large portion so I could use it for other meals. I also had a bottle of mezcal, and Damien mixed up a couple of mezcalitas using the fresh oranges from one of my little citrus trees.

Damien dampened the glass rims with an orange slice, then dipped them in chili lime salt. He added mezcal, fresh orange juice, fresh lime juice, and a little orange liqueur then garnished the drinks with an orange wedge.

He slid one over to me. "Try this. It has a nice smoky citrusy flavor."

I tasted the drink, then ran my tongue over my lips, licking some of the chili lime salt. It was delicious. "Mmm. That's so good." He watched me lick more of the salt off with hooded eyes.

We grabbed our plates and drinks, then headed out to my back patio to eat like we'd done it a hundred times before. I turned on my firepit and we ate in front of it. When Damien finished, he leaned back in his chair and took a drink then let out a long exhale.

"Thanks, sweetheart. I needed this."

His endearment made my heart rate speed up, and it took me a second to answer.

I smiled at him. "You're welcome. I needed this too."

We sat and talked a little more about Noah's reaction to Connor pressing charges, and what our workweek looked like. Finally, we went inside and straightened up the kitchen.

When everything was done, Damien turned to me and leaned against the counter. "Harley, I didn't want to say anything this weekend because of Frankie. But we need to talk."

My stomach flipped a little, and I wondered if Damien was finally going to brush me off. Spending so much time with me probably put a cramp in his social life. Or maybe he needed to drop Shanda's case because he was too busy.

"I thought that's what we were doing." I smiled nervously.

He shook his head, then reached out and took my hand, drawing me into his body. "No, Legs. I want to talk about you and me. And this."

He leaned in and brushed his lips across mine. Just the barest touch. I froze at the feel of his lips on mine. It had been so long since I'd kissed anyone, I was afraid for a split second I'd forgotten how. Then he rubbed his nose across my cheek and kissed my neck. My thoughts flitted away, and I shivered and inched closer to him.

Cupping my face, he tipped my lips up and kissed me deeper. Maybe I wasn't cramping his social life after all. He slanted his mouth across mine and slid his hands around the nape of my neck.

My hands moved around his torso, and then slowly slid up his back while we kissed. I could feel all the wonderful muscles there, from his lats to his deltoids. And holy shit, he felt so hard beneath my hands. I wanted to touch him without his shirt on.

Damien's tongue slid across my lips, and I made a soft sound in the back of my throat. He parted my mouth and pushed inside. Then he walked me backward until I hit the wall, his front plastered against mine. I stood on my tiptoes to get closer to his mouth. He sucked at my tongue, and I whimpered.

His hands roamed down my sides, and he took hold of my waist and tugged me into him. I could feel his bulge, and I rubbed against him. Finally, he pulled his mouth from mine, and I tried to draw in air.

He laid his forehead on mine. "Holy fuck. I didn't know we'd set each other off quite like this."

"Is *this* what you call talking?" I panted.

He grinned, and his damned dimple popped, making my ovaries flutter. He kissed me again, then nipped my lower lip. "No. But it's a hell of a lot more fun."

He'd pinned me against the wall and nestled his thigh between my legs. I could feel his hard length against my stomach, and I rolled my hips against him experimentally.

"Fuck, sweetheart. Don't do that unless you want to end up on your back in the middle of your kitchen floor the first time."

"I can't help it. You feel so good, and it's been so long."

He slowly pulled back as if it pained him, then took hold of my shoulders.

"Harley, how long has it been?"

My silence was deafening in the quiet kitchen, and I turned my head to the side.

He took hold of my chin and turned my face back to his. "You don't date, and your mom said you haven't been with anyone in a while."

"I haven't," I answered flatly.

"I'm not a good person, because that turns me the fuck on." He leaned in and bit the tendon in the side of my neck. I gasped and arched against him. "And I don't give a shit if you don't want to date. You and I are going to be doing a lot more than just dating." He reached up with his thumbs and rubbed the undersides of my breasts.

"Oh, God," I moaned softly.

"We're so good together, Legs. We fit. And now that I know we set each other off like fucking fireworks in July, I can't walk away from this."

He was right. We did fit, and we set each other off. I wanted to wrap my legs around him and rub my core against him. But it wasn't that easy.

"What are you thinking? Talk to me." He squeezed me gently.

I sucked in a breath and tried to cool the heat coursing through my system. "Everything you say is true." He opened his mouth, but I held up my hand to stall him. "But I have... issues. And Baggage." I waved vaguely toward Ava's house.

"I know. It's part of what makes you so different. You're complex and independent. And compassionate. And so fucking hot."

A laugh escaped me.

He smiled. "It's a compelling combination, and I want to explore this."

So did I, God help me, so I slowly nodded my head.

"You look scared, sweetheart." He lowered his voice and whispered in my ear. "You should be. Because while we're settling into each other, I'm going to enjoy the hell out of getting to know every inch of your sweet, beautiful body."

My pulse jumped. His hair was slightly disheveled, and his gray-blue eyes were laser-focused on me. But I needed to get control of this conversation.

"I don't want just a hookup or a casual thing. If I wanted that, there are a dozen guys who would—"

"Don't even finish that sentence," he growled.

I held up my hands. "Okay. I think you know what I mean."

His jaw clenched, but he nodded.

My hands crept up to his face. "You matter. You could hurt me, so hell yes, I'm scared." I paused and gathered my thoughts. "Please be patient with me."

He let out a long exhale and laid his forehead on mine. "Okay, sweetheart. I can be patient. But that doesn't mean I won't cop a feel every chance I get in the meantime." He slid his hand down and squeezed my ass.

I grinned. "I'd be disappointed if you didn't." I reached down and grabbed his tight ass right back. He smiled and leaned in to kiss me again.

I had to kick him out a few minutes later, or we really would have ended up on my kitchen floor.

I finally texted Ava and told her I'd help put up her Christmas tree. She texted back a few minutes later.

Ava: Been up for days. Olivia's coming Thursday. Is yours up?
Me: Of course my tree is up.

Then I dragged my Christmas tree out of the garage and put it up. I'm sure Ava knew I'd lied because while I decorated my tree, she sent me an eye roll emoji back.

Olivia had been with me a couple of years ago when I'd bought my retro 1950s atomic starburst ornaments from a little boutique on Palm Canyon Drive. The decorations had been expensive. But they were quirky and bright, and reminded me of that day when we'd walked around Palm Springs together and I took her to some of my favorite spots.

As a peace offering before Olivia came for the holiday break, I invited Ava to lunch. We talked about a watercolor class she'd signed up for, and an upcoming golf tournament. We didn't talk about Gary.

"What kind of tournament is it?" I asked.

"It's a charity event. Grace set me up with her banker who needed a female partner to play in his foursome."

"So is it a date?"

Ava looked a little nervous, which wasn't like her. "I'm not sure, actually." She refolded her napkin in her lap.

"Well, whatever it is, I think he's lucky to have you as his golf partner. You have a mean putting game and you look great in golf shorts."

Ava gave me a genuine smile. "Why thank you, Harley." She shifted in her chair and leaned forward. "Speaking of shorts, are you still wearing those ratty cutoff sweats to bed? Because if you ever *do* decide to clear the cobwebs out of your vagina, those aren't going to help."

My favorite pajamas were worn-in cutoff sweats and old t-shirts that had been washed so many times they felt like tissue paper. It was my favorite outfit to wear after work and then to bed. And it saved on laundry.

"It's too weird to have my mom worry about my sleepwear and talk about cobwebs in my vagina. You're intentionally inflicting emotional distress."

Ava rolled her eyes at the legal term and held up her perfectly manicured hand. "I'm just trying to help. You need a pedicure too. And when's the last time you had a good wax job down *there*?" She motioned to my vagina with her salad fork.

The ladies in the booth next to us gave her a strange look, and I choked on my chicken salad and shook my head. "God, woman, will you stop obsessing about my privates? It's creepy."

"Maybe if you'd give it a little attention once in a while, I wouldn't have to worry about it," she shot back.

The ladies next to us were now openly staring. I wondered if Ava somehow knew about Damien, and that was why she brought up my sleepwear and getting waxed *down there*. My hour lunch break felt like it had lasted three hours by the time we finished.

Damien went with me to Frankie's service that evening. The service was short and most the people there appeared to be her family. Many of them looked like they'd lived a hard life.

If Damien hadn't been with me, the whole evening would have been depressing and sad. But I'd taken him to El Gordos for dinner afterward, and we'd talked and decompressed together.

"What's your best memory of Frankie?" Damien asked after our server set down our drinks and chips.

"Hmmm. Maybe how supportive she was of the other drug court participants. She cheered everyone on and seemed to internalize every setback." I took a chip and scooped up some salsa. I closed my eyes and hummed. I loved their salsa.

Damien sat back and smiled. "Good?"

"Mm hum. So good." I chewed and swallowed. "Or it might be that day last season when we were playing your team, and she gave me a decent set. She was *so* excited."

Damien took a chip and loaded it up as well. "No offense, but she was a pretty bad player. She looked scared every time the ball came close to her."

I sipped my margarita and nodded. "Yeah, I called her our black hole. But her serves were so unpredictable, that we'd usually score several points off them because no one knew where the hell they'd land. Including her."

He smiled and laid his arm on the table. I reached over and grabbed it.

"Looking back on that match and knowing you now, I'm sorry I hit you." I was bad at apologizing, and I just wanted to get it over with. "It wasn't on purpose, but I was mad and nailed it as hard as I could. Your face just kind of got in the way."

Shaking his head, he put his hand over mine. "That's a pretty half-assed apology, but I'll take it. I'm also sorry for whatever I said about your team. I was just trying to get under your skin and throw you off."

"That usually has the opposite effect on me."

He grinned. "Yeah, I noticed."

He turned his forearm around and took hold of my hand. Then he rubbed his thumb slowly across my palm, and my pulse skipped a beat. Holy shit, I didn't realize how many nerve endings were in my hand.

I cleared my throat. "What have you heard about Connor and his brother?"

"Connor asked us to change all the codes to his home, and he's supporting charges against Noah."

"Do you know if Javier quit?"

Damien shook his head. "I haven't heard, but I wouldn't blame him if he did."

"If I were Connor, I'd try to keep him. And I like Isa. She didn't seem rattled by what was going on, did she?"

"No, and I think she nailed Connor's balls to the wall." He studied my face. "I'm sorry it brought up what you've gone through with your mom."

I looked down at the table. "It reminded me of my shortcomings with Ava, so I think it was helpful in a way."

The server came with our food just then, and we ate in comfortable silence.

When we pulled up to my house later that night, he turned to me. "I want to come in, but if I do, I'll probably have you pinned to the wall and that sweet little black dress you have on up around your hips about three seconds after we clear the front door."

My vagina spasmed, and I clenched my legs together. "Oh, God. Is it possible to have an orgasm from just dirty talk?" I asked rhetorically.

He grinned and kissed my hand.

Damien followed me to the front door, and my stomach fluttered. I felt nervous and a little awkward. He wrapped his arms around me and hugged me close, then gave me a slow, sweet kiss. I got lost in the kiss and nipped his mouth, then licked his lips.

We kissed and made out for a few minutes on my front porch like horny teenagers. I'd forgotten how good it felt to touch and be touched by someone. He hummed low in his throat and finally pulled me closer, then ran his hand slowly up my stomach and cupped my breast.

The contact made me gasp in his mouth, and I pushed into his hand. He slid his other hand down my thigh then slowly lifted my leg and wrapped it around his hip. My dress slid up, and my panties were plastered against the zipper on his pants. I could feel his thick erection rubbing on my crease, and I rocked against him.

He pulled his mouth back and slowly let go of my leg. His hand didn't seem to want to let go of my breast though, and he gave it another squeeze then rubbed his thumb across my hard nipple before he released me. I shuddered and held onto his arms for a moment to keep myself standing.

"Fireworks," he said in a low, husky voice.

I nodded, then cleared my throat and stepped back a little. "You made what would've been a painful evening into a much better one. So thank you."

He gently took my face in his hands, and I held my breath but didn't move away. My heart was thudding, and my emotions were all over the place.

"You're welcome, sweetheart. I'll see you tomorrow."

I blindly unlocked my door and stepped inside. Gary walked into the living room and sat down next to me, probably wondering why I was just staring at the front door for a good minute after I'd closed and locked it.

If that was what a kiss at the front door turned into, we'd probably set the bed on fire when we got there. He was right, we were like fireworks.

Chapter 20

Shanda still hadn't surfaced. I had three preliminary hearings in front of Judge Conrad Wednesday morning. Two of my three clients showed up on time, but Shanda was still missing. The preliminary hearings were all scheduled at nine, and the court called them one at a time while everyone else waited their turn.

Jason was there with his attorney, and he stared at me with a smug, greasy expression. I glanced his way once but didn't make eye contact or show any recognition.

My other two clients planned to waive their preliminary hearings since the prosecution had met its low burden of probable cause at that point. I was anxious and worried, and I wondered for the hundredth time where Shanda was and if she was safe.

"Well, hello Harley. You look perky and attorney-like today." Trevor was one of the newer prosecutors, and he'd been hitting on me for a while. I loathed him.

"Hello, Trevor. I'm not sure what to do with your comment. And since I *am* an attorney, I hope I look like one. Are you handling my cases or is Evan?" *Please let it be Evan.*

Trevor frowned a little. "It's Evan." He eyed my legs and then my chest. What a putz.

"Are you going to be around at lunch?" he asked.

I just stared at him. He had to know me eating lunch with a prosecutor alone was a horrible idea. "I'll be somewhere for lunch," I finally said. "I'm going to talk to Evan." I walked by him without a backward glance.

Trevor wasn't taking my hints, so I'd gotten blunt and borderline rude with him. He was handsome and dressed well, but he seemed so smarmy and fake.

What really made me dislike him though, besides him hitting on me, was how he treated the court staff. That alone was enough to put him on my shitlist. And then there was the bet.

Eventually, my other cases were called, and my two clients waived their right to a preliminary hearing, got their next hearing date, and were free to go.

Judge Conrad looked down at me over his spectacles. "Your third client, Shanda Briggs, doesn't appear to be present. Is she planning to be here today, Ms. Emerson?"

"I don't know, Your Honor. I'd like to wait until the end of your docket to see if she makes it."

"Fair enough. But if she isn't here by the time I get through my calendar, I'll issue a bench warrant."

I nodded and sat back down as the bailiff called the next case. I checked my phone again. There weren't any texts or phone calls from Shanda, but I noticed there was a text message from Damien that was only a few minutes old.

Damien: Shanda coming. ETA 15 mins.

I closed my eyes and breathed a sigh of relief.

Me: Did she say anything?

Damien: No. Just found her this morning.

I looked around the courtroom. Jason and his attorney were still there, along with four other defendants. Between cases, I walked over to Evan, the senior prosecutor, and whispered in his ear. Evan Harman had been a prosecutor for almost as long as I'd been alive.

He was even-tempered and unflappable. His bushy gray eyebrows made him look vaguely surprised all the time, and sometimes there were food stains or crumbs on his white dress shirt or tie. I vastly preferred him to Trevor any day.

"Evan, Shanda Briggs is on her way here. I haven't been able to talk to her, so I don't know what she wants to do."

He glanced at me. "Do you need some time before we go on the record?"

"Yes, and I don't want Jason Ulrich in the courtroom when she gets here. I'll also be requesting the court bifurcate their cases and handle them separately from here on out."

He looked over at Jason and his attorney. "Okay. I'll ask the bailiff to call them next."

"Thanks. I'm going to talk with her out in the foyer when she gets here."

He nodded and I grabbed my belongings, then walked out of the courtroom. I hoped Jason and his attorney would think I'd given up on Shanda and was leaving for the day.

In the hallway, I dialed Damien's phone and waited by the elevators. He didn't pick up, but less than a minute later one of the elevator doors opened and he and Shanda walked out.

"Oh, thank you, God," I breathed out. Shanda looked pale and scared, but she also appeared healthy and clean. She wore purple scrubs, and she'd dyed her hair a teal blue color. It looked better with her skin tone than the orange color.

I opened the door to one of the small conference rooms in the foyer area and waved them inside.

When Damien walked by me, I spontaneously gave him a big hug. "I owe you, big time. Can you stay, or do you need to get going?"

He grinned and tucked a stray strand of hair behind my ear. "I've got a few minutes." He glanced down at my cream silk blouse and gray pencil skirt. "You look nice, Ms. Emerson."

"Thank you, Mr. Andreasen. Really. Thank you." I hugged him again, then I turned to Shanda. "I'm so glad to see you. I like your hair, and your piercings look better."

She raised her eyebrows. "That's it? You're not going to yell or give me shit?"

"We'll save it for later because we've only got about four minutes. Is it okay if Damien stays while we talk? He's an investigator, and he's working with me on your case."

She looked over at him. "He told me. He also said I'd get a bench warrant and the police would probably find and arrest me if I didn't show up today. He got me a Lyft here then followed us over."

I turned to him. "The PD's office will reimburse you for the ride."

He shrugged. "Don't worry about it."

Shanda interrupted us. "Is what he said true, or was he just blowing smoke up my ass?"

"It's true."

Shanda glanced at Damien. "Okay. He can stay."

I sat down next to her. "All right. The last time we talked, you saw the video showing Jason driving the car. The prosecutor has seen it too. I think it's in your best interest to admit you lied, but we let the prosecutor know you did it under duress. He's likely to drop the more serious charges against you."

Shanda sat down slowly at the small conference table in the room and looked up at me. "What's duress?"

"It means you were threatened or under pressure to answer a certain way."

She nodded. "I haven't seen Bertie in a month. I thought if I stayed away from the apartment, and my stepdad told Jason I'd run away and hadn't been home, she'd be safe."

"If I can tell the prosecutor that Jason threatened you and Bertie, he'll probably drop most of the charges against you—except the meth charge."

Shanda slumped a little. "Okay."

"Is that what he did?" I asked.

"Yeah." She sighed long and low. "He said neither of us would make it to our next birthday if I told anyone about the drugs and the wreck."

I ground my molars, thinking about that asshole smirking at me in court.

"Where have you been staying?" I asked.

She looked over at Damien.

He nodded. "Tell her."

She sighed again. "At the Sunny Palms assisted living center."

Well. That hadn't been what I was expecting. "You live there?"

"Yeah, and I work there too. They like having me there at night and they pay me a little more. It's a shitty room and doesn't have a window, but it's way better than home."

That was probably true, especially with her stepdad living at the apartment and drug users coming and going.

Relief swept through me. "It sounds like a good setup."

She shrugged. "They can tell the families they have 'onsite staff' there. I get meals too."

"Has it been working out so far?"

She dropped her eyes and looked down at the table. "Yeah, and the families don't know that the 'onsite staff' is an eighteen-year-old homeless meth head."

Shanda didn't look like she'd been using meth. In fact, she looked good. "That's total horseshit, and we both know it. I've represented 'meth heads.' You're not one—yet. You still have all your teeth and brain cells. Although you won't if you keep using it."

She jerked her shoulder. "I haven't been using. I only did it with Jason."

She seemed relieved that I didn't believe she was a meth head. I dreaded telling her Jason might still be in the courtroom.

"Shanda, here's what's going to happen. I'm going to negotiate with the prosecutor and request what's called a plea in abeyance for the meth charge and see if he'll dismiss the rest."

"What does that mean? Speak English."

I nodded and explained it to her.

"Does the prosecutor usually agree to the plea thing?" she asked.

"No, but I think he'll do it with you."

She nodded. "Are you going to ask him today?"

"Yes, but he'll want to make sure you're not using." I leaned forward. "Jason and his attorney were in the courtroom when I got your text."

Shanda straightened up, and fear flooded her face. "Oh, fuck. I do *not* want to see him."

I nodded. "The prosecutor agreed to call his case when I came out to find you. I think he's gone by now, but we'll make sure before you go into the courtroom."

Damien touched my shoulder. "Do you want me to see if he's around and let you know when he leaves?"

I nodded gratefully. "Yes, please. He's about my height, mid-thirties, brown hair. He's wearing a short-sleeved pink shirt, and his attorney is wearing a blue suit with a yellow tie."

Damien nodded, then stepped out.

I turned to Shanda. "Did you have to take any drug tests to get your job?"

"Yeah. I took one before I started, and two since then." She smirked. "I think my piercings and orange hair made them a little nervous."

I was cautiously optimistic. "Do you have copies of those test results?"

"No, but I can ask for them."

"Okay. Let's get those."

I pulled out the bus pass and a gift card to a secondhand clothing store I'd picked up at the public defender's office, hoping she'd show up today. I wordlessly handed them to her, along with another one of my business cards. She looked at them, glanced up at me, then stuck them in her pocket.

Damien came back. "Jason and his attorney just got on the elevator. The bailiff said there's one more case and then the judge will adjourn for lunch. You need to go in soon."

I nodded. "We'll continue this hearing and set a date and time for the next one. We should have an agreement by then."

Shanda groaned. "Another hearing? Why are there so many hearings? I don't want to keep taking time off work. Can't we just take care of this today?"

I put my hands on my hips. "We probably could have, but since you've been ghosting me for the past month, I haven't been able to do anything with your case. You need to stay in touch and *not miss your appointments.*"

"Okay, I was scared. Geez."

"No more." I pointed a finger at her. "Let's go before Judge Conrad decides to throw your scrawny butt in jail."

That got Shanda moving. We went in just as the last defendant and his attorney were leaving the courtroom. Damien slipped onto a bench behind us. Judge Conrad wasn't happy, but after I spoke briefly with the prosecutor, we quickly went on the record.

The judge looked down at us. "Ms. Emerson, I see your client finally made it. Tell me why I shouldn't just issue a bench warrant, take her into custody, and reschedule her hearing."

Shanda sank down in her seat next to me. I patted her shoulder and addressed the judge.

"She's sorry for being late, Your Honor. Shanda is gainfully employed and just came from work, as you can see from her scrubs. This hearing should be quick. My client is waiving her right to a preliminary hearing today, and we're asking the court to set a pretrial date. We're also requesting that Ms. Briggs' case be bifurcated from that of the co-defendant, Jason Ulrich, and their hearings be set on different days from now on."

Judge Conrad turned to Evan. "Your Honor, Ms. Emerson and I have spoken, and the State stipulates to the bifurcation. We should be able to reach a resolution by the next hearing."

Judge Conrad nodded enthusiastically. The more stipulations the attorneys reached, the fewer hearings and oral arguments he had to sit through. We finished up quickly.

Trevor, the younger prosecutor, had stayed in the courtroom and he stood next to me as I gathered my belongings. "That was close. I hope you read your client the riot act about being so late for her hearing." He nodded his head toward Shanda.

"We got it done," I said shortly, then turned to Evan. "I'll get a hold of you in the next few days and send you a copy of some drug tests she's taken over the last month or so for her employment."

Evan nodded. "That will help."

"I'd like to discuss dismissing the charges, or a plea in abeyance on a reduced charge based on her age and extenuating circum-stances."

Shanda and I walked to the partition, and Damien stepped up and opened the short swinging door. Trevor stood there watching us. When I walked through last, Damien put his hand on the small of my back.

Trevor's eyes narrowed, and he snorted. "Why would the pros-ecutor's office give her a plea in abeyance? She's got felony charges, and she and her boyfriend are lowlifes."

Shanda froze next to me.

Evan glared at Trevor. "This isn't your case. And it's not appropriate or professional to call the defendants denigrating names. I'll see you back at the office."

Evan turned to Damien and gave him a firm handshake. "Detective Andreasen, it's great to see you again. How are things?"

Shanda leaned into me. "Detective? I thought you said he works for you."

"He's a *former* detective, and he works for himself now," I whispered back.

Damien shook his head. "I haven't been a detective for a while. It's great to see you. How's your family?"

"Good. Sammie's in college now."

Trevor looked at the two men greeting each other like old friends, then turned and stomped out of the courtroom.

Evan shook his head when Trevor was out of earshot. "Harley, I'm sorry he keeps bothering you. It's not appropriate, and I plan to talk with him. You've become a challenge to some of the single men around here, and he's competitive."

My face flamed a little.

Damien glared at Evan. "It needs to stop. And she's mine."

I blinked at Damien in surprise, and my insides fluttered.

Evan grinned and hit him on the shoulder. "You were always smart." He turned to me. "Harley, I'll look for those drug test results. See you later."

We followed him out, and Shanda let out a long breath. "I've been dreading that for so long."

I turned to her. "Please don't miss the next hearing. Do you have a working cell phone or an email you can access? I'll need to talk to you before then."

Shanda looked a little sheepish. "I get your emails and texts."

I stopped and stared at her. "Why didn't you respond?"

"Because I wasn't planning to come to court today."

"Well, that was a shitty plan. If you don't stay in touch with me, I'll have to withdraw from your case, and we're so close to resolving it."

"I know. I'll respond from now on. But please don't tell anyone where I am." Her gaze darted out over the parking lot. "I don't think Jason's done with me yet."

Chapter 21

I watched Shanda climb onto the bus and scan the pass I'd given her. "She looks so young and alone."

Damien took my hand. "When I found her at the assisted living center, she was talking with a few of the residents and staff members there. I think she's okay, at least for now." He walked me to my car as we talked. "What's going on with that younger prosecutor?"

I avoided his eyes. "Absolutely nothing."

"Don't bullshit me, Harley. I know you're not interested, but he hasn't quit. Now what's going on?"

"He doesn't like rejection, and he's an asshole. I've got it handled."

He studied my face carefully. "Does that happen to you a lot?"

"Why do you ask?"

"Why are you avoiding my question?" he persisted.

I nibbled on my lip and looked away.

He took hold of my chin and turned my face back to his. "Evan's comments reminded me of what your coworker, Wendy, said a while back about you being a challenge. Has dating you turned into some kind of a competition?"

My eyes widened in surprise and dismay. He was sharp, and I realized he didn't miss much. I'd have to remember that.

"Tell me," he persisted.

"It's more like a... bet."

His nostrils flared. "A bet?"

"Yeah, a bet." I stopped talking, but he shook his head.

"Harley, tell me."

I lifted my chin. "I only know because a bailiff heard Trevor and a couple of other attorneys talking about it after court one day. The bailiff told me that since I didn't go out with any of them, they decided to make having sex with me into a fucking bet. The first one wins." My voice broke a little, and I sucked in a breath.

I hadn't realized until then how furious I was about it. After the bailiff told me what he'd heard, I'd second-guessed a lot of my friendships with any unattached males, and I became less friendly with certain work colleagues. It was a relief to be able to talk with someone about it.

Damien's jaw locked. "Have you told anyone?"

"Who would I tell? It hasn't affected my practice, and no one's said anything to my face. I'm handling it. If Trevor hits on me again, I'll probably say something to his supervisor. And the bailiff told me if I ever needed a witness, he'd back me up."

Damien gathered me in his arms. "Damn it, Legs. We need to have a long talk about what else you aren't telling me." He laid his cheek on the top of my head. "I'm sorry, sweetheart."

He always smelled so good, and when he held me I got butter-flies in my stomach, but I also felt... cherished. I wished we weren't in the middle of the parking lot of the courthouse. "It's fine. I've lived through worse things."

He pulled back and looked down at me. "Come over for dinner tonight."

I smiled and started automatically nodding, then remembered Olivia was coming. "Can you come to my house instead? Olivia's coming tomorrow, and I need to get a few things done."

"Yeah. I'll come by around seven."

When seven finally rolled around, I was a bundle of nerves. I'd used the extra adrenaline to clean my house and change the sheets. Damien came right on time, and when I heard the doorbell, my adrenaline spiked. But he was scowling, and he had Zeke with him.

"What's going on? Is everything okay?" I asked.

"No," Damien said shortly. "Connor's brother tried to vandal-ize his house. Connor called us a few minutes ago and asked if I'd come out and help him. I want to introduce him to Zeke, so he feels comfortable with either of us. We need to go but I wanted to see you first."

Zeke grinned. "Hey, Harley. I would've told Connor to shove it. Just remember that."

Damien reached out and smacked Zeke on the chest without looking at him.

"She's mine, fucker." He stepped closer and leaned down to whisper in my ear. "I'm sorry."

I grabbed a hold of Damien's shirt and looked up at him. "It's okay. I know a little about what Connor's going through, and it's nice that you care about your clients. Do you need help?"

He shook his head. "I think he needs moral support and maybe help handling the police. He pays us a fuck load of money, so I feel obligated to go. I also like the guy."

"Okay. You're welcome to come by afterward—if you want. You know my code."

He nodded. "It'll probably be late, but I'm taking you up on that. Is it okay if I leave my truck in your driveway?"

"Yes, of course." He leaned in and sniffed my hair, then he tipped my chin up and gave me a hard kiss on my lips. I wrapped myself around him and kissed him back.

Holy shit, he was a good kisser. He had just the right slant and pressure, and his lips were firm but soft. I whimpered a little into his mouth.

"I hate you right now," Zeke muttered behind Damien. "I'll be in the truck."

We broke apart at his voice, and I panted like I'd just run a few miles.

"I'll see you tonight, no matter how late it is. If it's after eleven, I'll let myself in."

I licked my lips and nodded. He clenched his jaw, then turned around and walked to Zeke's truck.

It was after midnight when I heard Gary woof softly and then felt a hand on my shoulder.

Damien whispered in my ear. "I'm sorry it's so late."

"It's okay. I'm glad you came." My voice was raspy with sleep. "You're welcome to stay. There's a new toothbrush on my bathroom counter, and clean towels on the left rack."

He froze above me, and I was suddenly wide awake. "I thought we'd just sleep, but if you don't want to stay—"

"No, I want to. I was just surprised I didn't have to talk you into it, that's all."

I relaxed into my pillow and closed my eyes. "Okay. Good."

He didn't say anything for a minute. Then he squeezed my waist. "Harley, tonight we'll sleep. But if you let me into your bed, from now on it won't be to just sleep." He leaned over and murmured in my ear. "I'm trying to be patient. But I feel like a fifteen-year-old again. I want to fuck you every time I'm near you."

I was suddenly wide awake. I sat up, and he sat down on the bed next to me.

Letting out a long breath, I grasped his arm. "Yes. I feel the same." I rubbed my sternum. "But I need to tell you a few things. And I know it's late." I felt him tense next to me. "It's nothing bad. But... It's been over five years since I've been with anyone."

He sucked in a breath. "Shit, sweetheart. Why so long?" He put his arm around me and pulled me to his side. "I knew it'd been a while. But five years?"

"You know about my fiancé, Ryan." He nodded. "After he died, I just... couldn't. And then I went to law school, and it's not smart to start anything there."

"And the fucking bet," he finished.

"Yes." I sighed.

"How did he die?" he asked quietly.

I slowly leaned forward and put my elbows on my knees. The familiar guilt and regret slid through me, and I cleared my throat. "We were coming back from one of my volleyball tournaments late one night. Ava was in a bad place again, and Olivia was a senior in high school and had gone out of town for some school function or something. I thought I needed to get back to check on Ava, so we didn't stay overnight."

He ran his hand down my back. "What happened?"

I sat up and turned to look at him in the dark. "Ryan said he was fine to drive. He'd had an energy drink, and he *seemed* fine. But he didn't wear his seatbelt sometimes, and to this day I still don't know why he didn't have it on that night."

We'd had a couple of heated discussions about it while we were together, and he'd gotten better about wearing it. But I couldn't remember telling him to put it on that night. It was my single biggest regret that me reminding him might have saved him.

I continued. "He must have drifted into oncoming traffic, or the other driver drifted into us. No one knows. The other driver was an older gentleman who was coming back from his grandson's birthday party."

"You don't need to finish," Damien murmured, rubbing his hand down my back.

"It's okay. I was dead asleep in the passenger seat, and the next thing I knew I was jerked back by my seatbelt and the airbag. It was bad. I think the other man died on impact, and Ryan was partially ejected." I swallowed.

Closing my eyes, it all came rushing back. The smell of the powdery substance in the airbag. The feel of the seatbelt strangling me in the dark. The red and blue lights from the emergency vehicles, and the EMTs working over Ryan's body.

But I knew from the way his skull was crushed on one side, Ryan was already gone.

I continued in a halting voice. "I dislocated my shoulder, cut my cheekbone, and suffered from whiplash and a few other cuts. The cars made impact, then spun. And somehow, I was spared."

Damien pulled me into him. "That explains the scar." He cupped my cheek. "I'm so fucking sorry, sweetheart."

He didn't tell me not to feel guilty or blame myself. He didn't say things happened for a reason, which I'd particularly hated. Everything happened for a reason, and some of those reasons were downright shitty and senseless sometimes. Damien just sat with me in the dark and offered silent comfort.

Eventually, I pulled back and shifted to look at him. "It's been a long time, and I'm doing much better now." Maybe that was stretching it a little, but I was in a better place.

"Thank you for telling me. It also explains a few things about you that didn't make sense before."

I cocked my head. "Like what?"

"Like why a smart, sweet, beautiful, athletic attorney with a successful practice isn't already taken."

"Hmmm, thanks. I think?" I blushed in the dark. "I've thought the same thing. You had a long-term girlfriend, and I know you've... dated since then. But you're not with anyone either."

"I haven't been celibate, but nothing like Sebastian. Since I broke things off with my old girlfriend, there hasn't been anyone serious."

He nuzzled my hair and held me to him for a moment. "You need to get back to sleep, and I'm beat. I keep an overnight backpack in my truck, so I have a few things already. I'm going to get ready for bed."

"Okay." I laid back down.

He kissed my forehead then grabbed his backpack and went into my bathroom. I listened to him getting ready, and before I knew it, I'd drifted off to sleep again. I woke up briefly when he pulled me to him and wrapped his arms around me. I snuggled next to him, and we fell asleep tangled together.

The next morning, I woke earlier than usual. My back was warm and there was an arm across my chest. When Damien felt me stir a little, he gently drew my hair to the side and kissed the back of my neck. Then he licked my earlobe, and I shuddered and arched into him. He was already hard, and he nestled it against the crease of my bottom. He ran his hand up under my tank top and cupped my breast.

"Oh, God, that feels so amazing," I moaned softly. My breasts swelled and my nipples grew hard under his fingers.

I felt his nose glide into my hair. "Yes, it does."

He slid his other hand down my stomach and pushed me deeper into his cock. Then he growled softly in my ear, "I want to spend the morning getting to know your beautiful body and wrapping those flexible as fuck legs around my waist while I drive deep inside you. But we both need to get up, and we need to have our shit completely worked out first."

"What shit?" I sounded breathy. I reached back and ran my hand up his thigh and grabbed his butt cheek through his briefs.

He slid a hand down and palmed my center. "I promised you I'd be patient."

My mind went blank, and I started panting. "I changed my mind."

"Are you on birth control?"

Damn it, he was right. "No. But I will be by the end of the day."

He smiled into my neck and rubbed his length against me again. "I don't think it works that way. I got checked last week; I'm clean. I can use condoms if you don't want to get on birth control."

"I do. And my last OBGYN appointment was two months ago. I'm also good."

"I know you are." He slid my sleep shorts off and lifted my top leg to spread me open. Then he slid his fingers across my core. I'd never admit it to Ava, but after her jabs about my cutoff sweats and my needing a wax, I'd taken a couple of hours of personal time and bought some new underwear and sleepwear.

"Hmm. You feel like the best fucking wet dream I've ever had." He ran his fingers over my bare clit and gently rubbed me. I pushed into his hand and gasped. It'd been so long since anyone else had touched me like that.

He took a nipple between his fingers and rolled it. My mind emptied and my insides clenched with need.

I reached between us, pushed down his briefs, and palmed his pulsing cock. It felt hot in my hand, and when I latched onto it with my damp fingers, he groaned into my neck. I pumped him a few times, and he rolled my nipple even harder.

When I looked over my shoulder at him, his lips found mine in a deep, wet kiss. He worked my clit and nipple, and I fisted his cock.

He ripped his mouth away. "That's it, honey. A little tighter—aw, fuck!"

He pushed into me again, trapping my hand and his length between us, and I could feel him grow even harder. Damien latched onto my neck and nipped me there while he worked a finger inside my passage. Then he pushed two fingers in. My vagina was tight, and his hands were big, but I was wet and slick. I whimpered at the intrusion, and my body locked. The small bite of pain ratcheted up my pleasure, and I let out a sob.

He stroked my breast with his other hand. "It's okay, sweetheart. I have you."

After the first thrust with his fingers, my hips moved to meet him. He rubbed my clit with his thumb, and my fingers clenched around his length even tighter. I felt the beginning of an orgasm low in my belly.

I moaned deep in my throat as Damien drove his fingers harder inside me. I pumped my fist on his shaft, and we both let go at the same time. White flashes exploded behind my eyelids. He groaned into my shoulder, biting me as he climaxed all over my hand.

It took some time to catch my breath. We were a sticky mess, but we lay together for several minutes before either of us moved.

He groaned. "Shit. We'll probably fuck each other to death before we get this heat out of our systems."

"It'd be a great way to go." I let go of him.

"Yeah, it would be. Let's go get showered. You're leaking all over me."

"It's your semen, so *you're* leaking all over *me*."

"True. And I've got more where that came from." He wrapped his arm around me and squeezed my breast, then we rolled out of bed and started getting ready for the day.

We showered together after breakfast, and he thoroughly washed me, then rubbed my clit with his fingers and then his cock. He pulled me in front of him with my back to his chest, and I panted and pushed my bottom back into his groin while he worked me into another orgasm.

"Fuck, honey. I can't get enough of this."

As he stroked me, he murmured some of the dirty things he wanted to do with me while he rammed two fingers in and out of my core.

"Oh, God, your fingers feel so big. It feels so good," I sobbed.

"Then my cock will make you delirious." He chuckled wickedly. "And when we do fuck, I plan to keep you under me for hours."

His filthy words and his fingers had me coming all over his hand as my body bucked under him.

When I caught my breath and came down from my high, I turned around and picked up a washcloth to scrub his shoulders and back. While I slowly and meticulously scrubbed him, I bent down and bit one of his ass cheeks.

He looked over his shoulder in surprise. "Did you just bite me?"

I smiled. "Yep. I've been wanting to do that for a while. Now turn around."

He slowly turned around, and I took his long, thick length in my hand. I leisurely stroked and cleaned his shaft and testicles, then washed them off and knelt in front of him, drawing him into my mouth. Damien watched me with hooded eyes as I worked my lips over his length, then slowly slid his cock down my throat. He didn't know I didn't have a gag reflex.

I pulled back, then slowly licked up and down again and sucked on his tip. He jerked but didn't pull out. I worked him back into my throat, then slid his shaft in and out of my esophagus. I came up for air a few times, then pushed onto his shaft again as I swallowed around him.

He clenched and fought not to come. He finally pulled out and stared down at me, stroking my face. "Did you just deep-throat me for five fucking minutes without gagging once?"

"Yes."

"Harley, do you have a gag reflex?" he asked slowly.

"No." I grinned up at him.

His head rolled back, and he looked at the ceiling. "Ho-ly fuck. I've died and gone to heaven." He gazed back down at me. "How long can you go?" His voice was low and husky.

"As long as you want, I think. But you're big and the problem might be my throat getting rubbed raw."

His hand cupped my jaw, and he leaned down and kissed me, slipping his tongue inside my mouth. "You're a fucking unicorn, you know that?"

"Because I don't have a gag reflex?"

"That and a million other reasons. Do you want me to pull out, or can I come down your throat?" he growled.

I pumped his cock a few times. "I don't have a lot of practice, but you can come down my throat."

"How many people know about this?" he asked.

"Just you. And Olivia." Ryan had also known, but I didn't say that out loud.

He leaned down and kissed my mouth again. "Good, let's keep it that way," he said against my lips.

Then he stood and slowly worked his cock into my mouth again.

He stroked my face while he thrust inside me. "Shit, sweetheart. Watching you take my cock down your throat is one of the hottest things I've ever seen."

I flushed at his words and felt my nipples contract. He worked himself into the back of my throat again and gritted his teeth.

Staring up at his face and watching him fight for control made my vagina clench and my nipples pebble into hard points. I felt vulnerable and powerful all at once.

He reached down and cupped my breasts, then played with my nipples as he thrust in and out of my mouth. After stroking himself there for a few moments, he sped up his pace, then pushed all the way in and pulsed down my throat. He groaned long and low as he came, and my vagina spasmed at the sound.

Connor pulled me up and wrapped his arms around me. "Fu-uuck me. Your mouth should be considered a national treasure."

I barked out a breathless laugh and smacked his side.

Chapter 22

When I drove up to the passenger pickup at the Palm Springs airport Thursday night, Olivia stood on the curb waiting for me.

I jumped out and hugged her, then lifted her up and spun her around.

"Harley! What are you doing?" she laughed.

"Just throwing my back out." I set her down, then helped stow her luggage in the back seat. She gave Gary a few pets, then got in and looked me over. I'd been lounging around at home before picking her up, and I was still wearing my cut-off sweats and a ratty t-shirt.

"It looks like you've owned that outfit since high school."

I looked down and shrugged. "I've owned *most* of it since high school."

"Ha! I knew it!" Olivia leaned back and let out a long, audible exhale. "I'm so happy to be done with school for a while, and to be here with you. I don't even care if we watch one of your shitty indie movies tonight."

"You're nicer than I am because I *do* care about watching one of your horror movies."

She turned to me. "It's Christmas. Maybe we can pick something a little more uplifting."

"I'm good with that. But I think Ava invited us over for dinner," I reminded her.

Olivia grimaced. "Crap, I forgot. And I haven't eaten anything since breakfast."

Ava was a terrible cook, and she usually overcooked everything. We used to joke about it with my dad when he was alive. And then I'd taken over the cooking after he died. I wasn't a great cook either, but I knew how to grill and that had probably saved us.

"Have you and Mom talked at all since Thanksgiving?" Olivia asked.

My shoulders tensed. "Yes."

"About anything important?"

"I don't know. We went to lunch the other day, and I'm still going over to her house a couple of times a week to make sure it's clean and she's okay."

"Has she forgiven you for Gary's defection?"

"She threw Gary away by not taking care of him," I countered. Gary's head swung up to look at me when I said his name. "And I mostly leave Gary at home now when I see her."

We pulled up to my house.

"How do you think she's actually doing?" she asked.

"I think she's hanging in there, one day at a time."

Olivia nodded and looked out the window. "What do you think about getting her a kitten for Christmas?"

I mulled it over. "I think it'd be better to get her a full-grown cat. They're more self-sufficient."

Olivia nodded. "There are self-watering and self-feeding bowls we could try."

"Huh, it's a good idea. Let's think about it while you're here. There's a nice animal shelter in south Palm Springs, and I'm sure they have plenty of cats for adoption."

"Mom said she's seen a guy around your house lately. How come you haven't mentioned anything?" she asked.

"It's probably Damien. He's an investigator and I've been working with him on a case. He's going camping with us tomorrow."

"Is he one of Sebastian's friends?" she asked.

"Yes."

"Is he *your* friend?"

"Yes," I said.

"Is he your *special* friend?"

I rolled my eyes. "You're so funny. How old are you, twelve?"

"You know what's even more funny? You're twenty-eight and you don't have a boyfriend."

"Shut it, Ollie. And it's complicated."

Her eyes rounded, and she pointed her finger in my face. "Oh, my God! You *do* have a boyfriend."

"I love you more than life itself. But first, get your finger out of my face. And second, you're a nosy bugger and you've got a big mouth." Olivia rolled her eyes but didn't deny it.

Ava called Olivia about two minutes after she put her stuff in the spare bedroom.

"We'll be over in a few minutes. I just barely walked in the door," she told Ava.

Olivia paused, and I could imagine Ava giving her a guilt trip about staying at my house for the first part of her vacation. Olivia usually split her time between us when she visited Palm Springs. She also planned to be with Ava over Christmas Eve and Christmas Day.

"Mom, we've already talked about this," Olivia said. "I'll move over to your place on Christmas Eve. I want to spend time with Harley too." She paused, then sighed. "Don't ruin my first night here. We want to come over, but I don't want you bringing this up if we do." Olivia paused and listened for a minute. "Okay, we'll be over in a few. Love you too."

Olivia had somehow gotten stuck in the middle of the conflict between Ava and me, and I wasn't sure how to make it easier for her.

"You know you can stay with her the whole time. I don't want you to ever feel like you have to choose between us."

Olivia shook her head. "I *want* to stay with you. It's more relaxing and peaceful here. And she needs to stop being so pushy and unreasonable."

I sighed and arranged my hair in a quick knot. "She's not the only one with issues in our relationship. I have a short fuse with her, but I'm trying to do better. It's a work in progress."

"You shouldn't have to rearrange your life to be her safety net, and then put up with her nitpicking and moodiness on top of it."

She looked away for a moment. "Maybe it's time to let her make her own choices—just let natural consequences take their course."

"I've thought about it, and about selling this house." I looked around. "Dad's memory seems to keep me here. But maybe it's time."

We tabled the discussion and walked next door to Ava's house. She must have been watching for us because she was waiting with her front door open.

"Olivia! I've missed you so much." She gave Ollie a long hug and kissed her on the cheeks several times.

She turned to me. "Harley, do you have any lemon? I made halibut but forgot to buy one."

"Yes. I'll go grab it."

I went back to my house and got the lemon. I also took a few minutes to eat a little snack. When I got back to Ava's house, it smelled like overcooked fish. Olivia opened some windows and tried to air out the kitchen. She gave me a wide-eyed look.

"Your patio looks so inviting. Can we eat out there?" I asked.

"Oh, what a great idea," Olivia piped up. She surreptitiously waved her hand in front of her face.

Ava shrugged. "I guess we can eat outside."

During the meal, Ava peppered Olivia with questions about her plans after graduation, and we laughed about one of Olivia's roommates trying to wax her boyfriend's bottom and accidentally giving him second-degree burns.

Ava was aghast. "You mean he let her wax his privates, and she'd never waxed anyone before?"

Olivia shook her head. "Nope. And he's kind of hairy. I think they'd planned to wax his entire back along with his butt crack."

I winced, and my bottom clenched in sympathy. "Is he okay? It seems like the skin is sensitive down there."

Olivia shook her head. "I don't know. They were planning a trip to Mexico over the winter break. That's why they were waxing."

Ava picked up her wine glass and pointed at us. "This is a good lesson. You should leave beauty treatments to the professionals, ladies."

Ava didn't bring up Gary, and I didn't complain about her drinking, so everyone got along at dinner. Olivia and I went home afterward and watched a Scottish zombie Christmas musical called *Anna and the Apocalypse*. It was one of the strangest Christmas musicals I'd ever seen, and Olivia didn't hate it because it had zombies in it.

Besides Ava's overcooked fish, it had been an enjoyable night. I had to work tomorrow, but there was a rec volleyball game on Saturday morning against Damien's team, and we were going camping on Saturday night with Damien and my friends. I was confident Olivia and Damien would get along just fine.

On Saturday morning, we played Damien's volleyball team. It should have been our second match against them, but we'd officially forfeited the first one because of Frankie's death.

The match reopened fresh wounds, and my competitive spirit was gone. I just wanted to get it over with. But halfway through the first set, Kevin of all people called for a time-out.

Then he chewed our asses out. "What in the fuck are you all doing? Are we just going to give up? Huh? Is that what we learned from Frankie? And from treatment? We just give up?" He didn't wait for an answer. "And you, Harley. Do you think Frankie would have wanted you to just roll over and let those self-righteous assholes win?"

"I'm not a self-righteous asshole," Zeke called from across the net. "Just a regular asshole." I stuck my middle finger up without looking over at Zeke. He laughed.

Kevin lowered his voice. "I fucking hate to lose. But I'd rather lose knowing we didn't just give up, bend over, and let them dry-fuck us in the ass."

We waited for Kevin to continue, but he looked at us expectantly.

Jaime cringed. "Dude, that's gross."

"Really?" Tiana stared at Kevin. "That's how you're going to end your speech?"

Kevin shrugged. "Yeah."

I held up my hands. "Okay, Kevin. We get your point. You may have gone a little too far with that last visual. But we get it."

Kevin nodded and stepped back.

I studied my team. "Kevin's right, and I'm sorry. This isn't what Frankie would have wanted." Leaning in, I lowered my voice. "We're all going to have to hustle. And don't shank your serves, for Hell's sake." I went on to give a few more pointers and even went over some strategy with Kevin and Josh.

"Just get the damned point if you can. It doesn't have to be pretty."

We lost the first set. But during the second set, Kevin and Josh started working together, and we scraped out a win. By the third set, a switch seemed to flip in Kevin, and he was on fire.

He still fed most of the bumps and sets to me, but for the first time I was able to focus more on offense.

After Kevin gave me a particularly well-placed bump off one of Zeke's serves, Damien glanced incredulously at me. I just shrugged because I didn't know what was going on either.

We won the third set by four points, which was a huge margin for us. The team erupted, and both Jaime and Josh slapped Kevin hard on the ass. He was still mean, but he seemed happier than I'd ever seen him.

Damien shook his head and walked over to me. He grabbed my waist and pulled me into him. "That was the strangest, most disturbing pep talk I've ever heard." He studied Kevin. "Did he really say something about getting dry-fucked in the ass?"

I grimaced. "Yep. Instead of motivating us, I think he scared us into winning."

Chapter 23

A few hours later, Olivia crossed her arms and tried to stare Damien down through the rearview mirror as we drove to Joshua Tree.

Damien met us at my house after the volleyball game so we could drive together. Brock and Zeke were going together as well, and Sebastian would bring Laurel and Martina. We planned to meet at the trailhead, and Zeke had gotten our overnight camping permit.

Damien looked down at my tight black yoga pants and grinned appreciatively. I'd texted him to let him know I was now officially on birth control.

He wrapped an arm around my neck, then pulled me in for a quick kiss. I pressed against him, and he rubbed his thumb across my lower lip.

"You ready?" he asked softly.

I smiled. "Yes. Damien, this is Olivia, my sister. She's a little shit sometimes, so please take that into account."

Olivia shook her head at my introduction. "Hi, Damien. I'd say it's nice to meet you, but I'm reserving judgment."

Damien's lip twitched. "Good to know. It's easy to tell you two are related."

Olivia smiled like he'd just complimented her. We gathered our gear and threw it in the back of his truck. It had been a while since I'd been camping, and I missed it. The desert and mountains were therapy for me, and I craved getting outside and away from the crowds and noise sometimes.

On the way out to Joshua Tree, Olivia grilled Damien. "How old are you?" she asked.

"Thirty-three next month." I'd have to find out his exact birthdate.

"How long have you lived in Palm Springs?"

"Around eight years."

"Are you divorced?" she asked.

"No."

"Are you currently married?"

Damien smirked. "Still a no."

"Harley said you and a couple of your friends own a security and investigation firm. Do you make a decent living?"

I cut in. "Ollie, that's none of your business. Just stop with the fifty questions already."

"I think the saying is twenty questions."

"Yeah, but you're already way past that," I retorted.

She smirked at me. "Are you afraid you might hear something you don't like?"

"No, I'm afraid I'm going to reach back and strangle you, and Ava will be furious because it's only your second day here."

Damien turned to me. "I'm fine with the questions, Legs. If she asks me something I don't want to answer, I'll let her know."

"Okay. But if she gets too nosy, *I'll* stop her."

He grabbed my knee and squeezed. "Fair enough."

Olivia leaned back and started in again. "Who's watching your business while you three are away?"

I piped up. "Objection, it's not relevant."

Olivia leaned forward. "It *is* relevant. I want to know if he's a responsible business owner."

Damien smiled. "We're paying two of our employees overtime to be on call."

I hadn't known that, but I was glad they'd all come.

Olivia hummed, probably trying to think of more questions. "Do you own your own home, or rent?"

Damien glanced back at her through the rearview mirror. "That's a question an accountant would ask. I own a home and have a small short-term rental on my property."

Olivia grunted in reluctant approval. "How many siblings do you have?"

"My younger brother, Brock, and two half-siblings I don't know very well. They're ten and twelve years younger than me and live in Austin. You'll meet Brock today."

"Have you had any serious girlfriends?"

Damien shrugged. "A couple."

"Has Harley told you she's been engaged before?" Olivia asked.

I shifted uncomfortably in my seat.

"She has. She also told me about the accident." He looked over at me.

Olivia nodded and looked out the window. "Have you and Harley had sex?"

I cut in. "That's none of your business, and you're done."

Olivia didn't object.

Damien studied Olivia through the rearview mirror. "Now it's my turn to ask you a few questions."

"Okay." Olivia didn't sound concerned, but him asking the questions made me nervous.

"You're twenty-three, is that right?" he asked Olivia.

"Yes."

"Are you planning to move to Palm Springs when you graduate?"

"Kind of," Olivia replied.

"What do you mean, kind of?"

"I've been talking to an accounting firm in LA, and they said they'd let me work remotely most of the time."

"So you'll be commuting?"

"Yes," Olivia answered.

"Does Harley snore?" he asked.

Olivia grinned. "No, but she talks in her sleep sometimes."

"Good to know."

Olivia finally asked the dreaded question. "How did you and Harley meet?"

I groaned and Damien started laughing.

"What?" Olivia asked, leaning forward again.

Damien tried to stop laughing and cleared his throat. "We play city rec volleyball in the same league—on different teams." He didn't elaborate.

"Harley takes her volleyball very seriously." Olivia watched him.

Damien nodded. "Believe me, I know."

"Spill, Andreasen," she demanded.

He shook his head. "You're going to have to ask Harley."

Olivia huffed and sat back. "She never *voluntarily* tells me anything. She's like a damn vault."

We met the group at the trailhead, and I introduced them all to Olivia. Everyone said hello except Sebastian, who just grunted.

Brock studied Olivia. "She's like a Mini-Me version of you, Harley." Olivia was shorter than me but had similar coloring.

"No, she's not. She's a lot smarter than I am, she doesn't like most sports, and for some godawful reason she loves horror movies."

Zeke looked at her more closely. "I've never met a woman who likes horror flicks."

Olivia shrugged. "Then you need to get out more because I know quite a few. If they're done well, horror films take more talent and creativity than most drama or action films. Harley loves foreign indie films, the weirder and more esoteric the better. I can't stand most of them."

Zeke nodded and turned to Damien. "There's Harley's one major flaw. I told you, every hot woman has one."

I rolled my eyes. "That's a major flaw? Really?"

Zeke grinned and just shrugged.

We loaded up our packs and got on the trail. Olivia turned out to be the slowest and least experienced hiker. She'd spent a lot of time in school and working over the past six years, and it appeared she didn't get out on many hikes or do much cardio. I knew she liked Pilates and yoga, but we needed to talk about her endurance.

"Is this pack supposed to weigh this much?" she whined, huffing a little.

"You have the lightest pack out of all of us, and I'm carrying your tent. Suck it up, buttercup," I shot back.

Damien looked back at me. "You really are a *Lord of the Flies* hiker." He turned to Olivia. "The trail isn't as sandy about half a mile in. It gets easier from there."

We'd started on the Boy Scout trail to avoid all the sand at the beginning of Big Pine, but even this trail had its fair share.

"Thanks, Damien. Hopefully, *you* won't leave me behind if we run into a bear."

I sighed in exasperation. "It's the desert. We might see a rattlesnake or maybe a coyote. But no bears."

Olivia stopped abruptly. "Rattlesnakes? Why didn't you tell me this before?"

Zeke snickered. "People rarely die from rattlesnake bites, and they're more afraid of you. You might lose a foot if you get bit, but you probably won't die."

She glared at him. "That makes me feel *sooo* much better."

Damien pointed to Sebastian ahead of us. "The people in front are more likely to get bitten. It's rare, but it usually only happens if someone startles a rattlesnake."

"But the coyotes do like to pick off stragglers," Zeke added.

When Zeke glanced back at her, Olivia wiped nonexistent sweat from her brow with her middle finger. Zeke started laughing.

Olivia seemed to find her rhythm, and we hiked steadily for the next few hours. The trail went by rock formations, large groves of Joshua trees, and the huge dead pine tree the trail was named after.

We only ran into two other groups of hikers, and neither had overnight packs. Laurel pulled out her camera and stopped to take a few photographs later in the day when the lighting got softer. She looked comfortable with her camera, and she used it with familiarity and ease.

I'd walked behind Damien for most of the hike, and it was a nice view. Olivia caught up with me and whispered in my ear. "Quit looking at his perfect bubble butt."

I didn't turn around or break stride. I also didn't quit staring. "No."

"Yes. You're creeping me out."

"No, I'm not. And I don't like that you also noticed he has a perfect bubble butt."

"How can you *not* notice? They *all* have amazing butts. Admit it," she said.

"I admit nothing."

She laughed behind me. "It's made the hike so much more enjoyable."

Damien stopped abruptly in front of me. He looked at us and shook his head, then took my hand and drew me off the trail a little. He nodded at Olivia when she stopped next to us.

"Go ahead. I want to talk with Harley for a minute."

She gave him a knowing look. "Okay. I have a clearer view now anyway." I looked up the trail. Zeke and Brock were hiking ahead of us.

She walked past, and I turned to Damien. "What's up?"

He smirked. "Voices carry in the desert."

I stared at him, not knowing where he was going. "And?"

"And you can look at my ass all you want, but not at theirs."

My face flushed. "I wasn't."

"I heard you two talking." He looked like he wanted to laugh.

Oh, Lord. He'd heard us. And were we really having this conversation? "It's been pretty much yours since we started hiking. I can't vouch for Olivia though."

He went still for a second, then bent down and murmured in my ear. "We're sleeping in the same tent tonight."

My eyes glazed over. "Okay."

He ran his hands down my arms, then pulled me to him. "I fucking *need* some alone time with you."

We both glanced up the trail. Everyone had stopped to watch us. Martina was talking to Laurel and grinning. Zeke and Brock were staring, and Sebastian's arms were crossed. He looked impatient.

Only Olivia wasn't watching us. She'd gotten up on a large rock and was looking around at the ground nervously.

I sighed. "I know. Me too."

He studied me. "Fuck it," he muttered then grabbed my shoulders, bent his head, and gave me a long hot kiss—in front of everyone. His mouth was delicious, and I forgot we had an audience. I moved closer to him and grabbed his forearms. He cradled my face in his hands and slanted my head a little for better access. After a few seconds, he pulled back. My face felt flushed, and I was lightheaded.

Olivia made gagging noises. "Just stop, okay? I already need therapy. Don't make it worse."

Damien looked me in the eye, his lips twitching. "No more looking at anyone else's bubble butt."

I winced. "Crap. You really did hear us."

He grinned. "I did."

We both turned and started up the trail. "Olivia started it," I said. "She probably needed a distraction from thinking about bears and rattlesnakes. And how heavy her little five-pound pack is."

"I heard that, and it's heavier than five pounds," Olivia said loudly. The group started walking again too.

"Okay, more like six pounds," I conceded.

We stopped a while later when we'd found an area with a flat surface and a wide rock plateau we could use to sit on and eat our meals. Then we got to work setting up camp and pitching our tents.

Olivia looked at her tent, and seemed to have no idea where to start. I planned to help Damien pitch ours, then help Olivia with hers, but Zeke beat me to it.

"I can pitch your tent," Zeke told her as she struggled to unfold the green fabric.

"No. I don't want you to *do* it for me, big guy. I want you to teach me so I can do it myself."

"You sure? I bet I can pitch it in under three minutes."

Brock walked over and watched Olivia struggle to pull the folded poles out of the small nylon bag. "I bet I could pitch it in two and a half," Brock bragged.

"Listen, Bear Grylls and Ray Mears, I'm so impressed you all could pitch this little two-person tent in three minutes or less. But

I want to learn how to do it myself. Just because I haven't been able to spend a lot of time outdoors doesn't mean I'm an idiot."

Brock folded his arms. "You thought there were bears around here."

She glared at him. "So? I bet you have no idea how to navigate title twenty-six of the U.S. tax code, or what the accrual principle is, or even what ACCG stands for."

Zeke looked down at Olivia with his hands on his hips. He was at least a foot taller and almost twice as broad. "I know you're not an idiot. You're graduating in accounting this spring, for hell's sake."

"Thanks, Zeke." She turned to look at Brock. "ACCG is the acronym for accounting."

Brock shrugged. "I didn't know that. I don't know the tax code either, thank God, but the accrual principle is—"

Olivia slowly turned her head to look at him. She looked like the possessed little girl in *The Exorcist*. Damien and I both stopped working to watch them.

Brock held up his hands and backed away. "She's all yours."

Olivia turned back to Zeke and held up a folded-up pole. "Okay, big guy. Show me how to build this motherfucker."

Zeke's lips quirked, and he took the pole. "Alright 'little girl.' And the term is pitch this tent, not build this motherfucker. First, you need to find a good spot."

Then Zeke methodically showed Olivia how to pitch a tent. The process took longer than three minutes, but Olivia knew how to do it herself when they finished.

She stood back to admire their work and tapped Zeke's arm. "Thanks, big guy."

He grinned and gently put his arm around her. "You're welcome, little girl."

We lucked out with the weather, and the temperatures were in the mid-fifties. But all of us added a jacket or another layer when the sun went down. Brock and Sebastian pulled out a couple of backpacking camp stoves and we started the meal, then we sat around the camp stoves and ate freeze-dried pasta and stewed dried fruit for dinner. We cleaned up and watched the stars slowly come out as the light faded.

I pulled out the two chocolate bars I'd stashed in my backpack and broke them into pieces, then passed them around for dessert.

"I've got the perfect pairing for your chocolate." Martina grabbed a bottle of tequila and some little metal condiment cups out of her pack.

"Who brings a bottle of tequila on a hiking trip?" Laurel asked.

"I think the better question is who *doesn't*? Does this mean you don't want any?" Martina wiggled the bottle at her.

"No, I want some. Thanks for packing it in." Laurel smiled and then poured a small cup. She took a sip and made a face.

Martina laughed at her. "You know wine, but you suck at drinking tequila. Here, like this." She threw her shot back, then smacked her lips.

I winced. "I've had a few shots of tequila in my time, but never without a chaser," I admitted, raising my little condiment cup. "Cheers, everyone. To a beautiful starry night with some of my favorite people."

We nibbled on chocolate, drank tequila, and looked up at the night sky. I'd gotten my sleeping bag out, and Damien and I sat next to each other on it. Olivia was on my other side wrapped in her bag.

She peered up at the sky in awe. "I've never seen such a starry sky." She finally spread her sleeping bag out on the rock so she could lie on her back and look up.

The Milky Way was a bright swish of stars scattered across the dark sky, and the brighter planets shimmered and glowed at us.

Laurel sighed next to Sebastian. "It's so quiet in the desert, especially at night. I've always loved how peaceful it is."

We talked softly for a while and gazed up at the constellations until people started slowly getting ready for bed. I finally got up and brushed my teeth, cleaned my face, and wiped myself down a little with some baby wipes.

Damien got ready for bed as well. He'd zipped our bags together while I said goodnight to Olivia. She was drifting off when I left her.

Damien lifted the edge of the bag when I crawled into the tent.

"Come here, and I'll keep you warm."

I slid inside and snuggled up next to him, so we faced each other. His body heat seeped into me, and I felt lazy and content.

"Thank you for putting up with all of Olivia's questions and crazy comments today," I murmured.

"It wasn't a big deal. She's just watching out for you." He brushed a few strands of hair out of my eyes. "She's funny, and almost as crazy as you are."

"Ollie *is* a little crazy, isn't she?"

He chuckled. "I thought I was going to lose it when she gave Brock that scary, serial killer look."

My hand slid around his neck. "It's been a great day, hasn't it?"

He leaned in and kissed me softly. "Yeah. And it's going to be an even better night."

Damien ran his hands under my shirt and pullover and slid them up to cup my breasts. I'd taken off my bra when I'd gotten ready for bed.

"Fuck, honey. You're killing me," he whispered against my mouth. He swiped his thumbs across my nipples, then kissed up my neck. I moaned softly.

"We're going to have to be quiet. Sound travels out here. Can you be good, or do I need to stop?"

"I can be quiet," I murmured.

We kissed and stroked each other for a few minutes, then he pushed my shirt up and brought his head down to my breasts. He nipped and licked at my nipple thoroughly, then he switched to the other nipple. When he pulled my areola deep into his mouth and sucked, my neck bent back, and I grabbed his forearms.

Damien worked my breasts until I was panting, and my slit was leaking moisture. He finally came up for air, and I licked my palm then slid my hand down and found his swollen, pulsing cock under his sweatpants. When I wrapped my hand around him and started slowly pumping his shaft, he arched into me and swore. I couldn't quite reach all the way around, so I slid my other hand down and circled him with both my damp palms.

"Can *you* be good, or do I need to stop?"

He kissed me, and I felt him smile. "Oh, I can be good." Then he slowly pulled my yoga pants off my hips and gently fingered my clit.

I sucked in a breath and blew it out slowly. "Oh, God. I need you inside me right now," I barely whispered into his ear.

"Then I can guarantee you I won't be quiet. And neither will you," he whispered back.

"I don't care right now."

He shook his head. "I don't want anyone else to hear what you sound like the first time I drive my cock deep inside you. That's only for us." I pulled in a breath at his dirty words, then nodded into his neck. Because he was right.

We played with each other for a few more minutes, and then when I started begging him softly, he rolled me to my side and spooned me from behind. I felt his cock slide between my legs, and he rubbed himself through my slit while he played with my clit. I cupped his shaft underneath as he glided it between my saturated center. He gripped my chest tightly, latching onto a breast, and pushed his hips into me.

My heart pounded, and I could feel my pussy pulsing with each heartbeat. Damien's breathing sped up, and I knew he was getting close. I was a little lightheaded and my clit felt so swollen and sensitive.

When my hips started thrusting back to meet his and I began to orgasm, he pulled my head to the side and covered my mouth with his. He bit my lower lip, then smothered the soft sounds coming out of my throat as I came. He continued to rhythmically slide his shaft between my thighs, and a few seconds later he forcefully arched into me and silently climaxed between my legs. I lay there panting and trying to catch my breath.

He eventually stirred and leaned over and whispered in my ear. "I haven't even been inside your hot little pussy yet, but I'm already fucking addicted to it." I shivered and wondered what it would be like when we finally had sex. He groped around and found his micro towel, and we cleaned up the best we could.

I was sticky and wet between my legs, but I didn't care. Endorphins were floating through me, and I could feel his heat warming my back. He gathered me into him, and I fell asleep with his lips brushing the top of my head.

The next morning, I woke up alone. Damien's side of the sleeping bag was cold, and I missed his body heat. I groaned softly and sat up. My thin sleeping pad had done little to soften the hard ground beneath us.

It was cold, so I got dressed and bundled up, then crawled out. Olivia was still in her tent, and everyone seemed to be sleeping. Damien sat looking out across the expanse, and he'd already put water on a camp stove to boil. When he saw me, he propped his knees open and motioned for me to sit between them. I was still a little sleepy and cold, and he looked warm and inviting so I sank in front of him and leaned back against his chest.

"Good morning," he murmured in my ear. Zeke and Brock were both still burrowed into their bags, and I could see just a little tuft of Zeke's hair poking out.

"You feel warm and hard."

He chuckled. "You make me that way. What are you doing up so early?"

"I got a little cold. What are you doing up?"

I felt him shrug. "I usually get up early. I was also having a hard time keeping my hands off you."

My backside wiggled even closer to him, and I started breathing a little heavier. He moved my braid over and kissed my neck.

"You and I need to find some alone time. Not in between emergencies or family, or on a camping trip with half a dozen other people around." He rubbed his cheek on mine, and his whiskers felt ticklish against my skin.

"Yes, we do." I reached back and patted his cheek. "I was just wondering what your whiskers would feel like on... other parts of my body."

He'd bent over me and was nipping my ear when Olivia poked her head out of her tent and yawned widely.

"What're we having for breakfast? I'm starving."

Damien tightened his arms around me and groaned softly. We reluctantly pulled apart and got moving. We made instant coffee, then whipped up breakfast. Damien and I made pancakes and re-hydrated scrambled eggs, and Brock and Olivia cleaned up. Then we packed up and got ready to go.

"I don't know why instant coffee always tastes like shit, except when I'm camping," Brock said.

Martina nodded. "Then it tastes like *the* shit."

"Did you know the word 'shit' is one of the most versatile words in the English language?" Zeke asked.

Brock shook his head. "I didn't know that, but it sounds like you're going to tell us."

"It's true, smartass. Think of all the meanings that word has. There's the standard 'bullshit,' meaning something's a lie, there's 'horseshit' which means unfair—"

Martina held up her hand. "My personal favorite is bat shit."

Sebastian shook his head. "Not a big surprise there."

Zeke ticked off several more. "There's Jack shit, deep shit, a shitstorm."

Olivia cut in. "I've always liked ape shit. Oh, and chicken shit."

"There are a few good sayings too. 'When the shit hits the fan,' or 'I don't give a shit,'" Martina added.

I grinned. "Holy shit, you guys are like a bunch of twelve-year-olds."

"Good one," Laurel yelled from up the line.

When I looked back at Damien, he was shaking his head at all of us. "We definitely need some alone time, Legs."

Chapter 24

I felt restless and needy as I tried to figure out how Damien and I could schedule some alone time. The work week before Christmas was always busy since the courts usually shut down between Christmas Eve and New Year's Day.

My private practice had also taken off in the last year or so, and I seemed to be getting more referrals than ever. Sariah and Yun kept telling me I needed to give up the public defender work and do all private practice, but I just couldn't bring myself to do it. I felt a sense of purpose when I could help some of those clients.

On Monday night, Damien took Olivia and me to Laurel's Martini Monday Christmas party. We walked in and heard the "Hawaiian Christmas Song" playing. Laurel's gigantic Christmas tree was adorned with plush superhero characters tucked into the branches in various poses, and a bright red cape had been wrapped around the bottom, doubling as a tree skirt. I was pretty sure Willie and Lennie had picked out the tree decorations.

Through her floor-to-ceiling windows that faced the back of the house, I could see some of the palm tree trunks had been wrapped in colored lights. There were a couple of extra-large red and white striped candy cane floaties drifting around in her pool too.

I noticed Martina standing in the backyard talking with a tall, stocky man who had thick muscles and a craggy, sharp face. He appeared to be in his mid to late thirties. For once, Martina wasn't smiling, and she looked a little angry and pissed off. I wondered if I could pry the story out of Laurel or Zeke.

I knew everyone else there, and when Damien stopped in the kitchen to talk with Sebastian, I walked over to say hello to Grace and Sheila.

"Thanks again for taking care of Gary for me last Saturday."

"It was no problem. How was your hike?" Sheila asked.

"Really nice."

"Nice and hike are two words that should never be in the same sentence," I heard Ramone say from behind me.

I smirked. "It *was* nice."

Olivia hummed a little beside me.

I turned to her. "What?"

"We ate freeze-dried pasta for dinner and instant coffee and rehydrated scrambled eggs for breakfast."

"So? You hike long enough, and everything tastes good."

Ramone held up his finger. "Maybe not *everything*."

"It's sleeping on the hard ground that gets me," Sheila said.

Grace shook her head. "I'd only walk that far if there were eighteen holes of golf involved."

Olivia pointed at me. "Harley also didn't tell me there were rattlesnakes or coyotes out there."

Grace shrugged. "It was smart of Harley to omit that part."

"I didn't purposefully *not* tell her." I threw up my hands. "It's the desert. It's their natural habitat."

"And all that sand and dirt, with no running hot water or a bathroom? No, thank you." Ramone shuddered.

I put my hands on my hips and turned to Olivia. "Did you like *anything* about the camping trip?"

"The night sky was amazing. I've never seen that many stars before. And I liked learning how to pitch a tent. Okay, there were some good parts."

I rolled my eyes. "Glad to hear you liked *something*."

"My favorite part was hanging out with you and your friends." She turned to Grace and Sheila. "You should've heard Zeke's commentary about how versatile the word 'shit' is."

Grace laughed. "That man has some interesting ideas."

Ramone stood there in thought for a moment. "You know, he's right. There's bullshit, and a crock of shit—"

"Don't start!" I protested. "You don't want to go down that rabbit hole."

Scott, Laurel's neighbor, walked up. "Are you talking about how many meanings have been attached to a variation of the word, shit? It's pretty interesting."

"I can't go through this conversation again without a drink first." I left them and walked over to Laurel who was at the kitchen bar with the martini ingredients lined up in front of her. I remembered her various Halloween-themed martinis and wondered what she'd dreamed up for Christmas.

"What strange and amazing flavors did you decide on?"

She smiled happily. "I'm glad you asked. We've got peppermint martinis." She pointed at the beautiful but empty martini glass rimmed with crushed candy cane.

"I've also got a sugar cookie-flavored martini with vanilla vodka and amaretto." She pointed at the glass with red and green sprinkles around the rim.

"And a white Christmas martini with white chocolate liqueur, heavy cream, and vanilla vodka. It's a pure white chocolate martini."

I looked down at all the decadent, sugary ingredients. "Those sound delicious, but I'll have to visit the dentist tomorrow."

She grinned. "There's also a traditional eggnog martini. And finally, we have a tart but slightly sweet cranberry orange gin martini with just a hint of cinnamon. That one's Sebastian's recipe; he made it for us at Thanksgiving."

I nodded. "That last one sounds intriguing. I'll try that."

Damien and Sebastian walked over while we were talking.

Sebastian started making my drink. "Good choice. The rest will put you into a sugar coma."

"Who's the guy in the backyard with Martina? She doesn't look happy," I asked.

Laurel glanced at Sebastian. "His name's Iz Nixon. He and Scott own The Cockpit over on Arenas and Indian Canyon Drive."

"The gay bar with the over-the-top karaoke night and Sunday drag brunch?"

"Yes. That's the one."

Sebastian smiled. "The first time Laurel heard Scott and Iz owned The Cockpit, she asked Scott if it had an aviation theme."

I shrugged. "We do have an airplane museum, and there's the Marine Corps Air Ground Center in Twentynine Palms."

Laurel gave Sebastian a disgruntled look. "See? It was a simple mistake."

"It was sweet, just like you are." He wrapped his arm around her waist and drew her closer, then kissed her neck.

Laurel curled into him. I was too keyed up and had to look away.

"Martina didn't look happy out on the patio with him. But she hasn't ripped his balls off yet. What's the story?" I asked.

Laurel tugged her ear. "I know a little, but not all of it. Martina's adamant about not dating until she's been divorced for at least a year, which was in August."

Watching them out on the patio, I nodded. "That's smart. It's probably not a bad idea to get your head together and give yourself a little time after a breakup or relationship. And it's better for Iz as well."

Sebastian glanced at Damien and his mouth flattened, but he didn't say anything.

Laurel sighed. "Iz has other ideas though."

There was more to the story, and I could feel a strange undercurrent between Sebastian and Damien.

Sebastian finished shaking my drink and poured it into a chilled glass. Then he cut off a small section of orange rind and lit a match to warm the skin up a bit. I could smell the fragrant oils in the orange rind release as it heated up.

It was a work of liquid art. I picked up the glass, gave Sebastian a toast, and took a sip. A faint hint of cinnamon, and the tart cranberry and tangy orange flavors mixed with the gin.

Damien watched me lick my lips, and his eyelids drooped.

"Holy shit, this is *so good*."

Olivia slid into the stool next to me. "See? Shit *is* an amazing, magically diverse word."

"Please don't start. I'm having a transcendent moment here with my drink." She rolled her eyes, but I simply handed the glass to her.

She took a sip, and her eyes went wide. "Well, damn. That *is* good."

On Tuesday during juvenile drug court, Judge Perez reminded the kids to be vigilant during the holiday break.

"The holidays are a fun time, but they're also stressful. And stress is a trigger for most people. Tell your family and friends if they're causing you stress. Let them know what triggers you."

"So if my mom makes me let Aunt Lupita kiss me on the lips, I can tell her having my mean, sweaty, and stinky aunt's lips on me is a trigger?" Roland asked.

Wendy palmed her forehead, and I bit my tongue.

But Judge Perez answered in a serious tone. "Yes, that could be a trigger." He looked at my clients. "Some family members behave badly, and sometimes they're the worst triggers we have."

Roland leaned back in his chair with a small nod. "Okay."

Judge Perez pointed at him. "That doesn't mean you can be disrespectful. But don't be a people-pleaser if someone makes you uncomfortable. Your family should protect and support you."

I thought of Shanda's family and her mom forcing her to live with an abusive stepfather and drug user. Then I thought of Frankie and her family. Some kids were dealt such awful hands when it came to their parents and family.

That evening, Olivia and I finally agreed to watch an episode of *The Witcher* together since she wanted a horror movie, and I wanted a foreign film. We made margaritas and ended up binge-watching four episodes. The characters had fantastic chemistry together. Their chemistry was so good in fact, I was crawling out of my skin with sexual frustration by the end of the night.

The next morning, Damien walked out of the gym as I pulled into the parking lot. He waited for me to park and climb out, then he plastered his sweaty body against mine and kissed me, long and deep. I mindlessly glided my hands around his shoulders, then pulled him into me. He finally ended the long, wet kiss and leaned back to look at me.

"Legs, you're killing me. This weekend you're coming over. I don't care if it's for two hours, or two minutes at this point."

"I need more than two minutes." I held him to me one more time before letting go. "Olivia's going to stay with Ava on Christmas Eve, and we'll probably have dinner together, but after that I'm free."

He sighed. "I'm driving to my dad's house in Carlsbad with Brock to spend Christmas Eve. But we'll be home late in the morning."

"Okay." I gave him a hard kiss and bit his lower lip then tried to pull back.

He chased my lips and grabbed my face to hold me in place while he thrust his tongue inside my mouth again. I wrapped my arms around his waist and smashed my breasts against his sweaty torso. Damien pushed me up against my Sequoia again, then glided his hand down the back of my thigh. He started to pull my leg up when his cell rang. He sighed and stepped back.

"I have to go. So do you. And this isn't exactly the best spot to be making out," he admitted.

"Get your phone call. Christmas Day." I squeezed his hand.

"Yeah. It'll be the best fucking Christmas present ever."

Later that afternoon as I walked into my office, I noticed I had several texts. One was from a client letting me know she'd paid off her court fines. The other two were from Olivia and Ava telling me they were going to drive out to Desert Palms for the evening and go shopping then see a movie. Olivia told me not to wait up.

"Thank you, God," I muttered and pulled up Damien's number, then shot him a text.

Me: Are you free tonight? Olivia and Ava are going out for the evening.

He texted back two minutes later.

Damien: A Xmas miracle. Hell yes—come over when u get off work. Plan to spend the night.

He sent another text with the code to his house if I arrived first. When I got to my office, I ruthlessly culled what wasn't urgent and sent out a few emails then headed home to grab an overnight bag.

Gary had been enjoying having Olivia home all the time, and she'd already taken him out for a hike that afternoon. He gave me a little tail wag, and I gave him a belly rub then fed him dinner.

I quickly showered, shaved everywhere, and changed into my favorite little purple wraparound dress with a soft cream cardigan over it. I even had on a new matching underwear set. After packing an overnight bag and my work clothes for the next day, I scribbled a note to Olivia telling her I wouldn't be home until tomorrow. On impulse, I grabbed a bottle of wine and a few treats. Anticipation and anxiety coursed through me. I hoped having sex was like riding a bike, and I remembered how everything worked.

Chapter 25

It was after six by the time I made it to Damien's house. He didn't answer the door and there weren't any lights on, so I plugged in the front door code he'd texted me and let myself inside.

I wandered into the living room. "Hello?" I called.

His house was dark and quiet. I went into the kitchen and put the wine and treats in the fridge then looked around a little bit. His house didn't have a bachelor pad feel to it, and there were even a couple of healthy succulents on his kitchen windowsill. His décor was contemporary and comfortable.

Resisting the urge to snoop through his bedroom, I sat at his kitchen bar and reviewed emails on my phone while I waited for him to come home. I was about five emails in when I heard his garage door open. My heart sped up and anxiety and something else drifted through me. We'd fooled around, but I hadn't had sex in a long time, and I was a little anxious.

He walked in and stared at me sitting there at his kitchen bar. Damien had two bags of takeout food with him, and he put them in the fridge, then threw his keys on the counter. He walked over to me and swiveled my stool, so I faced him, then he spread my thighs and stepped between my legs.

"You have two choices. We can fuck now and eat later—then fuck some more, or we can eat now and fuck later."

"There are a lot of fucks in that sentence, Dimples."

"I know." He grazed my cheek with his mouth and ran a hand up my leg, pushing my dress up as he went.

"I like your dress, sweetheart. It gives me fast access to some of my favorite parts." His hand at the back of my waist pushed me closer to him, spreading my legs even wider.

"I vote for number one."

"Good choice." He grabbed my ass with both hands and lifted me. "Straddle me."

I wrapped my legs around his waist, and he walked us to his bedroom. The friction between my legs as his jeans rubbed against me made my insides clench. The room was in shadows as he laid me on the bed.

He reached over and turned on his bedside lamp, then leaned over me. "I want to see you."

Damien dipped his head and captured my mouth in a hot, wet kiss. While our tongues tangled, he ran his hand up my thigh until he found my thong and pulled it down my legs. He leaned back and glided my dress up to my waist, then looked down at my bare, wet center.

"Your pussy is fucking perfect. Spread your thighs for me, sweetheart."

My face flamed, but I slowly spread my bent thighs open even wider. It felt so naughty to have both of us dressed, except my skirt pulled up around my waist. He leaned over and ran his finger through my slit, then slipped inside me.

"Oh, God." I arched into his hand. He added another finger and pumped in and out a few times.

"You're so damn wet. I can hear how much you want my cock."

I tried to close my thighs.

"No, I love the sound. Keep them open for me." While he fingered me, he reached down and unbuttoned the top of the sundress with one hand then spread the fabric open so he could see my pink lace bra underneath.

My hand ran up his thigh, and I cupped his shaft through his jeans, rubbing his length.

Pushing against his fingers, I moaned softly. "I want to see you, too."

He finally stood up and pulled his shirt over his head, then he undid his jeans the rest of the way and slid them down his thighs. He quickly took off the rest of his clothes. His thick shaft was hard and long. We'd need to go slow the first few times.

I sat up and fidgeted with my cardigan. My skirt was still pushed up around my waist and my bodice was opened down to my navel, but I still had my cardigan on. Damien ran a hand along his length and watched me.

Leaning over to kiss my neck, Damien then trailed his mouth down to my chest as he peeled the cardigan off my shoulders. He slowly licked the swell of my breast while he slid the sundress down my arms and unsnapped my bra.

He pulled my bra off and bent to suckle my breasts until I was panting heavily, and my hands were tangled in his hair. His whiskers tickled and scraped my nipples, and I angled my chest to get closer to his mouth.

"Your mouth feels... like heaven. Please don't stop."

"It's a beautiful sound hearing you beg me, Legs."

His mouth traced down my ribcage to my navel as he peeled my sundress off. Then he went lower and licked up the inside of my bent thigh. I whimpered and felt him smile against my leg. Finally, he circled my clit with his tongue, and I jerked against his mouth. As he scraped his whiskers across my clit, I made a long, broken sound.

The feel of his whiskers and tongue on my clit felt so good, my eyes slammed shut and I shuddered underneath him. When he licked my nub and flicked his tongue across it, I arched restlessly into him. I grabbed onto his shoulders to keep him in place. Damien glided a finger back into my passage, then slid another in and pumped them slowly while he licked me.

He studied me with heavy eyes. "Pinch your nipples, sweetheart. Play with yourself for me."

I hesitated, then slowly took both my nipples between my fingers and pinched and rolled them. My face flushed, and embarrassment and heat crawled through me as he watched.

"Now that's a beautiful sight." He bent down again and sucked my bud into his mouth. I rolled my hips while he pushed a third finger into my vagina. The fit was tight, and an orgasm started building. He licked my folds, then bit down softly on my clit. My climax hovered and built, and when he sucked me deep into his mouth, it barreled through me, and my hips lifted off the bed.

"Oh, God! Damien, please." My head flew back as he flicked his tongue over me. When my shudders stopped, he crawled up my body. My anxiety was long gone, and I ached to feel him inside me.

"You were made for me, sweetheart. I love every fucking thing about your body."

I smiled up at him lazily, then reached down and stroked his hard, swollen shaft. "And I love everything about yours. But I'm not sure you're going to fit."

He smirked and rubbed his nose against my cheek. "There's one way to find out."

Kneeling between my legs, he pulled my thighs far apart and lifted my bottom with both hands. Then he started working himself inside me as he focused on my face. My head fell back, and I closed my eyes and panted.

He reached down and stroked my jaw. "Look at me. I want to watch your face the first time I'm inside you."

I opened my eyes and looked at him. His shaft was big, and he was having to work to fit inside me. Sweat glistened on his chest, and I moaned long and high when he finally gave three hard thrusts and bottomed out inside me. He paused to let me adjust.

"You feel so fucking good," he murmured as he knelt over me. He finally started driving his hips back and forth, holding me up to meet his thrusts. Then he drew my legs up around his waist and stopped after several hard thrusts as his control slipped. I moved my hips against him.

"Careful, Legs. Or I'm going to come inside you a lot sooner than I planned."

My hands gripped his forearms, and I flexed my vagina around his pulsing shaft. He rolled his hips and leaned over to put his forehead against mine.

"You don't listen very well, do you?"

"Did you say something?" I asked in a husky voice, and he smiled then bit my lower lip.

Damien started slowly impaling himself in me again and rubbed my clit while he thrust. He pulled my legs out from around his hips and stretched me wide. I felt the stretch.

"Zeke was right. You're flexible as fuck." He drove deep inside then pulled out and slammed back in again and again.

My eyes rolled back, and I put my hands above my head to brace myself against his headboard. My mind emptied, and my hips pushed up to meet his. He leaned over and licked and bit at one of my nipples while he played with my clit. Then he pinched the other nipple between his fingers and pulled. I felt another orgasm building low in my stomach.

"Please, I can't hold back," I gasped.

"Then don't. Come with me."

He rammed into me harder and faster, and I held my breath. My body jerked with each thrust. I'd never been taken this hard and deep before, and my vision blurred as I tried to process all the sensations.

A second orgasm built low in my belly, and a few thrusts later I came all over him. He pumped his cock, then slammed inside me, bruising my pelvis. He groaned low and deep as he came. It took several moments to stop pulsing around him, and he buried his face in my hair.

"Your sweet, tight pussy is quite the ride, Legs."

I turned my head and kissed him on his ear, then wrapped my arms and legs around him.

"Did you just compare my vagina to an amusement park ride?"

"It's so much better," he mumbled, still laying on top of me.

We stayed in bed until late into the evening, then we cleaned up and warmed up the burritos he'd brought home from La Perla's for dinner.

"Do you want to soak in the spa?" he asked after we ate.

"I didn't bring a swimsuit."

He grinned. "Even better. Although your little green pinup suit gave me blue balls for a few days afterward. It was nice soaking in your spool, but it was fucking torture not to drag you onto my lap, pull your suit aside and drive my cock up inside you."

My eyes got heavy and I shuddered at the image he put in my head. The next time I used my spool, I knew I'd be thinking about that.

His backyard was private, and I remembered the tall Ficus hedge that lined most of his fence. I tipped my head and looked at him standing there in sleep shorts and nothing else. He looked tousled and sated.

"Do you use your spa often?" I asked.

"A few times a week."

I straightened when I remembered what Martina had told me about Sebastian and his hot tub. My insides clenched a little, and jealousy washed through me.

"What's that look?" he asked.

My first impulse was to let it go or deflect, but I knew it would eat at me. "Sebastian has a hot tub." I didn't know exactly how to ask him if he used his spa to get laid. And how often.

He narrowed his eyes and set his drink down carefully. "How do you know about Sebastian's hot tub?"

"Martina and Laurel told me. They said he usually didn't use it alone before he met Laurel."

Damien studied me carefully. "Did anything happen between you and Sebastian?"

My head jerked back a little. "No!"

He let out a long sigh. "I shouldn't have asked."

"You're right, you shouldn't have. There's never been anything like that between us, and I wasn't in a good place." I went quiet.

"Tell me."

My shoulders hunched, and I looked away. "I'd just found out about that stupid fucking bet. And I'd sworn off men in general."

Damien rubbed his neck. "I'm sorry. The fact that you know him, and you brought up his hot tub. Well, let's just say he's gotten his money's worth out of it."

"Have *you* had a lot of sex in yours?"

He leaned against the counter and folded his arms. "Some."

"Okay." My stomach squeezed, but I tried to keep my face neutral. I'd asked, so I couldn't be too upset.

"Then I realized I didn't like bringing random women home. It felt too intimate." He paused. "And not just in a sexual way."

My insides relaxed a little. I knew what he meant because my house and backyard were my sanctuary too.

He motioned out to his back patio. "My rental has its own small patio area with a little hot tub, and I've put up some sound barriers so we can all have our privacy. My backyard is one of the few private places I have."

"I get it. I shouldn't have asked either."

"I'm glad it bothered you enough to ask. So, do you want to use the spa before we hit the sack?"

My shoulders relaxed. "Yes, if you're still up for it."

He grinned, showing off his dimple. "I'm pretty sure I'm up for it."

I smirked and rolled my eyes.

We grabbed a couple of towels and the wine I'd brought. It was chilly, and when my bare feet hit the concrete, I shivered a little. He pulled off his shorts and slipped into the hot, bubbling water.

When I pulled my dress off, he leaned back with his arms on the spa ledge and watched me with hooded eyes. "You look so fucking good standing there in the moonlight with nothing else on. I've always loved your body, and especially those legs."

I smiled down at him, then ran my hands up over my rib cage to my breasts. I cupped and lifted them as if offering them up to him. "Most men seem to like these better."

He smiled wickedly, then stood up and waded over to me. "Oh, sweetheart, I like those too. And your body is a work of art. But your legs—they're a masterpiece."

My vagina spasmed, and I felt my breasts grow heavy. He reached over and slid his hand up the inside of my thigh, then delicately stroked my clit. I was slick and ready for him.

"Your sweet, tight little pussy is a masterpiece too, Legs. Now come here so I can worship it."

I swayed toward him. He held his other hand up and helped me step into the water. Pulling me to him, he reached down and brushed a strand of hair off my shoulder.

"You offering up your tits like that makes me want to slide my cock between them and fuck them. Hard."

My breasts tingled, and my insides clenched. I took his hand and guided him to the side of the spa, then pushed his shoulders down until he sat on the ledge.

"How about if I take you down my throat first, then we can get to the tit-fucking part?"

He grinned slowly and his hand squeezed mine. "You're playing out every dark, depraved fantasy I've had about you over the past year."

"We've only known each other for a few months."

"Even before last fall, I had a few dirty fantasies about you. I didn't know about your oral skills though."

Smiling up at him, I sank to my knees. He stroked my cheek, then ran his hands down to my breasts and thumbed my nipples. I took his shaft in my fist and slowly sank my mouth over him.

His thighs flexed, and I heard him take a sharp breath. I thoroughly and methodically licked my way up and down his length before sliding him into the back of my throat. I teased him and pulled back, then played with his tip. He groaned and thrust his hips.

His cock slid partway into my throat, then he stopped. He massaged my breasts, then started pinching and tugging my nipples between his fingers. I arched into his hands as the bite sunk into me and my insides spasmed. He slid his cock slowly the rest of the way down my throat, and my eyes closed.

Damien stroked my jaw. "No, sweetheart. I want your eyes on me, so you know exactly whose cock is lodged deep in your throat."

My heart sped up at his dirty words. My mind went hazy with need and my body seemed to hum. I slid my mouth up and down on his shaft, his size stretching my lips. I swallowed several times before pulling off enough to catch my breath. Pushing back down on him, I worked him inside my throat again.

"Your mouth and throat feel like fucking paradise," he rasped out.

After several deep strokes, he reached down and took hold of my shoulders, pulling me off his cock. "I'm going to blow if you don't stop, and I'm not done with you yet."

He bent me over the ledge of the spa, putting my hands on the deck.

"Stay there," he commanded.

Then he ran his hands up and down my buttocks and squeezed and kneaded them firmly. I pushed toward him, silently begging for his cock.

He gave me a light slap. "Not yet. I want you dripping and begging for it."

Sliding a finger inside my passage, he bent down and bit my ass cheek.

"Ah!" I rose up a little, but he planted his hand on the small of my back and rubbed the bite.

Damien spread my thighs even further apart, then licked up and down my slit. He pulled my hips up until I was on my tiptoes, then he nibbled and bit at my clit.

"That feels so good," I moaned.

He pulled off and glided his hand up and down my back. "Do you want me to fuck you, sweetheart?"

"Yesss," I groaned as I pushed back at him.

"What's the magic word?"

"Now," I gasped.

He chuckled and reached down to stroke me again. "I'm pretty sure that's not it."

"Right the fuck now."

He laughed and squeezed my swollen, sensitive clit. Then he shoved two fingers into my soaking wet passage. "Try again."

I pushed my hips back onto his fingers, trying to find some relief from the ache inside me. "Damien, please!"

"There you go. That wasn't so hard, was it?" He patted my hip, and I growled at him.

Positioning his cock at my opening, he drove up inside me in one hard thrust.

My head flew back, and I cried out softly.

"You feel so damn *hot*," he rumbled. Then he grabbed my shoulders to hold me still and pistoned in and out of me, pushing me back onto his rock-hard shaft again and again. I could feel him hitting me deep inside, and pleasure and a little pain rolled through me.

"I'll have to get between your breasts tomorrow," he said breathlessly. He reached down and stroked my clit as he hammered inside me. I threw my head back and panted breathlessly, feeling my toes start to curl as an orgasm built.

He stroked me again, and my vagina clenched around him. I came with a long low wail. Damien leaned over me, turned my head, and caught my wail in his mouth as he shoved inside me one last time. Then his body locked, and he came hard.

When we recovered a few moments later, he stroked my back and stood up straight, taking me with him. He pulled out, then picked me up and settled me on his lap on the spa bench. I curled around him, and let out a long, contented exhale.

"I think I'm addicted to your mouth and pussy, Legs," he said after a few minutes.

I laid my hand on his chest and smiled. "Good, Dimples. It's only fair."

We finally made our way back inside, cleaned up together, then twisted around each other in his bed. We talked about our families, work, and whatever else came to mind until we drifted off to sleep a little while later.

Early the next morning, I woke on my back with Damien kneeling between my thighs, licking my clit and sliding a finger inside my passage. I reached down and grabbed his hair, then rocked into him. He sucked on me for a few more minutes, then crawled up my body.

Damien cupped the side of my face and skimmed his thumb across my cheekbone. "I want to fuck your beautiful breasts. You up for a little revised sixty-nine?" I'd have been up for anything when he asked me like that.

I grinned sleepily at him. "Yes. This is a delicious way to wake up."

He smiled, then rolled me onto my side. He positioned himself on his side with his face next to my pussy. We got ourselves situated between a few gropes and laughter.

I grasped his cock and slid it into my mouth to get it wet and slippery. Then I pulled it out and slid his shaft between my breasts, pushing my mounds together. He thrust in and out of the tight wet space I'd created. Then he pulled my hips to his mouth, peeling my lips back, and flicked and lapped at my clit.

My pussy was sore and a little sensitive from all the sex we'd had the night before, but I loved the feel of his mouth and warm breath on my clit. My mind drifted, and I felt bliss and endorphins slide through my body as we worked each other.

A few moments later, he started thrusting between my breasts in earnest. He bit and nibbled on my clit and slid a couple of fingers inside me. My pelvis clenched, and I squeezed around Damien's fingers. He drove deeper inside me and continued to rhythmically lick my clit. My back locked as I came all over his fingers and mouth.

His thrusts became more erratic until he pushed into my chest one last time and covered my breasts with spurts of hot semen. I lay there for a minute, catching my breath and savoring the afterglow of my climax. When Damien rolled over on his back, I haphazardly wiped myself off with his sheet. We lay sprawled together across his bed for a while, both of us a little dazed.

I lay there basking in the afterglow of sex with Damien, thinking about how good my life was right then. Maybe the holidays were actually going to be fun this year. Then I started worrying, wondering if I'd just jinxed myself.

Chapter 26

Olivia and I spent Saturday morning together since she planned to stay at Ava's house for the rest of her trip.

We did an online yoga session together and when the video ended, I turned to Olivia. "I know you love yoga, but there's just not enough movement or resistance for me to call it exercise."

She rolled her eyes. "That's because it's not just exercise, dummy. You increase your flexibility, and gain energy and balance."

"Did you just call me 'dummy'? Didn't the yoga instructor just say we need to set our good intentions for the day? How's that working for you?"

She shrugged. "It usually works fine unless I'm around you. Yoga can help you center yourself and regulate your emotions."

"I get all that, but sometimes it feels like doing one of Ava's golf mediation and affirmation sessions instead of working out."

"Don't be a hater. Just because you're not dripping with sweat and sore the next day, doesn't mean it isn't a workout."

"Hmm. I'm pretty sure it *does* mean that."

She shook her head. "Fine. You do you."

We got cleaned up, then took Gary on a walk to the local coffee house for breakfast.

"I love your neighborhood." Olivia looked around as we walked over to Paws for Coffee.

Several homes sported festive holiday decorations—done Palm Springs style—and the neighborhood was quiet and peaceful the day before Christmas. While we ate, we talked about Ava.

"Have you asked her about us easing off on monitoring her?" I asked.

"I tried. But she wasn't in the mood to talk about it. I did talk to her about a cat though."

"What did she say?" I asked as I reached down to give Gary a scratch behind his ears.

"She seemed receptive to it, but she wants a kitten. Then she started looking up different expensive cat breeds online. I hope we didn't open a can of worms."

"The last thing she needs is an expensive breed that requires a lot of care and fussing over."

Olivia nodded. "Maybe we can take a trip to the shelter and have her at least look at the cats there."

"Good idea. Let's plan on it Tuesday or Wednesday during my lunch hour."

"Do you work on Monday?" Olivia asked, sipping her latte.

"No. Sunday is Christmas Day, so the official holiday is Monday. Why?"

"What are you planning to do?" she asked.

"Not hang out with you and Ava."

She gave me the stink eye. "You can't abandon me just because I'm moving over to her house."

"I won't. Why do you say that?"

She squinted her eyes and pointed at me. "You plan to spend next week playing grab ass with Damien, don't you?"

"What? No!" I scratched my right eyebrow.

"You *are lying*, right to my face. You just scratched your eyebrow."

I shook my head. "No, I did not. And if I did, it doesn't mean anything."

"Big fat lying liar. Scratching your eyebrow is your tell."

I rolled my eyes at her. "My tell? What are you, a professional poker player? And you need to stop. I'm not going to abandon you."

She rolled her eyes. "Sure, Lying Liar McLie Face."

I reached over and flicked her forehead.

"Ooouch! Why do you *do* that?" she whined, rubbing her head.

"Because sometimes you act like a five-year-old. I *am* going to spend some time with him over the next week. I can't be with you all the time, we'd murder each other."

"Fine," she grumbled. "But you need to come over to Ava's house sometimes—besides just Christmas Eve. I'm not sure I'll still be sane and functioning by the end of my trip if you don't."

"I'll hang out with you," I promised.

"And Ava," she added.

"And *maybe* Ava. She gets under my skin, and I have a lot of pent-up resentment for that woman. But I'll try."

Olivia got serious and studied me. "Har, I know you do. And God knows you have more than enough reason. But sometimes I worry you're hurting yourself by holding onto all that. You need to find a way to let it go."

I looked out across the back patio area. "I'm not sure I even know how." I worried again that Olivia was getting dragged into the middle of my conflict with Ava.

She nodded and took a sip of her coffee. She looked sad, and I didn't know how to make it better.

I tried to change the subject. "Have you been seeing anyone in North Carolina?"

"No. But what's going on with you and Damien? He's the first guy you've brought around since Ryan."

I looked down at the crumbs on my plate. "He's different. He's kind and patient, and his friends and work colleagues like and respect him."

She smirked. "Yeah, and he's hot, has a great bubble butt, and a dimple. That doesn't hurt either, does it?"

I pointed a finger at her. "Quit looking."

"I'm not lusting on him, but I'm not dead either."

"Okay, fair enough." I smiled. "I also trust him. Damien would never make a bet with his friends about sex."

"That's a very specific and bizarre reason to trust him." Olivia leaned forward. "Harley, did that happen to you?"

My eyes shifted away.

"Harley," she said sharply.

I sighed. "Ollie, I should have told you a while ago, but something happened at my work." I finally told her about the bet. She was sputtering and red-faced by the time I finished.

"You have got to be fucking *kidding* me! Who does that?" she was practically yelling, and a few customers glanced over at her.

"Is that a rhetorical question, because it's obvious there are more than enough men who'd do something like that."

"Well, they shouldn't, damn it. It makes me so mad!" She studied me closely. "How have you not nut-punched any of these assholes yet?"

Olivia knew I had a temper, and it wasn't exactly a secret I had a few run-ins when I'd played college volleyball.

"When I first heard about it, I *did* want to nut-punch them. I was devastated that some of my colleagues—people I worked with every day—would do that."

Olivia nodded jerkily. "Very normal reaction."

"But then I got thinking. I could cause a big stink and try to get them in trouble, but I'd probably appear weak in a profession that isn't kind to people who aren't tough. And when you swim with attorneys all day, you can't appear weak."

"The saying is, 'when you swim with the sharks,' I believe," Olivia corrected me.

"Same thing. That's a disservice to sharks though."

She smirked, then sighed. "Have you done *anything* about it?"

"Yes. I've worked my ass off to be the best damn criminal defense attorney I can be. And I make sure I'm always courteous and professional with the court staff and other attorneys."

She nodded. "Dad would come back and haunt you if you weren't."

"True, and it was a good lesson he taught me. A court bailiff is the one who told me about the bet. So that's my best revenge I think—to make them look petty and cruel."

She slowly nodded. "You're taking the high road. Damn it, the high road is *so hard*."

I smiled. "It's gotten under their skin."

"Does Damien know about it?" she asked.

I grimaced. "Yes. He was in court the other day and saw one of them asking me out and harassing me. He wanted to rip the guy's balls off when I finally told him."

"Good! I can't believe you didn't tell anyone before now."

I rolled my shoulders. "They'd just deny it if I tried to get them in trouble or fired. I'm handling it on my own."

She didn't like it, but she let it go. "If you ever want a partner in crime to go break some kneecaps or slash some tires, I'm your ride or die."

I grabbed her hand. "I know, Ollie. That's one of the many things I love about you."

I planned to meet Damien at his house for a quick lunch—and other things—on Christmas Eve before he and his brother took off to spend the night with their dad in the afternoon.

He texted me a few minutes after I left his house yesterday morning. My vagina had still been pulsing, and I buzzed with leftover endorphins from our morning in bed.

Damien: You've been gone for 10 mins, and I already want you again. Lunch here tomorrow before I take off?

Me: What exactly will we be eating?

We'd eaten leftover burritos for breakfast because Damien was out of groceries. I doubted he'd picked any up in the meantime.

Damien: Each other first, and then whatever I can scrounge up.

I smiled and shook my head. The man was obsessed with my lack of a gag reflex.

Me: This isn't really a lunch date, is it?

Damien: No. I want your ass back in my bed one more time before I leave.

After I got back from breakfast with Olivia that morning and wrapped a few gifts, I made chicken salad sandwiches with some leftover grilled chicken to take to Damien's house for lunch. I thought we'd both need the food afterward if we had a repeat of Thursday night.

But on the way over, I got an unexpected call from Shanda's neighbor.

"Is this Harley Emerson, Shanda's attorney?" the man asked in a shaky voice.

I got a sick feeling in my stomach. "Yes. Who is this?"

"I'm Walt, her neighbor. I talked to you when you were here one day."

"Hi, Walt. What's going on?"

"It's Shanda. She came back to her mom's apartment a few minutes ago, and her stepdad is screaming at her. I'm pretty sure he's also high as a damn kite. I don't think Shanda's mom is home either."

I scrubbed my face and wondered what to do.

Walt kept talking. "Ms. Emerson, I'm afraid for Shanda *and* Bertie. Shanda's mom leaves Bertie alone with that stupid crack-head all day, and we've seen her wandering around the second-story walkway a couple of times in just a dirty diaper."

"By herself?"

"Yeah."

"Does Mikey still get visitors?" I asked.

"Yes," Walt clipped. By visitors, I meant drug buyers.

"Do you know who Jason Ulrich is?"

Walt paused. I was afraid he wouldn't tell me or maybe hang up on me.

"Yeah. I've heard of him. He's one of the druggie guys who come around the apartment sometimes."

"Have you seen him there lately?" I pressed.

"Last night. While Shanda's mom was gone."

Well, fuck, this was worse than I thought. I'd hoped the no-contact order would've kept Jason away from the apartment.

It sounded like Walt was pacing, and I could hear screaming in the background. Before I knew what I was doing, I swung my vehicle around and aimed it toward Shanda's apartment complex.

"I know this is a lot to ask, but will you call DCFS and make an anonymous complaint about what you've seen regarding Bertie? Legally DCFS can't tell anyone who you are when a person makes a referral. Your identity is protected."

He scoffed a little. "We both know it'll probably leak out. Secrets have ways of getting out."

He was right, and I didn't want to lie to him by denying it. "Please, Walt. Bertie isn't old enough to protect herself. She needs us. When I get off the phone, I'm going to call the police and hope like hell they beat me there. Would you rather call them?"

He sighed. "No, I'll call DCFS. Just be careful. Drug dealers have long memories, and they aren't good folks."

Nothing like stating the obvious. "I will, Walt. I'm hanging up now. Please call them."

Chapter 27

I quickly called nine-one-one. My heart pounded, and my hands went clammy.

"You've reached nine-one-one. What's your emergency?" the dispatcher asked.

"My name's Harley Emerson. A two-year-old child and an eighteen-year-old girl are in a domestic violence situation." I rattled off the apartment.

"What's the danger?" the dispatcher asked.

"The stepfather is high, probably on meth, and appears to have assaulted the older daughter. His first name is Mike, he goes by Mikey, but I don't know his last name." I didn't know if Shanda had been assaulted yet, but it was only a matter of time.

"I don't know about the younger one, but I could hear her screaming. Her mother, Charlene, isn't home and I don't believe anyone else is in the apartment."

"Do you know if the stepfather has a gun?"

"No, I don't think so." I hoped like hell I was right.

"Stay on the line, please." I could hear the dispatcher making the call out to the nearest units. It sounded like I would get to the complex first.

"Ma'am, we have a unit on its way. Are you outside the apartment?"

I pulled into the parking lot and quickly found a spot. "No, but I'm at the complex."

"Do you still hear screaming?" he asked.

"Hold on, let me see."

"Ma'am, please don't approach the apartment. If the stepfather is high and already agitated, he could be dangerous."

I was sprinting to the apartment by that time. "I understand." And I did understand, but I wasn't going to stand by while Shanda and Bertie got the crap beat out of them.

Outside the door, I heard a man shouting and a baby crying inside. And then I heard a smack.

I tried the knob, and when it turned I shoved the door open with a loud thud. Shanda sat huddled on the couch, and she had a bloody cut under her eye and a mark on her cheek. Bertie had latched onto Shanda's waist, with her head buried in Shanda's stomach. Mikey stood over them with his arm raised.

"If you hit her again, I will kick your fucking ass," I growled.

Shanda turned to me, her eyes wide and glassy.

"What the fuck are you doin' in my house?" Mikey's words slurred a little.

"You're assaulting two *children*, you stupid piece of shit. Shanda's bleeding and there's a large red handprint on her face." I lifted up my phone so the dispatcher could hear.

Shanda started easing to the side with Bertie in her arms. There was a wrapped Christmas present on the floor next to Mikey. It looked like he'd stomped on it a few times.

I continued talking. "You also appear to be high. You've got sores all over your face, you have bad teeth and an ugly sunken sallow complexion. It's not a good look." I had no idea what his teeth looked like, but the rest was true.

He narrowed his eyes. "Who the fuck are you?"

"Shanda's attorney. You've met me before, but I'm sure you don't remember."

Mikey was completely focused on me now. Shanda slipped around him with Bertie in her arms, staying off to the side.

"Shanda, can I come in?" I was already standing inside.

She looked at me like I was crazy. "Yes?"

I turned back to Mikey. "I've been invited inside. Now I'm going to walk outside—with Bertie and Shanda. And you are not going to touch either one of them. *Ever again.*"

Mikey rushed at me. He didn't give me any warning, but he was high and uncoordinated, and I quickly stepped to the side. He plowed into the small kitchenette behind me and fell on his ass. I wanted to stomp on his face while he was down, but I had a good idea of what charges I'd be facing if I did. But I *really* wanted to.

Mikey groaned and started slowly gathering himself to get back up.

I could hear the dispatcher on my phone calling my name.

I put the phone to my ear and started talking. "Shanda has a bloody laceration under her eye and a big red hand impression on the side of her face. Bertie looks like she hasn't been bathed in days and is clinging to Shanda like a spider monkey, but otherwise, she appears to be unharmed." I sounded like a damned robot even though my heart was beating fast.

"What about the assailant?" the dispatcher asked.

"He's still struggling with a chair. And losing. He tried to body-slam me, but I stepped out of the way. I'd rather not be the one to try and subdue him when he gets up and goes after me again though. Where are the officers?"

Just then I saw movement at the door, and two officers strode in.

"They just walked in, thank God. I'm going to hang up now." I turned off my phone and faced them.

Shanda put Bertie down next to her and stepped behind me. The cut under her eye was bleeding a little.

"We got a call about a domestic disturbance," one of the officers said.

I pointed at Mikey. "He was yelling at Shanda here, and then he assaulted her and had her trapped on the couch with Bertie in her lap when I came in."

The female officer turned to Shanda and started assessing her and Bertie for injuries. The other officer walked over and squatted down by Mikey. Just then my phone rang.

I looked down and saw it was Damien, so I took the call. "Hey. I don't think I'm going to make lunch."

He paused. "You okay?"

"Umm, kind of. I got a call that Shanda's stepdad was beating the shit out of her, so I came over to her apartment."

Damien's voice grew sharp. "You're over there right now? Are there any officers there?"

"Yeah. They just walked in."

"What's the address?" he asked.

I told him the name of the complex and the apartment number, but I couldn't remember the exact street address.

He sighed. "I know the complex. I'll be there soon."

"I'm not going to say no. Thank you." Relief flooded me. I could handle the situation without him, but it would be better to have him here.

Mikey got to his feet. "She fucking walked into my house and started threatening me." He pointed at me.

I stepped forward. "I'm Shanda's attorney. I was notified Shanda was in danger, so I called the police, then came over to see what I could do."

The female officer looked at Shanda. "I'm Officer Schroeder. What's your name?"

Shanda glanced at me, and I nodded. I was proud of her that she'd checked with me before she started talking to the officer. Maybe a few things I'd told her had gotten through.

"Shanda Briggs. I live here on and off with my mom and little sister. He's the freeloader."

Officer Schroeder pointed down at Bertie. "And who's this?"

"Bertie. She's my little sister."

The officer pointed at Shanda's face. "What happened to you?"

I wondered briefly if Shanda was going to lie again. I'd have to kick her ass, then talk some sense into her if she did.

But Shanda straightened. "I came home to check on Bertie and see her for Christmas. My mom lets this ass wipe watch her when she goes to work. He was mad at me for getting his drug dealer in trouble, so he hit me in the face, punched me in the stomach. Then he slapped me."

"You bitch! This isn't even your house. You don't belong here!" Mikey yelled, spittle flying out of his mouth.

The other officer turned to Mikey. "Sir, let's go outside so I can get your side of the story, okay?"

Mikey puffed up his chest and swayed a little bit. "This is *my* fucking house. I'm not going anywhere."

The female officer stepped forward. "I'll take Shanda outside. We can take Bertie with us."

I walked over to the kitchen sink. There were dirty dishes everywhere, and the countertop was crusted with dried food and gunk. I grabbed a wad of paper towels and wet them down.

Shanda scooped Bertie up. She laid her head on Shanda's shoulder and wrapped her arms around Shanda's neck. A lump formed in my throat. We walked outside and went over to the picnic table by the swing set in the middle of the complex.

Two EMT's walked up, and Officer Schroeder filled them in. Bertie was still wrapped around Shanda and didn't look like she wanted to let go.

I turned to Officer Schroeder. "I have some food and a blanket in my car. Don't start questioning Shanda until I get back."

The officer stared at me. "I've never met an attorney who makes house calls."

"I'm not in the habit. But this one's different."

I ran to my vehicle and grabbed a blanket and cooler with the lunch I'd packed. When I got back, Officer Schroeder had taken photos of the cut and marks on Shanda's face, and the bruise on her stomach.

Shanda adamantly refused to let the EMTs work on her. "It's not an emergency, and I can't afford it. I don't think it's too bad."

They couldn't force her to accept treatment, so after a few minutes they packed up and took off. I understood, but it made me angry that an eighteen-year-old had to forgo medical treatment because she thought it was too expensive. Running back to my vehicle, I grabbed my first aid kit.

I handed her all the bandages and antibiotic ointment I had and dabbed at her cut.

"Keep the edges of your cut together if you can. The butterfly bandages work the best. If you're careful, it may not scar."

Damien walked up while Shanda and Officer Schroeder were talking, and I was feeding Bertie.

He put his hand on my shoulder and nodded at the officer. "Schroeder, it's good to see you. I'm glad you're on this call."

Officer Schroeder smiled. "Hey, Andreasen. Good to see you too. I didn't know she was yours." She inclined her head to me.

Damien squeezed my shoulder. "We're getting there. I'm still easing her into it."

"You know she's a criminal defense attorney, right?" Schroeder asked.

Damien grinned. "Someone's gotta work for the dark side." He looked down at Bertie in my lap. "Who's this?"

I bounced her lightly on my knee. "This is Bertie. She's Shanda's little sister."

Bertie reached up to give Damien a handful of soggy, smashed bread. Damien leaned over and pretended to eat it. Bertie giggled and pulled her hand back.

Then Damien looked over at Shanda and stood up straight. "What the fuck happened to your face?"

I slipped my hand into his and squeezed. "Mikey hit her when she came to check on Bertie and give her a Christmas present. And you can't say the f-word in front of Bertie."

Damien scrubbed his hand over his face. "He's high, isn't he?"

"He's always high." Shanda sounded defeated.

After Officer Schroeder finished talking with Shanda, she went to find her partner. The DCFS worker arrived a couple of minutes later.

"My name is Raina Fletcher. I'm an investigating DCFS worker. Are you her mother?" she asked me, pointing at Bertie.

"No. My name's Harley Emerson, Shanda's public defender. Shanda's not a minor, so she's not under DCFS jurisdiction."

Shanda explained to the worker what had happened.

Damien stared at Shanda when she finished. "That fucker punched you in the stomach too?" Shanda looked like she wanted to cry, and he leaned over and squeezed her shoulder.

Just then Officer Schroeder and her partner came around the corner with Mikey in handcuffs. He was swearing and stumbling. It didn't look like his interview had gone well. Good. I hoped the fucktwit spent some quality time in jail.

I pulled Shanda aside. "Are you going to be okay?"

She looked at Bertie. "Yeah. I'm glad DCFS is involved now that I'm eighteen and they can't do shit to me. I've been worried thinking about Bertie here alone with that asshole and his friends."

Shanda took Bertie from me and sighed. "I don't think my mom likes you. It might be better if you're not here when she gets home."

I nodded and dug into the small backpack I used as a purse, pulling out a Target gift card I'd planned to give Olivia for Christmas.

I handed it to Shanda. "Officially, this is for you to buy an appropriate court outfit. That way I can give it to you and not violate any attorney rules. Unofficially, Merry damn Christmas. Go buy you and Bertie something."

She teared up a little. "Thanks. I'm not sure what would have happened today if you hadn't come." Then she closed her eyes and pulled herself together.

I lightly punched her arm. "Don't tell anyone, but you're one of my favorite clients. Hang in there. And let me know if anything like this happens again."

Shanda smirked. "That's not saying much since all your clients are criminals. But thanks—for everything."

Damien walked me to the parking lot and pulled me in for a hug. "That wasn't exactly how I'd hoped to spend the afternoon, but I'm glad you were there." He glanced around. "This isn't the best neighborhood. Will you call me first if you ever have to come back?"

"I'm fine."

He stared at me. "Promise me. Out loud."

I raised an eyebrow. "Okay. I promise."

He fingered a strand of my hair, then hugged me tight. "I need to go pick up Brock. I wish like hell I wasn't going out of town tonight so I could fuck you under your Christmas tree. Now *that* would be a great Christmas present."

I laughed and squeezed him back. "I'll take a rain check on that."

Chapter 28

Olivia and I gave Ava a round of golf at an exclusive golf course in La Quinta as one of her Christmas gifts. The course was one of the nicest in the area, and Ava loved playing there.

We'd made previous plans to play on Christmas Eve, so when I got home after the incident with Shanda, I hurried to get ready. I usually enjoyed playing golf, but Ava was one of my least favorite golf partners. She tried to coach me whenever I made a bad shot, and she became moody and temperamental if she was playing poorly. But since it was Christmas, I sucked it up. The course was surprisingly busy for Christmas Eve.

"I just love this!" Ava gushed as we loaded our clubs in the cart. "Golfing with my two beautiful girls on Christmas Eve. And the day is just perfect."

She wasn't wrong. The temperature hovered in the mid-sixties, and the sky was a brilliant blue against the greens and the palm trees. The air smelled like fresh-cut grass.

We were all golfing fairly well and having a nice round. But the foursome of middle-aged men in front of us had two bad golfers, and they were taking forever. They also didn't show any indication of letting us play through.

Then the group behind us caught up, and the group behind them caught up as well. When the foursome in front spent ten minutes with the beverage cart, Ava started fretting.

"They should see there are three or four groups behind them and take a hint. I bet it's because we're women and are better than them," Ava complained.

A few minutes later when the slow foursome was still huddled around the beverage cart, I pulled out my phone and called the clubhouse. I got the golf marshal on the line and explained the situation. Ava was starting to get worked up, and I wanted to avoid a scene.

"Did you ask them if you could play through?" the marshal asked.

"No. They don't seem to care they're holding everyone up, and they spent the last ten minutes getting drinks from the beverage cart. Everyone is at a standstill."

The marshal sighed. "I hate groups like that. Yeah, it's probably better if I approach them."

A couple of minutes later we saw him ride his cart over to the group. We watched as he talked to them, and one of the men started waving his hands around and shouting.

The marshal pointed a finger in his face and the other three men stepped in and pulled their irate golf partner back. A couple of minutes later, the marshal rode over to us. "Play on through. I'm going to have the next two groups do the same." He looked back at the culprits. "Just ignore them if they say anything to you."

So we played through. When I stepped up to putt, I heard the man who'd been giving the marshal a hard time call me a "stupid bitch" under his breath.

It was a relatively long putt, and I was about to hit the ball when I heard him. I narrowed my eyes, breathed out, and focused. I was using my go-to chicken stick club, and I felt good about the shot. Maybe Ava's golf meditation wasn't such a waste of time after all. As soon as I hit the ball, both Ava and Olivia started walking toward me. We all knew it was probably going to drop.

"Lovely shot," Ava praised.

"Nice putt," Olivia added as my ball rolled into the hole.

"Thanks, ladies." I turned slowly and stared down the man who'd called me a stupid bitch. I looked him up and down. Then I noticed one of his golf buddies smile and give me a quick thumbs up. My lip twitched, and I nodded briefly at him. Okay, they weren't all assholes.

The holes ahead of us were empty thanks to the men behind us, and the rest of our round went smoothly. When we finished up, we loaded our clubs and headed home. All in all, it had been a nice afternoon.

We prepared Christmas dinner at Ava's house. Olivia had put seasoned red potatoes and garlic chicken in a slow cooker and left it cooking while we golfed. I'd brought a salad and a loaf of fresh bread, and Ava pulled out a bottle of white wine.

"It smells so good," Olivia moaned as we set the table. "I'm getting used to all this delicious food. It's going to be tough when I get back to school."

Shaking my head, I glanced at her. "You can cook for yourself."

"Says the woman who only grills," Olivia shot back.

I smirked. "You say that like it's a bad thing."

We finished putting the food on the table, then sat down and devoured the meal. Golfing must have made us all hungry. While we ate, we talked about Dad and past Christmases.

"Do you remember that Christmas we went to the beach after we opened our presents? And Dad put up the volleyball net in the sand?" I asked.

Olivia nodded. "Yeah. That was a fun day."

Ava pointed at me. "What *I* remember is your father wrenching his back when he dove after one of your spikes. Hudson was in pain for a week afterward."

My lips curved into a satisfied smirk. "Yeah. And he missed it."

Ava looked up at the ceiling and sighed.

We watched a feel-good Christmas movie after dinner, then I said goodnight and headed home. As I walked toward my house and spied my Christmas tree twinkling through the curtains, I remembered Damien saying he wanted to fuck me under my tree. My stomach dipped, and I wondered what he was doing with his brother and dad.

Then I thought about my own dad and brother and tried to guess what we would have been doing tonight if they'd both lived. I also worried about Shanda and Bertie, and I wondered how they'd spent Christmas Eve.

As I walked into my house, my phone buzzed in my back pocket, and I pulled it out.

Damien: Merry Xmas. How about dinner at my place tomorrow night?

Ava and Olivia had invited Sheila and Grace over for Christmas day dinner. I'd bowed out, hoping Damien and I would be getting together.

Me: I hope Santa finds you. Dinner sounds nice.

Damien: Santa already gave me my present--you in my bed, the spa, and my bed again. And let's not forget the shower.

Me: You're making me all hot and bothered. Go be with your family. I'm going to take a cold shower.

Damien: Now I need a cold shower too. Good night, Legs. I'll talk to you tomorrow.

His text caused my vagina to spasm a little. I missed him, his mouth, and his hands on my body. My house suddenly felt too small, and I wandered into my backyard. Gary followed me outside and watched me pace. I was restless and charged. We'd only been together for a short time, and I already missed Damien when he wasn't around. I worried about the fallout if things went south.

The adrenaline from earlier in the day hadn't worked itself out either, so I decided to take Gary for a quick run over to the park and back. I knew it wasn't smart to run alone at night, but I needed to get some energy out and the gym was closed. I grabbed my mace and whistle, put on a light-colored pullover with a hood, and headed out.

Gary started wagging his tail and wiggling his body when I pulled his leash out. While we ran, I let my mind drift.

When I was in high school, I had a few short-term boyfriends. But between school, volleyball, and trying to hide Ava's addiction, none of them lasted. Then in college, I met Ryan my freshman year, and we were together until he died. After he passed away,

I found myself talking to him out loud sometimes when I was alone.

He'd always been a good listener, and he didn't try to solve my problems or minimize my concerns. As time passed, my habit lessened until I couldn't remember the last time I'd talked to him like that.

Grief is a peculiar thing. Sometimes it's powerful and overwhelming, and sometimes it's a quiet ache or memory that brushes by like a soft wind.

When I was half a block away from my house, I noticed a car turn slowly onto my street. My hackles rose and my instincts kicked in. There was something suspicious about the dark tinted windows and slow speed. I quickly pulled my hoodie up over my head.

The car slowed way down in front of my house, and my heart rate sped up. I squinted at the license plate but could only pick up the last three digits--SFW.

The car seemed to slow down even more when it was close enough for the driver to see me. I walked between a parked car and the gutter so I wouldn't be an easy target and turned my head away so the headlights wouldn't blind me. After it passed, I heard the car speed up and continue down the street.

When I got closer to my house, I quickly glanced back to make sure the car was out of sight before I went inside. It might not be anything, but the whole incident made me jumpy and uneasy.

Chapter 29

On Christmas morning, I brought Gary with me over to Ava's house. I decided I was done walking on eggshells, and I wanted him around after the strange drive-by last night.

Olivia met me at the door and smothered Gary with affection. "How's my favorite guy this morning? Are you having a good Christmas?"

He wiggled happily and danced around her. When she turned around, I noticed the Grinch's face smiling malevolently from the butt of her green and red striped pajama bottoms.

"Nice ass, Cindy Lou Who." As a child, Olivia loved the Jim Carey version of *How the Grinch Stole Christmas*. We'd watched it together so many times, we used to quote some of the lines to each other.

"Thanks. Where's *your* Christmas spirit, Scrooge?" She looked at my clothes. I had on gray leggings and a black pullover.

"It's in my heart. I don't have to wear it on my butt."

She shook her head. "Ava's still asleep. She stayed up watching another Hallmark movie after you left. I made coffee and was going to toast a bagel."

I followed her into the kitchen. "Did you notice anything strange last night after I left?"

"Like what?"

I shrugged, a little embarrassed. "I don't know. Maybe cars passing by slowly, or anyone around the neighborhood who looked suspicious?"

She studied me. "I didn't. Tell me why you're asking."

"It's probably nothing, but I thought it'd be good for you and Ava to know." I told her about the incident at Shanda's house, Jason the psycho drug dealer, and the car I'd seen in the neighborhood.

"Why were you running at midnight on Christmas Eve?" she asked.

I shrugged defensively. "I don't know. My mind wouldn't shut off, and I felt restless."

Olivia nodded slowly. "Holidays get to me too sometimes. I'm not sure we need to tell Mom about the car. She's already kind of weird about you being a criminal defense attorney."

"I'd rather not tell her. But on the off chance it's something we need to worry about, I thought you should know."

She stuck another bagel into the toaster. "Does that kind of thing with Shanda happen a lot?"

"Domestic violence incidents? Yes, they happen all the time. But I'm usually not in the middle of it. I learn about it after charges are filed and I'm representing the defendant."

She rubbed her forehead and sighed. "I hate to say this, but I think Mom has a point about you being safer as a real estate attorney."

"I wasn't cut out for that. It's too sedentary and boring. Criminal defense is rewarding and interesting. It also involves actual people."

Olivia squinted at me. "You just made my point."

I grinned and shrugged. Ava walked in a few minutes later. She glanced down at Gary who was lying next to me and tensed a little but didn't say anything.

"Good morning, you two. Harley, you have black on and it's Christmas Day. Where's your Christmas spirit and holiday fashion?"

I rolled my eyes. "I don't have any Christmas clothing. Why should I buy something I can only wear a few times a year? Unless it's pajamas. And if they're comfortable, I'd wear them in July."

"I know you would," Ava said. "That's the problem."

We jabbed at each other and chatted during breakfast, then we opened a few gifts by the Christmas tree. I walked back home with Gary around noon.

A couple of hours later, Damien let me know he'd made it home.

Damien: Just got home. A few work issues came up. Don't know about tonight.

My stomach clenched a little when I read his text. I wondered for a split second if he was trying to distance himself after he'd gotten sex.

My heart throbbed when I thought about Trevor's bet. I tried to objectively analyze Damien's text and then sent what I hoped was an appropriate reply.

Me: No worries. Another time.

I walked out to my backyard and gazed at the white flowering rose bushes lining my back fence while I thought about Damien. My phone buzzed with an incoming text.

Damien: You up for a drive out to Palm Desert again?

My stomach unclenched, but a little of my anxiety remained. I struggled to understand the roller coaster of emotions I'd experienced from a couple of innocuous texts. I *liked* Damien, and he already had the power to hurt me. My heart ached a little at the thought of him brushing me off like he'd done to the hostess at Jonathan's birthday brunch. I tried to shake it off and texted him back.

Me: Sure, unless it'd be better for you to go alone.

My phone rang a minute later. Damien's name popped up on my screen.

"Merry Christmas," I answered.

He paused before responding. "You too, Legs. Everything okay?"

"Yes. I just got home from Ava's house, and we had a nice morning. How about you?"

"It was good, but you sound a little off. Talk to me."

I didn't know how to respond. "I'm fine, really. We had a nice Christmas Eve and Ava behaved herself. Then we had breakfast together this morning and opened a few gifts. How was your Christmas?" I tried to keep my voice light.

He sighed. "It was fine, but I'd rather be with you today. I'm sorry. The last thing I want to do is work."

"It's okay. You don't have to apologize."

"I want to. My first thought when I woke up this morning was to get the Christmas shit out of the way so we could get on the road."

I smiled. "I'm sure your dad loved that."

"He didn't know. But Brock did. In between spending time with you and having Christmas dinner, I planned to fuck you senseless in about twelve different positions."

My stomach dipped, and my face went hot. "Okay."

"First, I want to bend you over the back of your couch, then have you on all fours under your Christmas tree—"

My insides jumped and my nipples tightened as I visualized what he'd just described. "Okay! I get it. This is kind of new to me, and I thought maybe you needed some space. Anyway, I'm fine."

He growled over the phone. "Harley, I'm so fucking far from needing space it'd probably scare the shit out of you."

I rested my head on the back of the couch, feeling a little over-whelmed. "I'm not very good at this. I'd like to go with you to Palm Desert... and then try those twelve different positions after we get back."

He exhaled slowly. "All right. Good. I'll pick you up in an hour or so. I need to make a few phone calls first."

"It'd be easier if I came over there and we could leave from your place." His house was closer to Palm Desert, and he'd have to drive out of his way to pick me up.

He paused. "You don't mind?"

"Not at all. I wouldn't have offered if I minded."

"Okay. Thank you. And will you plan to spend the night?"

More of the tightness eased in my chest, and I smiled. "Yes. I'll see you in an hour or so."

We made it out to Connor McCoy's house early that evening. Connor himself answered the door. His hair was a mess, and his eyes looked a little bloodshot.

"Hey. Thanks for coming out on Christmas Day. I'll make sure it's worth your while." He shook Damien's hand, then turned to me. "Hi, Harley. I'd say it's good to see you again, but I'm a little gun-shy after the last time you were here."

I quirked my head. "Why?"

"You didn't pull any punches about Noah. You were right, by the way."

I shook his outstretched hand. "If you don't want my opinion, don't ask."

Raising his eyebrow, Connor kept a hold of my hand. He was a tall, arresting man with dark hair and a rugged, battered face. Damien came up behind me and wrapped his arm around my chest.

Connor let go and his lips twitched. "Right. Damien, I told you my car was vandalized last week when it was parked at the arena. Early this morning, someone took a blunt object and beat the shit out of the keypad to the front driveway gate. Javier also found more damage to the fence."

Damien took my hand as we followed Connor into his beautiful living room.

"Javier didn't quit then?" Damien asked.

Connor winced. "No. But his daughter isn't happy."

I studied him. "I liked Isabella."

"That's not surprising. You two are a lot alike." Connor turned to Damien. "My daughter is living with me now."

Damien nodded. "You're concerned about the vandalism escalating with her living here."

"Exactly. Elodie's only five, and she's already been through a lot. I'm glad I found out about Noah before she came."

Damien nodded. "Let's look at the damage and get some photos. Then we'll call it in. I'd recommend putting up security cameras around your entire perimeter and in all your vehicles at this point. You may also need to get a personal bodyguard for a while too."

Connor sighed. "No to the bodyguard, but I'll implement your other suggestions."

I heard small feet pattering on the floor and looked up to see a dark-haired little girl coming down the hall toward us.

"Elodie, these are my friends Damien and Harley." Connor held his hand out to her.

She stopped abruptly when she saw us. "Hi, lady and guy."

Elodie wore red stretch pants with candy canes and an orange and black striped t-shirt. Her long, messy hair was pulled back in a crooked ponytail. It looked like she'd probably dressed herself that morning. I waved back.

Damien smiled. "Hey, Elodie."

She looked so small and a little lost standing there in the doorway.

Connor patted the seat next to him. "Els, come sit by me."

She walked over and gingerly sat down, clasping her hands in front of her. She resembled Connor except for the broken nose.

Connor put his arm around her, and she leaned into him. "I need to show them a few things outside. Are you okay inside alone for a few minutes?"

Elodie looked around at the large room. "I guess." She didn't sound too confident.

I raised my hand. "I can hang out with her if you'd like."

Connor looked relieved. "You wouldn't mind?"

"No, as long as Elodie is okay with it."

"You can stay with me," Elodie said quickly.

Connor gave me a grateful look, and Damien and Connor headed outside.

I turned to Elodie. "How long have you lived here with your dad?"

She shrugged. "A long time. Maybe a week. Or a day?"

"How old are you?"

She held up four fingers. "Five."

"Huh. I've got a friend in Palm Springs with twin brothers who are around your age, I think. Do you have any friends around here?"

She hung her head and rubbed her pant legs. "No. Daddy doesn't know any kids."

The neighborhood was gorgeous, but it didn't seem like the type to have many kids in it. Most of the residences in Connor's neighborhood were probably second or third homes and used as golf retreats.

I thought about Lennie and Willie. "Maybe I can talk to my friend and see if you can meet her twin brothers."

She looked up at me. "Can you help me find some friends?"

"I can try." I pulled out my phone. "Sit here."

I sent Laurel a quick text. Over the next half hour, Elodie told me about her Grammy in Vancouver, her dance class, and her worry about making friends.

"Have you met Javier yet?" I asked.

She smiled. "Yes. He's my best friend. And guess what?"

"What?"

"He has candy sometimes. And one time he gave me a cookie."

Javier obviously knew how to win a five-year-old's heart. "Would you like to meet his daughter?"

She nodded. "Is she my age, or old like you?"

Ouch. "Closer to my age, but she's awesome."

Elodie put her hand on my thigh. "Okay. 'Cause you and Javier are my only friends so far."

My heart broke a little. "Do you have any leftover Christmas candy we could take to Javier and Isabella? She's probably over at his place right now."

"I think so. There's lots of stuff in the kitchen. We could see." She looked up at me with those big dark brown eyes.

"Great. Let me teach you the fine art of regifting. And let's go see if we can find you another friend."

Elodie gave me a lopsided, gap-toothed smile, and I could see her resemblance to Connor. I imagined Damien's little girl or boy, standing there with a big grin and a dimple, and my heart squeezed painfully.

Chapter 30

Damien glanced over at me as we drove away from Connor's house. He shook his head, then started chuckling.

"What?" I asked.

"You can't help yourself, can you?" He took my hand and kissed it, then nipped the tip of my index finger.

I shivered slightly. "What do you mean?"

"Helping Elodie. Having Isa and Javier over at the house. And a Christmas Day feast laid out when we got back."

"You guys were gone for almost two hours. We got hungry. It's obvious Connor needs help with Elodie, and Isa is great. Except for the fact she can't stand Connor, it's a match made in heaven."

We made it back to Damien's place a little while later. When we walked into the kitchen through the garage, he laid his phone, wallet, and keys on the counter, then took my backpack from me, peeled my jacket off, and backed me into the fridge. Bending down, he nuzzled my neck, then drew his tongue up the shell of my ear. I shivered and wrapped my arms around him, twisting my hands in his hair. He slid his leg between mine and nudged them apart.

"It's only been two fucking days, but it feels like a month since I've been inside you." He murmured a few of the dirty things he wanted to do to me, and my knees went weak. He rubbed his thigh against my cleft, and the friction made my head spin. Running his hands up my ribcage, Damien took off my shirt, then gathered my wrists above my head.

He looked down at my red lace bra and groaned. I stood stretched out and exposed to him, and my breath came in short pants. He rubbed his chest against my swollen breasts and kissed me hard and long. My senses were surrounded by him, and I wanted to drown in his touch and masculine, spicy scent. He leaned down and sucked and licked at my cleavage, and I loved his impatience and his need to touch me. I'd been struggling with the same urges since I left his bed.

He unsnapped my bra and lifted it up over my outstretched arms. Then he cupped my breasts and rolled my nipples between his fingers.

My thoughts scattered, and I arched into his hands. "I want to touch you, too."

He smiled wickedly, then bent down and pulled my nipple into his mouth, sucking hard on one and then the other. When he finally came up for air, I was rubbing myself frantically on his thigh and my hands had come down to slide into the back of his jeans.

He smiled while he kissed me. "No, keep your hands up for me."

I reluctantly put my hands back up and pushed into him. He pulled his own shirt off, and reached down to undo my jeans. He slid his hand inside and cupped my wet slit under my panties. "Kick off your shoes. I need to be inside you."

It took me a second to process what he was asking, but in the meantime, he'd bent down and efficiently tugged off my shoes and socks then pulled my jeans and panties down my legs. He helped me step out of them then stood up and wrapped my legs around his waist.

"I want in."

A desperate need spread low in my belly, and I nodded. He positioned his length at my opening, then powered inside me. My head flew back, and I brought my arms down and wrapped them around his shoulders, digging my fingernails into his back. His bare cock felt so good, even with the pain of him stretching me open to accommodate his size.

"Oh, God. Oh... God," I chanted. He pushed himself in and out a few times until he finally bottomed out inside me, and I felt the tip of his shaft hit against my cervix.

He gathered me in his arms, then walked us over to the countertop. Damien set me on top and brought both my legs out, so I was doing the splits along the edge of the counter. He pulled my hips forward a little, then buried himself deep inside me again.

"Keep your legs spread." He leaned me back and brought my core right to the edge, then thrust himself into me several times before having to stop so he wouldn't come.

"I've been wanting to do this since I watched you stretch out last year. You did the fucking splits like it was nothing. You don't know how many times I've jacked off to this fantasy."

"I need you deep and hard right now," I moaned, leaning back on my hands, and pushing my pelvis into his thrusts.

His depraved and wicked grin made my toes curl and my pussy spasm around his cock. He gave me several hard, deep thrusts and continued to pump in and out of me. My breasts jostled each time he shoved himself in, and I felt a climax start to build. He reached down and stroked my clit, then leaned over and drew one of my nipples deep in his mouth. He pulled and sucked on it. Then Damien bit down, and my climax rose and sizzled through me.

"Please," I begged mindlessly. He smiled against my breast until he felt my channel clamp down on his cock and ripple over him as I came. He propelled in and out of me several more times, then slammed his cock deep inside. He groaned long and low as he orgasmed.

Damien eventually pulled back when he felt his own semen dripping down his leg. "Fuck." He grimaced, grabbing a dish towel. "It's only hot when my semen drips down your legs."

I snickered and gingerly brought my thighs together. I groaned a little at my sore, abused muscles. "If you always give me a mind-blowing orgasm to go with it, the mess is a small price to pay."

He smirked and leaned down to kiss my neck. "I'm glad you think so, Legs."

We finally made it to his bedroom and started getting ready for bed. My backpack was still in the kitchen where we'd dropped it when we first got to Damien's house. I walked out to grab it, and I glanced down and noticed Damien had a couple of text messages on his cell phone sitting on the counter next to my backpack. I didn't think anything of it until I noticed the messages were from someone named Sadie.

Sadie: Hey, baby, it was so nice to see you the other day. I hope you're having a good Christmas. If you want me to come over again—

Sadie: I'm home tonight if you need anything at all.

The longer text was cut off, and I didn't know Damien's code so I couldn't pull it up and read the entire text. And I absolutely would have. I felt sick to my stomach and my heart slammed in my chest as I stared down at his phone. My hands shook, and I set my backpack back down on the counter.

He'd been talking to someone named Sadie on his phone at the dog park not long ago. I wondered who she was and if he was still seeing her. And still fucking her. It sounded like it. I wasn't stupid or naïve. My job made me cynical as hell and I had a reasonable bullshit meter. But I hadn't seen this coming.

I fought through the pain and confusion. We'd never talked about being exclusive. I'd just assumed we were on the same page. Maybe there was a reasonable explanation, but right then I just wanted to get away before I broke down.

My feet felt stuck to the floor, and my hands were shaking so much I had difficulty digging my phone out of my backpack to get a ride home. I leaned against the same counter he'd fucked me on a few minutes earlier and tried to calm down. I didn't know what to say to Damien, but I knew I didn't want to talk to him right then.

Damien called my name from the other room, and I started digging for my phone in earnest. My breaths were coming in short gasps, and I just wanted to get the hell out of there.

Right before I bolted for the front door, Damien walked into the kitchen. "What are you doing out here in the dark?" He reached over and turned on the light above the kitchen sink.

I flinched. My hair shielded my face from him. "I need to go home. I... I'll get an Uber."

He froze in the middle of the kitchen and studied me. "You drove over here. Your vehicle is outside. What's going on?"

Then I remembered I'd driven here earlier today. I wondered frantically if I could drive myself home in my current state. I could if the alternative was having him take me home. Or waiting here for an Uber.

My stomach lurched, and I wanted to double over in pain. "You have a couple of texts," I whispered. "Your phone was sitting next to my backpack." I finally looked up at him with pain-filled eyes.

He cocked his head and studied me cautiously, then reached over and grabbed his phone off the counter.

He looked at it, then swore viciously under his breath. "Let me explain."

I put up my hands. "When someone says those words, the next thing that usually comes out is a lie or an excuse."

He stepped closer to me. "I'm not going to give you either."

I felt my keys in the bottom of my bag. I pulled them out and held them to my chest.

"Who is Sadie?" I asked quietly.

He blanched but answered truthfully. "My old girlfriend."

"When was the last time you fucked her?"

He narrowed his eyes. "A couple of months ago."

I had to hand it to him, he promised me he wouldn't lie or make excuses.

I swallowed when I felt bile starting to crawl up my throat. "We never talked about... seeing other people, or what either of us wanted from this." I couldn't call it a relationship because I didn't even know what it was anymore. "I just assumed. That's on me."

Damien stepped toward me with his hands up, but I backed up hard against the counter.

"Don't you touch me right now," I rasped out.

He watched me carefully, then nodded and stepped back. "I'll take you home tonight if that's what you really want. But we're going to talk tomorrow. I want your fucking promise."

I shook my head. "I'll drive myself home. And I can't promise that. You spoke to her on the phone when we were at the dog park together. You've obviously seen her since then." I shook my head and whispered brokenly. "You didn't say a *word*."

"Harley—"

"I don't want to be with someone who isn't with me, one hundred percent. I should have made it clear before now."

He inched closer to me. "You're making assumptions right now that are dead fucking wrong. I told Sadie about you, and I told her that she and I were done."

I did not want to hear about his old girlfriend, who didn't sound like such an "old" girlfriend after all.

"You never said a word about her being back in your life. I told you things I've never told anyone." I swallowed and my eyes filled with tears. "I *trusted* you. And you fucked her *two months ago*."

My emotions were all over the place, and I just wanted to cry quietly in the dark for a while.

But he didn't get to watch me break down. "I can't do this right now."

He followed me with his eyes. "When?" he clipped.

I tried to gather my thoughts. They seemed to float around my head like dandelion seeds on the wind.

"We never talked about not seeing anyone else. You don't owe me an explanation. Maybe this whole thing is for the best. I have scars and baggage. I'm... damaged." A tear slipped out, and I silently cursed myself. "I need to go."

"Let me get your clothes. You're standing there in my shirt and nothing else."

I looked down and noticed I was naked except for his shirt. I nodded jerkily and avoided his eyes. He got my clothes and shoes, then cautiously set them on the counter and stepped back.

I turned my back to him and dressed quickly. Keeping my back turned, I stuffed my bra and panties into my backpack and turned around. I skirted around him to get to the front door.

"Harley," he said again.

I braced myself for more pain or humiliation. "Please. I need to go." My voice cracked.

"You're not damaged, sweetheart. This isn't fucking over, and we *will* talk. Fair warning."

I shook my head and bolted out the door.

Chapter 31

When I got home, Gary met me at the front door. I dropped my backpack, sank to the floor, and cried like I hadn't cried since Ryan's death. My heart felt bruised and beaten, and I felt so stupid. I'd done this to myself. Gary crept over and nudged my hand with his paw.

"Hey, big guy. Your mama is pretty dumb. Did you know that? You did, huh?" I talked to him softly for a while as I stroked him. He leaned into me and let me pet him until I finally dragged myself off the floor and got ready for bed.

Gary usually slept in his dog bed in the corner of my room, or sometimes on the living room couch. But tonight he jumped up on my bed and plopped himself down next to me. I wrapped my arm around him and gave him a few belly scratches as my mind replayed the night.

Tomorrow would be too soon to see Damien. My thoughts and feelings were in turmoil, and I needed to step back and try to get my emotions under control and gain some perspective. I picked up my phone from the nightstand and texted Olivia.

Me: I'm going exploring in the desert tomorrow morning. Do you want to come? Leaving at six.

Olivia: WTF, it's after one. Why are you up?

Me: You coming or not?

Olivia: You're leaving soooo early.

Me: Suck it up, buttercup. Bring your swimsuit.

Olivia: Okaaay. See u at the butt crack of dawn.

Almost two hours later, I finally drifted off to sleep. When my phone alarm chimed the next morning, it felt like I'd only slept for a few minutes. I rolled out of bed and stood up, and the night rushed back to me. I stooped over a little as anguish hit me all over again.

I resolutely pushed back the pain and turned on the bedside lamp. Pulling out some hiking clothes and a swimsuit, I got ready for the day. It was Monday and several of the hiking trails and preserves would be closed. But I'd heard Sariah and Yun talking about the Big Morongo Canyon Trail a few weeks ago.

It was also far enough away from Palm Springs that it was unlikely we'd run into anyone I knew. I was packing some lunch when Olivia let herself in the front door.

"Good morning, stinky head! Hi, Gary, how's it going?" She walked into the kitchen and put her backpack on the counter.

I looked up. "You're only thirteen minutes late."

"And those were thirteen beautiful minutes between me and my snooze button. Besides, it's not like we have anywhere we have to be."

Little did she know I wanted to get away from the house before sunrise. Damien was an early riser, and I didn't put it past him to show up at dawn to talk. I didn't know if I'd ever be ready to talk about last night.

When we took off, Olivia promptly fell asleep, so I used the thirty-minute drive to stew. Olivia was still asleep when we made it to the parking lot, so I texted Damien.

Me: I won't be around today. Olivia and I are going exploring, and I need some time.

After I'd sent the text, I pulled up my favorite hiking app and decided which trails we'd take. My phone vibrated with an incoming text as I closed the app.

Damien: I understand, Legs. But we're talking tomorrow. Be safe.

His text and him calling me Legs made me miss him and want to knee him in the balls all at once. I was confused and conflicted, and I needed to get my head together before I saw him again.

When Olivia woke up, we took off. The trail wove through California fan palms and desert shrubs, and a pleasant, pungent smell came off the creosote bushes.

Olivia glanced over at me. "Despite my charming personality, I have a feeling we're not out here just because you want to spend the day with me."

"You do have a charming personality—when you want something. And we talked about going on another hike before you went back to school."

She rolled her eyes. "You texted me at one in the morning, and we left five hours later. Who or what are you running from?"

Olivia had always been good at reading people, and she knew me better than anyone.

I slowed down and my eyes got a little watery. "I promise I'll tell you everything. Just not today, okay?"

Olivia looked a little spooked. We rarely got emotional with each other unless something serious happened, or someone died.

I grabbed her hand and squeezed it. "It's not life or death. Things with Damien were good until it all imploded last night. And I didn't see it coming. When I get my head around it, we'll talk."

She studied me, then nodded and squeezed my hand back. We stopped and ate lunch at one of the many benches along the trail, then headed back.

We both had our swimsuits, so at the last minute we decided to buy a couple of day passes to one of the little hotel spas in Desert Hot Springs. The pool and spa were heated by a hot spring in the area, and the plush mature desert landscaping made it feel like a little oasis as we quietly sipped our drinks and soaked in the spa.

Olivia turned to me. "Will you tell me what happened with Damien tomorrow? Sometimes you don't talk about things until months or even years later." She looked down at her drink. "I worry about you bottling things inside."

I sighed and leaned my head back. "Yeah. If you really want to hear it."

When the light started to fade and the temperature dropped a little, we cleaned up and headed home.

Damien hadn't tried to contact me since my text that morning. I missed him, and I missed talking to him about whatever interesting thing happened during our day. Lying in bed that night, I felt miserable and conflicted before finally drifting off to sleep.

Chapter 32

When I woke the next morning, the smell of coffee wafted through my little house. I rolled over and quickly sat up when I heard Damien's voice.

I took several deep breaths, gathered my clothes, and showered quickly. Damien sat at my counter drinking coffee and talking with Olivia when I came out a few minutes later.

My chest ached when I saw him, and I stopped in the doorway to gather my composure.

He looked up, and set his mug down. "Hey, sweetheart."

Olivia turned to me from the kitchen sink. "Look who I found on your doorstep when I came over this morning?"

"What are you doing here?" I asked Damien softly.

He crossed his arms and studied me. "We're going to talk. And Olivia was filling me in about Christmas Eve. Why didn't you tell me?"

I shrugged jerkily. "You don't need to worry about it. And I forgot. Besides, it was just a car."

"The fuck I don't have to worry about it. Tell me exactly what you saw, and then you and I are going to talk."

Olivia looked between us and sat her coffee mug down. "I just remembered I have... stuff at Mom's house."

I pointed at her. "No you don't, big liar."

"Yes, I do. Stuff like eating breakfast and waiting for you to come over and tell me what the hell's going on." She started easing toward the front door.

I didn't want her to leave. "Ollie, I need you. I found texts from Damien's girlfriend on his phone the other night. Will you please stay? I don't want to do this alone."

Olivia stopped in her tracks and stared at Damien. "You motherfucker," she whispered hoarsely.

He stood up, folded his arms, and looked at both of us. "It was my *old* girlfriend. You sure you want to do this with an audience, Legs?"

I involuntarily flinched at the endearment. "I don't want to do 'this' at all, Dimples."

"You didn't read the whole text, and you left before getting the entire story." He stepped toward me cautiously. "I won't lie to you, and I won't make excuses. But we both deserve for you to have all the facts before you decide anything."

Olivia stood there, watching us both carefully. I suddenly felt sorry for dragging her into this. I shifted uncomfortably and absently rubbed the scar on my cheek.

She watched me rub the scar and smiled sadly. "I'd do anything for you, Har. If you want me to try and kick his ass to the curb, I will. But if it were me, I'd want to hear what he has to say first."

I stared at him. My heart hurt and I didn't want to feel that kind of pain ever again. I'd had enough of it in my life, and I was heartily sick of it. But Olivia was right. I knew if I didn't hear him out, I'd always regret it.

Nodding slightly, I reached over and squeezed her hand. "Okay, I'll call you later. Love you."

She looked at Damien. "Don't lie to her and don't leave anything out. She deserves the whole truth." She walked out, leaving us alone.

Damien watched me. My body locked, as if bracing for more pain. He cautiously pulled his phone out of his pocket and pulled up his texts, then he slid it over the counter to me. After a moment, I picked it up and read the text chain.

Sadie: Hey, baby, it was so nice to see you the other day. I hope you're having a good Christmas. If you want me to come over again so we can continue our talk, please let me know. I understand you've moved on and I'm sorry I got so emotional. I only want the best for you. Even if it isn't me.

Sadie: I'm home tonight if you need anything at all.

He waited for me to look up at him. "She came to the office a week ago because I stopped taking her calls. I'd already told her I was seeing you and it was fucking serious."

I carefully set his phone back down on the counter.

He continued. "I told her before we hooked up in October that it was a one-time thing. Her grandma had just died, and Sadie said she wanted... some comfort."

My eyes narrowed. "Sebastian knew you'd gotten back together with her, didn't he? At Laurel's house on Monday. He knew."

"Goddamn it, I didn't get back with her," he bit off.

"Okay, that you'd started having sex again and talking with her," I amended.

He folded his arms and scowled. "He suspected we'd hooked up. But when Sadie came into the office and made a scene, Sebastian called me a fucking moron."

Humiliation and hurt slid through me knowing Damien's friends were aware of what was happening with Sadie, but I'd been clueless. Sebastian calling him a fucking moron made me feel a little better.

He rubbed the back of his neck. "Sadie started crying after I told her—again—there was no way I'd ever get back with her. Then I told her I was dead serious about you, and she started crying and yelling in the office."

He put his hands on his hips and shook his head. "When Zeke found out, he told me if I was really that stupid, he'd have to re-think our friendship."

I smiled faintly for the first time in a while. "I've always liked Zeke."

"She's my *old* girlfriend, Legs. I'm not fucking her or talking to her, and we haven't gotten back together. We split up almost four years ago, then she moved away. But she moved back a few months ago, and we hooked up. She thought it meant more than it did."

I stared at him. "How many times have you 'hooked up' since you broke things off?"

"Are you direct examining me, counselor?"

"Answer the question," I clipped.

His lips twisted. "Twice. Once not long after we broke up. She came in town to visit, and the other was two months ago." He gazed at me. "*Over* two months ago—right before Sheila and

Grace's party. I haven't touched or had sex with anyone but you since then."

I studied him. "Why didn't you tell me about her? If I would have known, seeing her texts wouldn't have been such a shock."

He sighed. "It happened before we got together. I didn't see a need."

My back went straight. "Those texts made it seem like you were still hooking up."

Damien watched me carefully. "I didn't want to give you an excuse to pull away. And you've been subconsciously looking for one."

I started to automatically deny it. But I stopped and thought about what I'd said to him after finding her texts. That I was damaged, and it was for the best.

My eyes slid away from his. "This thing between us happened so fast. I told you I have issues, and I didn't take the time to really analyze this."

"Yeah, I didn't want to give you the time because you would have analyzed it to death. For the past two years I've been watching you coach that crazy-ass volleyball team of yours and staring at your legs in those spandex shorts. And when I got to know you and got a chance to get in there, I fucking took it."

He stood up and grabbed my arms, then shook me gently. "We weren't together in October. We are now, and you know I'll be honest with you. You can trust me with your heart."

He leaned in, kissed my forehead, and held me for a moment. "But I'll give you some time if that's what you need." Then he turned and walked out.

Over the next few days, I didn't hear from Damien. Olivia and Ava carefully tiptoed around me. My mind dragged me back through my past, and the trauma lurking there.

On Saturday, we played our final rec volleyball match of the season against the older, retired team. They'd gone on a cruise together during the regular season and rescheduled the game.

By the end of the match, Jaime and Tiana were both watching me carefully. I saw them talking quietly afterward as I gathered my things.

Then they walked over, and Jaime crossed his arms. "What's up?"

"What do you mean?" I asked carefully.

Tiana shook her head. "Don't bullshit us, girl. You haven't yelled at any of us to do more cardio or get off our asses. You were actually *nice* today. You're scaring everyone."

I smiled faintly. "Sorry. I'll make sure to get back to my bitchy self by next season."

"Who pissed in your coffee this morning?" Jaime asked.

"I don't know what you're talking about."

Tiana raised her eyebrow. "You're a shit liar. Now spill."

My shoulders slumped, and I sighed. "No one pissed in my coffee. I'm just... scared," I finally admitted.

Tiana's jaw dropped. "What the fuck? Why?"

Jaime studied me. "It's that Damien dude, isn't it?"

"Maybe."

Tiana snorted. "It all makes sense now. Honey, it happens to most of us when we find 'the one.' What're you afraid of? That he's too sweet, too fine, or the sex is too smoking hot?"

I rolled my eyes and plopped down on the grass like a three-year-old. They sat next to me, and I spilled my guts. I told them about my dad and Ryan, Damien, his ex-girlfriend, and my fears.

Jaime stared at me like I'd lost my mind, and Tiana nodded and kept saying, "Uh-huh," as I talked.

When I finished, Tiana reached over and patted my knee. "I understand about the bitch ex-girlfriend thing. But Damien's right. If you two weren't together at the time, you can't hold it against him."

Jaime scooted away from me a little. "Now I know what crawled up your ass. It was your head."

Tiana and I both gasped, and I reached over and tried to slap his leg. He backed up even more and held up his hand.

"Don't tell me your shit if you don't want my opinion. I saw how he took care of you when you found out Frankie died. And most of us have a crazy-ass ex. Or three."

Tiana nodded. "That's true."

Jaime grinned. "But if you're too chickenshit––"

I gasped and jumped up. They got up as well, and Jaime danced away from my pinching fingers.

"Ouch, damn it! Quit pinching me! I'm just trying to help you, you crazy bitch."

I stepped back with a demented gleam. "You can call me a crazy bitch, and ask me what crawled up my ass, but if you ever call me 'chickenshit' again I'll tell your wife you really want to try pegging. And you have a foot fetish."

He held up his hands. "Okay, *puta loca*." He tilted his head. "How'd you know about pegging?"

Tiana started laughing.

Jaime threw his arm around my shoulder. "Go call him."

Chapter 33

Before heading home, I called Damien. He didn't answer, so I sent him a text.

Me: Tiana said I can't be angry since we weren't together. Jaime called me a crazy bitch. I'm scared but I want to try and make this work. Call me when you can.

Right after sending the text, I noticed an alert that my front yard camera had been motion-activated that morning. I wondered briefly if Damien had come by as I pulled up the footage to watch it. The footage showed a man in a black beanie and a black jacket walking up to my back fence and tossing something into my backyard. Then he turned and quickly walked away.

I squinted at the footage, not understanding what I was seeing at first. Then it hit me. The man had thrown what looked like a chunk of meat into my yard, and Gary spent a good portion of his day either sleeping or lounging around back there. I'd even installed a handy dog door so he could get in and out.

My hands were shaking, but I found Olivia's number and called her. "Please, God. Please, God. Not Gary," I begged as the phone rang.

Olivia picked up. "Hey, Harley."

"Ollie, someone threw a chunk of probably poisoned meat into my backyard this morning." I started shaking. "Have you been over to my house? Have you seen Gary?"

"Mother fucking son of a whore! Who would do something like that?" Olivia yelled. She took a deep breath. "Har, Gary's with us. Mom wanted to go to Paws for Coffee this morning. It was her idea to take Gary."

I put my head on my steering wheel and started bawling. Ava had saved him. My mother had saved Gary. The irony wasn't lost on me.

"Harley, are you there? Are you okay?"

I pulled myself together and wiped my eyes. "I'm here. Thank you. Tell Mom thank you."

Olivia went silent for a moment. "I'll tell her. We'll be home soon. When it's safe for Gary, we'll bring him over."

I called the police on the way home, and Officer Robertson met me less than ten minutes later. We studied the chunk of meat, and he took a few photos. It looked like some type of cheap steak and had blue crystals mashed into it.

Officer Robertson thought it was rat poisoning. "You're lucky your dog wasn't here when the perpetrator threw this over the fence." He bagged the piece of meat. "This looks like the type of rat poison that causes internal hemorrhaging. It's a terrible way to die."

I shuddered, thinking about Gary suffering like that.

He rubbed the back of his neck. "I'll ask around and let you know if I hear about any similar cases."

After he left, I hosed down the backyard and scrubbed the patio area where the meat had landed. I'd just walked out the front door to get Gary from my mom's house when Damien drove up.

He got out of his truck and studied my face. "What's wrong? Hey, we can work this out..."

I sobbed once then hugged him and buried my face in his neck, wrapping my arms around him. "Someone tried to poison Gary."

He jerked. "What the fuck? Is he okay?"

We walked back inside and I told him everything. "If you hadn't put the security cameras in, and if my mom hadn't decided to take Gary to the coffee shop, Gary would probably be dead or in terrible agony."

My doorbell rang, and Ava and Gary stood at the door. "Are you all right, honey?"

Handing Damien Gary's leash, I wrapped my arms around Ava. I laid my cheek on her head, even though I expected her to complain about her hair getting messed up.

But her arms slowly wrapped around me, and I felt a soft sob.

"We haven't hugged in..." She didn't finish, but I knew. We both did. We hadn't hugged since my dad died.

I finally pulled back. "Thank you. So much."

She tried to smile as she wiped a few tears away. "I was trying to be better about Gary. Well, anyway. I just wanted to check on you."

I leaned down and kissed her cheek. "Thank you for checking on me. And thank you for Gary."

Then I took Damien's hand. "Now we're going to clean out a few cobwebs."

Ava gave a startled laugh, then smiled slyly. "I'll be on my way then. Glad to hear you're finally cleaning out those cobwebs."

Damien looked at the closed door. "Do I want to know what 'cleaning out cobwebs' means?"

"Nope. But you can probably guess. I need to give Gary some love first though."

A few minutes later Damien pulled me to him, cupped my jaw, and kissed me, thoroughly fucking my mouth. I slanted my head and took him in. He groaned and sucked as heat curled through me. My ovaries tightened, and my nipples contracted to tight points.

He grabbed the hem of my jersey and pulled it off. Then hooking his thumbs in my shorts, he yanked them down. Damien pushed me down on the couch and laid me out.

Staring down at my body clad only in my sleek sports bra and a thong, he growled low and long. "Shit, sweetheart. You're a fucking sight."

Damien tugged my bra off, and when I lowered my arms to touch him, he put them back above my head.

"No. Right now you do what I say. You want the truth, Legs? I'm still a little pissed at you for running away and not talking to me. I get it. But I want my pound of flesh." He leaned down and bit the swell of my breast, and I cried out and arched into him. "So, you're going to be my good little girl and give me exactly what I need."

Before I could tell him to shove it, he leaned back down and took the other breast deep into his mouth. His tongue lavished and licked at my distended nipple, and I moaned and shifted restlessly.

He slid his other hand down, pulled my thong aside, then ran his fingers across my center. I bucked when he rubbed my clit with his thumb. My mind told me to bring my hands down, but my body hummed in pleasure and need. I kept my arms above my head.

Damien sucked on my other breast and continued to stroke. Then he shoved two fingers inside me and thrust in and out. When I started panting and squirming, he lifted up and yanked my thong off, staring down at me.

"Do you want me to fuck you?" he growled.

"Yes! God, I need you."

He smirked and clucked his tongue. "Not yet." Then he cupped my vagina.

I lifted my hips to him. "I need you inside me."

"You're going to be begging for my cock by the time I'm done with you. Now open your beautiful long legs and show me that wet, needy pussy."

I stared up at him, not fully registering what he'd said. My mind was full of white-hot need. He lightly slapped the inside of my thigh.

"Open."

I slowly drew my legs apart and showed him my core. His eyes drank me in for a moment, then he leaned down and licked my clit. When I started to bring my hands down to touch him, he bit my thigh.

"Up. Now." He grabbed my wrists and brought them back above my head.

Trailing his hands down my sides, he pulled my legs further apart and slid his fingers back inside me. Then he spread me there. His commands and touch sent currents of lust and need sliding across my body.

"I think you like being told what to do. You're dripping wet for me." He leaned in and bit the juncture between my hip and thigh hard enough that I gasped out loud.

He licked me there, then sucked on me. My hands started drifting down again, and he sat up and grabbed my wrists.

"Do you want me to tie you up? Would that help you remember?"

My hips shifted restlessly against him, and my back arched. He leaned down and bit my nipple. Pain and pleasure zinged straight to my clit, and I moaned.

"I wonder if I could make you come just by biting on your perfect pink nipples."

"I want you inside me," I begged.

"Say please, sweetheart," he murmured.

"Please put your cock inside me. Now!"

He grinned and climbed off me. Before I knew what he was doing, he pulled me up and dragged me to the back of the couch. Then he bent me over. Kicking my thighs apart, Damien stood between my legs.

He stroked my back, then pushed my head down. "Be careful what you wish for."

Positioning his cock at my opening, he grabbed my shoulders and shoved deep inside me in one long, powerful stroke. He used his hips and braced his foot to drive up inside me, and I cried out at the rough invasion. Damien stroked my sweaty back and gave me a second to adjust, then he slammed into me again and again.

The feel of his bare cock ignited me. I wailed as he battered against me every time he shoved himself inside. Dark pleasure spread through my veins, and my orgasm quickly built.

Damien braced a hand on my shoulder, pulling me back on his cock with each hard thrust. My breath caught in my throat. I was so close. He reached around and plucked and stroked my clit, and a climax exploded through me. I threw my head back and cried out as overwhelming pleasure and pain radiated through me.

He pumped in and out as I pulsed around his cock, then he slammed into me one last time and let out a low, deep groan. After a moment, he laid across my back and finally wrapped his arm around me, hugging me tight. Then he pulled us both up straight.

Damien was still buried deep inside me, and he stood between my legs. "You're *mine*, Legs. Don't run away again without talking to me first or the outcome won't be this pleasurable."

I turned my face and brushed my lips against his. "If you fuck your old girlfriend again, or anyone else, it'll be more than just a volleyball."

He grinned. "Deal. Now let's get you cleaned up."

Kissing my temple, he slowly pulled out, sending his warm semen spilling down my legs.

"After lunch, I'll give you something else to eat. I'm fucking addicted to watching you take me down your throat."

We'd just had sex, and I'd orgasmed so hard my insides felt sore and bruised. But I still shivered at the thought.

Chapter 34

The night before Olivia left to go back to school, we sat out on my back patio huddled around my firepit, drinking wine. Ava had already gone to bed.

After two glasses, I told her about my conversation with Jaime and Tiana.

She studied me. "Have you thought about talking to an actual therapist?"

I looked down at the fire. "Yeah, but I haven't had time."

She snorted. "You mean you haven't *made* time."

"That's probably true. I have my first appointment in two weeks."

Olivia smiled and raised her glass. "It's about fucking time."

"When do you think you'll be back?" I asked, blatantly changing the topic.

"I don't know. I need to start studying for my CPA exam, and I've got a few big projects this semester."

"I'm going to miss you, but I get it."

Olivia set her wine glass down. "You've been a little quieter since you and Damien worked things out. Are you sure you're okay?"

"Yes, I'm fine. We're fine," I answered quickly.

She looked at me with a raised eyebrow. "Uh-huh."

"We're getting there," I amended after a minute. "I... need to work a few things out. Hence the therapy."

She stared out into the twilight, then finally looked up at the night sky. "I love you, Harley. And I support you no matter what. But I think you should give yourself a chance to love someone again. He's right, you know. You're good together, and you've been happier than I've seen you in years." There was sorrow in her eyes.

"Thanks, Ollie. I'm going to miss the crap out of you."

When I dropped Olivia off the next morning at the airport, we were both quiet and melancholy.

"Text me when you get back to your apartment," I told her as we hugged on the sidewalk at the Palm Springs airport.

"I will. Please check in with Mom and Chippy. He seems like a hardy cat, but just in case. And be patient with Mom. I think she's really trying."

I nodded. "You know everything isn't magically fixed with her, but we've made some progress."

We'd taken Ava to the Palm Springs animal shelter, and she picked out a small male black and white shorthair with a cute little personality. She'd named him Chip, and he seemed scrappy and feisty, but I'd be checking on him regularly.

I pulled Olivia's suitcase out and set it on the curb while she grabbed her backpack. Then we hugged one more time, and she was gone. When I got back home, the house seemed quiet and lifeless without her.

I wanted to crawl back into bed and mope and sleep some more, but I knew from experience it wouldn't make me feel better. So I spent the next couple of hours taking Gary for a long walk, cleaning, and doing laundry.

Then I decided to drive over to Palm Desert and do a little shopping on El Paseo Drive for a New Year's Eve outfit. I wasn't a big shopper, but the weather was bright and sunny, and the flowers and holiday decorations were still up. El Paseo was always festive and cheerful.

For New Year's Eve, Damien and I planned to go to Cha Cha's for dinner, then to Scott and Iz's bar for their New Year's Eve celebration.

Damien called me while I was driving back to Palm Springs. "How are you holding up after dropping Olivia off?"

"I'm only a little moody and depressed. I should be good by tonight though." It felt good to have someone care that I was sad.

"It's okay if you're moody and depressed. I'll make you feel better tonight. What are you up to today?"

"I returned some work calls and did a few chores at my rental in between guests. That's all."

For some reason, I pictured him working with his hands and wearing a tool belt. "I like that you're good with your hands. Do you wear a tool belt while you work?"

I could hear a smile in his voice. "No, but I have a toolbox."

"Oh, I know you do."

He laughed. "You make it sound dirty."

"That's because what I'm thinking *is* dirty."

"I'm sleeping over tonight," he told me. "What I have in mind is going to take some time."

My toes curled. "Oh? What do you have in mind?"

"While I was at the hardware store today, I picked up some nice silk rope. It has a decent tooth, and the friction is good."

I paused, wondering for a split second why he'd tell me he bought rope. And then it hit me, and my vagina spasmed.

I cleared my throat and shifted. "What are you planning to use the rope for?"

"Not what, but whom."

"Oh, God," I breathed.

He laughed low. "Tonight while we're out celebrating, I want you to anticipate, and maybe worry a little, about what I plan to do to you."

"Why don't you just tell me?"

"Because you have a vivid imagination."

He was right. I did. And I worried, fantasized, and wondered about it all the way home.

Cha Cha's was an iconic poolside restaurant in Palm Springs. For New Year's Eve, lanterns had been placed around the pool and in the surrounding gardens, and gold balloons with streamers were tied to all the awnings.

Propane heaters around the tables kept the dining area reasonably warm. We ordered a bottle of sparkling wine and a couple of appetizers.

The black and gold dress I'd bought at a little boutique on El Paseo was short and clingy, and hugged my curves. The halter top tied behind my neck, and showed off my shoulders and a little cleavage.

When we sat down, I took off my wrap, and Damien's eyes grew dark and hooded as he studied me. I'd dusted my shoulders and chest with a little glitter and fixed my hair in a partial updo.

He wore black pants and an expensive white shirt with the sleeves rolled up. I wanted to lean over and bite his jaw.

"You look very fuckable in that dress, sweetheart." His hot gaze traveled over me as he poured our wine.

My insides clenched in anticipation and need. "And you clean up well too, Dimples." I took a sip of wine and gazed at him. We ate and drank for a few minutes, staring at each other while we made small talk.

He finally leaned across the table. "Come here."

I scooted forward and leaned in. He picked up my hand and turned it around, then slowly licked up my wrist. I shuddered and my panties grew damp.

He reached up and rubbed some of the glitter off my shoulder. "You look beautiful, but my favorite look on you is when you're naked and sweaty underneath me."

"It's edible."

"What's edible? I know your pussy and tits are."

I smiled a little. "The glitter is edible, and so is the lotion I'm wearing. Along with my, uh, pussy and tits," I whispered.

His nostrils flared, and he slowly tasted the glitter on his finger. "How hungry are you?" he growled.

I swallowed. "Hungry. But not for food."

"Good." He looked up and motioned to the closest server. "We need our check."

My breathing grew heavy. I wrapped my arms around my middle, trying to relieve the deep ache in my core.

"Fuck it." He stood up and threw money on the table and grabbed my hand. Just then the server came with the check.

"That should cover it. Keep the change."

"Sir, are you sure you don't want your change?" The server asked.

"Yes." Damien grabbed my wrap and dragged me out of the restaurant.

Pulling me to his truck, he practically threw me inside. When he climbed in, I leaned over and took hold of his shirt collar.

He turned in his seat and grabbed my face, then kissed and licked me until I was gasping for air. I was so gone, I blindly climbed into his lap. He eased his seat back and helped me straddle him.

"My windows are tinted, but anyone walking by is probably going to know what we're doing," he growled.

My hips rolled against his hard cock, and I rubbed myself against him through his pants. "I don't care. I want you inside me." Then I started undoing his belt and unzipping his pants.

He grinned and reached around to untie my halter top. I didn't have a bra on. "Your dress is perfect for a fast, dirty fuck."

He slid my top down and palmed both my breasts, then squeezed and pulled them to the point of pain. I arched into him and moaned.

I'd never had sex in a vehicle or in a public place before. Anxiety and hot lust slammed through me. Damien let go of my breasts and trailed his hand down to my clit, rolling and tugging on it.

My thong got in his way, and he yanked it off me with an impatient snap. My body jerked, and I heard it tear.

Then he pulled himself out of his pants and guided me onto his hard, thick shaft. "Fuck yourself on me. I want to watch you struggle to work your pussy over my cock."

I panted and rubbed myself on him, then reached down and positioned his large tip inside my opening. I put my hands on his shoulders and worked myself down on him.

"Look at my cock stretching you." He grabbed my head and forced me to look down and watch his cock thrust in and out of me.

Then he palmed my breasts again, pulling and pinching my nipples until I was gasping with the sting and pleasure. My knee dug into his seatbelt, and it was a tight fit. But I didn't care. A white hot haze of need had engulfed my mind.

He started thrusting his hips up to meet me. "Hold your dress up and rub your pussy, sweetheart. You're going to come for me while you fuck yourself on my cock."

I brought my hand down and did as I was told, holding up my dress and pleasuring myself so he could watch.

"You're so beautiful when you get this hot and needy."

His dirty words, my fingers buried in my clit, and the thought of us having sex in his truck all made my orgasm build. I drove myself down on him even harder, and my climax broke over me. I ground down and wailed softly while I came all over him.

He pumped in and out of me a few more times, then grabbed my hips tight enough to leave bruises, and drove up inside me, coming long and hard.

We sat there for a moment, panting, and locked together.

Then I looked at him with wide eyes. "I can't believe I just did that."

He smirked and leaned in to kiss my bare chest. Then he licked my shoulder. "You taste like vanilla and sex."

I shivered at the feel of his tongue on my skin, and I wrapped my arms around his neck. He grabbed my ass and rubbed the backs of my legs.

His cock was still buried deep inside me, I'd just orgasmed hard, and I still wanted more. "When I crawl off, your clothes are going to get wet," I whispered.

He leaned in and kissed and nuzzled my neck. "It was fucking worth it. I'm just glad my windows are tinted."

I sighed and rubbed my forehead in the crook of his neck. "Is it bad that I just want to go home and screw your brains out again?"

He laughed, and I could feel the vibration through his length still buried deep inside me. I shifted restlessly against him.

"I love the feel of your greedy little pussy wrapped around me." He bit my shoulder. "You're going to need to climb off though. Sometime tonight I want to take you home and tie you up. It's my turn to fuck *your* brains out."

I shuddered. He growled when he felt the vibration, and finally pulled me off him so we could get cleaned up.

He helped me re-tie the halter top on my dress, and we used a t-shirt from his overnight bag and a whole package of wipes to clean up. Damien had to untuck his shirt to hide the wet spots on his pants, and I tried to straighten my dress and repair my hair before we went inside The Cockpit. We'd decided to stop by since everyone was expecting us.

When we walked in and Martina and Laurel spied us, I knew they could tell we'd just had sex. Martina wiggled her eyes, and Laurel gave me a stupid smile and a thumbs-up. Even Isabella, our new friend, smiled knowingly when she looked at my messy hair and Damien's untucked shirt.

The music was low tonight so people could talk, and the bar was serving a light buffet. Silver streamers and party horns decorated the tables, and everyone had dressed up for the evening.

"Nice hairdo." Martina sidled up to me. "They call that style 'sex in the restaurant bathroom,' I think."

"Oh, shut it." I lightly punched her arm.

"Is that body glitter?" Laurel rubbed my shoulder. "I haven't worked up enough nerve to try it yet."

"Yes, and it's edible. Olivia gave it to me for Christmas."

Martina laughed. "I knew I liked her."

Isabella rubbed my shoulder too. "Does it feel any different from regular lotion?"

I shook my head. "No. And Damien seems to like it."

"Edible body glitter," Laurel murmured, studying my chest. "I'd like to try it."

I laughed. "I don't think Sebastian would mind. You can probably order some online."

"Order what online?" Sebastian asked as he walked up and handed Laurel a drink.

"Hair extensions," Martina said with a straight face.

"Why the fuck would she need hair extensions?" he asked.

Laurel took the drink and patted his stomach.

Then she absently ran her hand over his abs. "She's kidding. We were talking about edible body glitter."

His eyebrow rose. "Huh. I'd like to try that."

I poked Laurel. "That's what she said."

"Oh, God. Don't get started with the 'that's what she said' jokes," Ramone groaned from his spot at the table.

Martina laughed. "We weren't. We're discussing hair extensions and body glitter."

Ramone shook his head. "It sounds like you're planning to enter a teen beauty pageant."

Jonathan scrubbed his face. "God, I'm too old for this shit."

Ramone patted his arm. "I'll get you another whiskey."

Iz walked over and stood next to Martina. She scowled at him but moved closer. He leaned down and said something in her ear, and her eyes flashed.

While Iz and Martina argued and the rest of the group talked, Damien came over and wrapped his arm around my waist then nuzzled my ear. He turned me slightly and licked up the side of my neck.

"You taste like candy. I wonder what your pussy tastes like with that stuff on it."

I pressed into him. "Hmm, we can try it on you too. It'll be like licking a giant Blow Pop."

"Tell me when you're ready to go."

I swayed into him. "I'm ready to go."

He grabbed my hand. "We're taking off," he told the group.

"What? You just got here," Martina complained.

"Sorry, I have other plans tonight for Harley." Damien didn't sound sorry at all.

Sebastian smirked and tipped his beer bottle at him. Laurel smiled and Isabella waved. Only Martina scowled at us.

"Happy New Year everyone." I waved as Damien dragged me out of the bar.

Chapter 35

When we got to my house, I was buzzing with anticipation and a little fear.

We walked inside, and Gary greeted us at the door. I leaned down to pet him. "Hey, buddy. Are you having a good New Year?"

I stood up and looked at Damien uneasily. "Are you hungry? I've got leftover shrimp linguini."

Damien took my hand and pulled me into him. "No, sweetheart, I'm not hungry. For food anyway. Are you nervous?"

I shook my head, then changed my mind and nodded. "Yes."

He skimmed his fingers down the side of my face, then across my collarbone. "Good. But what I should have asked is whether your panties are wet."

Smiling, I touched his cheek. "I don't know if my panties are wet because you ripped them off in the truck."

"Huh. Let me see." He ran a hand up the back of my thigh, then slid his fingers across my wet center.

His touch felt so good, I shivered. "You may not know this about me, but I'm a little bit of a control freak. I'm not sure I can do this."

He tilted my head up with his thumb and forefinger and kissed my mouth. Then he licked my lips.

Damien took hold of my wrists. "You've been in charge and in control before you were probably ready. Of your mom, your sister, and even your own life. You need to let go and let someone else be in charge for a while."

I stilled at his words. The year after my dad died, sometimes the stress and fatigue were so crushing, I'd cry late at night into my pillow. I worried about finding my mother dead, losing our house, and losing what was left of my family.

Reaching around my neck, Damien untied my halter top again. He was right, this dress did give him easy access.

He ran his fingers over the swell of my breasts. "I'll make sure you like it, sweetheart. But if you're really afraid..."

He'd thrown down the gauntlet. Damien knew exactly what he was doing.

"I'm not afraid," I lied. My heart fluttered and my breath quickened, but I realized I wanted to do this with him. To give him control over my body.

"Good." He smiled and took my hand.

In the bedroom, he put his backpack down and finished taking off my dress and shoes. Then he sat me down on the bed and took my wrists, placing them so they faced each other.

"I'm going to tie your wrists together, bring your arms up over your head, then tie your hands behind your back."

My mouth dropped open. "Do you... what is this called?"

His lip quirked. "Some people might call it shibari, or Japanese rope bondage. We'll try it tonight and see if you like it."

I watched in fascination as he took the white rope out of his backpack. He pulled me to my feet, and expertly wrapped my wrists several times.

Then he wrapped the rope between my wrists and tied it off. The restraint suddenly made me feel vulnerable, but the pattern was precise and intricate, and looked sensual against my skin.

"You're doing so well, Legs." He moved behind me. "Now raise your arms up and bring your hands down behind your head."

He positioned me where he wanted me, then he brought the rope down behind my back. My elbows pointed to the ceiling and my breasts jutted out.

He moved in front of me and studied my face. "I'm going to wrap the rope around your chest, then tighten it up. Are you with me?"

I panted a little but nodded. He wrapped the rope around my ribcage several times, then brought it behind my back, looped it through, and tightened everything down.

He studied me with hot eyes, then slowly wrapped a length of rope around my breasts, crisscrossing it between my cleavage.

"And now I'm going to play with you. Kneel on the bed."

He took hold of the rope between my breasts and backed me up to the bed, then held me steady while I climbed on.

Damien started to get onto the bed too, but I shook my head. "You're still dressed."

He smiled. "I know. How do you feel kneeling there naked with your hands tied behind your head and your breasts so proudly displayed, while I'm fully clothed?"

"Annoyed," I spit out.

He smirked. "Uh-huh. Is that why you're panting and rubbing your thighs together?"

I hadn't realized I was doing that, and I froze. "It's frustration."

He gave me a hot, wet kiss then bit my lip. "So if I felt your sweet little pussy, it wouldn't be dripping wet."

"No," I lied. I knelt further back on my heels to get away from him.

He dragged me back up by the ropes. "You're lying." Slowly bringing his mouth to my chest, he licked up my right breast and bit my nipple. "Hmm. You taste like edible glitter and sexual frustration."

I wanted to grab his head and hold him to me, but my hands were immobile. While he lavished my breasts and tugged on the rope, his other hand trailed down to my center. His fingers found my core.

"Your pussy doesn't lie, sweetheart. It tells me you like being tied up," he said against my breast.

"Oh, God," I whispered when he shoved a finger inside me. My mind blanked, and I wanted to grind myself against his palm.

He traced my clit, then pushed two fingers back inside me. "Let yourself go. Let me play with you, and just feel tonight."

My head fell forward, and my anxiety drifted away as I started moving on his hand. I wanted to do what he asked and just experience what he gave me.

Damien bit down a little harder on the swell of my breast while he fingered me and played with my clit. I wondered if he wanted to leave marks on me.

When he started sucking, I knew that's what he was doing. He finally raised his head and studied me. My pupils were dilated, and my eyelids felt so heavy.

He undressed and stood in front of me, stroking his shaft. "I'm not going to deep-throat you tonight, but I want you to be a good girl and get my cock nice and wet."

Before I could decide what to do, he held me behind the neck and bent me over. Then Damien steadied me while he positioned me over his length.

"Open." He pressed his thumb against my chin.

I obediently opened even as my mind rebelled. And then he was inside my mouth.

"Suck, sweetheart."

I hesitated, and Damien gently slapped my breast. "Do you need a spanking tonight?"

Shuddering, I started sucking and licking. He massaged my breasts while I worked his cock.

"That feels so good. I need to bend you over and return the favor," he growled.

The thought of him licking my clit while my hands were trussed up behind me made my head spin.

He finally pulled out of my mouth. "Come here and sit on the side of the bed." Before I could move, he took hold of the rope again and pulled me to the edge. He seemed to like dragging me around by the harness he'd created.

I situated myself the best I could with my hands tied. Then he pushed my breasts together and leisurely ran his cock between the valley there, rubbing his length against the rope and the sides of my breasts.

A strand of hair fell over my face, and he let go of a breast to brush it behind my ear. Then he continued rubbing himself until he had to stop.

He backed up and pulled me off the bed, again by the rope, then turned me around. "Bend over, sweetheart. I'm going to eat you out, then fuck you hard."

I froze, and lust and anxiety slammed through me.

Damien nestled behind me and ran his hands up and down my waist, then cupped my breasts. "I'll take care of you."

Little by little, I relaxed against him and pushed back into his rigid cock. "I know."

He let go and stepped back. I let out a breath then positioned myself over the bed. I had to lay my torso on the bed first then turn my head sideways with my arms positioned the way they were. Damien watched me struggle to get into position but didn't help me.

His knee pushed between my legs, and he nudged my thighs further apart. Then he leaned over a bit and licked my left buttock. I almost reared up, but he put his hand on the small of my back.

Then Damien leaned in and sucked the inside of my thigh. His hands reached around and cupped my breasts, and he pinched and tugged on my nipples.

I shifted and pushed back against him. He worked his tongue and teeth over the backs and insides of my thighs, then he pulled my legs farther apart.

Then he sat on the floor and turned around, so his mouth was facing my pussy. "Come here," he growled as he pulled me into his mouth.

I was tethered and immobile, with my head on the bed and my hands tied behind my neck. He'd have to come to me, I thought.

The thought fled when Damien started licking and sucking on me. He held my ass as he ate at me, and I cried out and ground into his mouth when he bit down and sucked on my clit.

His tongue lapped at the sting. My body was awash in pain mixed with pleasure, and I felt my climax rise. Damien pushed two fingers inside me, and I clenched around them greedily.

He bit down on my clit again, and I cried out as an orgasm built with each lick and bite, then it tore through me. My body locked and my womb clenched as I came, long and hard.

When I came down, Damien stood up and crawled over my prone body. His cock nudged my pulsing center, and he pushed himself inside me. My head tried to rear up, but I was still immobile.

Damien stroked himself inside me and grabbed a hold of my waist as he sped up. My core was sore from clenching so hard when I came, but his shaft felt so good. He pulled me back onto him, shoving himself deeper with every thrust.

He slowed down and his hand slid around to my bottom. When he slipped a finger into my back hole, I froze and moaned softly.

"Shhh, I've got you." Damien slid his finger further in and let me get used to the feel. The sensation was strange and foreign, but when he slid another finger in the sting made my insides tingle, and I could feel another orgasm start to build.

He reached around with his other hand and stroked my clit until I was squirming underneath him, begging him to stop, then not stop. My pleas didn't make any sense.

When I started struggling beneath him as another climax threatened, Damien leaned over and whispered in my ear. "You're going to come with me this time, sweetheart. I'm going to fuck you and finger your ass until you do. And I can do this all night."

He pushed his fingers in a little further, and stroked my clit as he continued to piston inside me. The sensations were so intense, I came violently around his cock and fingers. This orgasm hurt a little, coming so soon on top of the last one, and my insides clamped down around his cock.

As I spasmed, Damien sped up, then slammed into me, coming deep inside me. My body slid forward on the bed, but I couldn't use my hands to hold myself in place. I gasped for air as he groaned behind me.

He lay on top of me for several seconds catching his breath, then he pulled out and undid the ropes. I moaned as the blood started flowing back into my hands and wrists. He went into the bathroom and washed up then brought back a warm, wet washcloth. Damien cleaned me up and massaged my shoulders and biceps, pulling my arms down behind me.

I lay there, letting him administer to me as my mind and body floated. Then he turned me over and pulled me into his arms. He sat on the bed with his back braced against the headboard and cradled me.

A few minutes later, when my breathing regulated and I came back to myself, I felt tears on my cheeks. Mortification and embarrassment scored through me, and I stiffened in his arms.

He nuzzled my cheek and hugged me closer. "It's okay, sweetheart. It's normal to be a little emotional after this kind of sex."

I sighed. "Damn it. I hate crying." I could feel his body moving beneath me as he chuckled, and I poked him.

He grabbed my hand and squeezed. "I can always hogtie you."

Laughing, I wrapped my arms around his waist. "And I know how to make a death look accidental."

He shifted me so he could see my face. "Legs, sometimes you scare me."

"Good, you should be nervous."

He laughed and hugged me again.

As I fell asleep tangled in his arms, I realized we'd probably been doing a lot more than kissing when midnight came and went. And I had no premonition of the danger ahead.

Chapter 36

The court was in full swing after the holiday season. I called Shanda at the beginning of the week to remind her about her hearing scheduled a week from Wednesday.

"How was your holiday break?" I asked her.

"After Mikey got kicked out of the house, I went home and spent my days off with Bertie and my mom."

I grinned. "Nice. How's Bertie doing?"

"She's teething. So she drools and whines a lot, but she's good."

"That sounds like a few teenage boys I used to know," I replied.

"Huh. You're funny." She didn't laugh at all.

I rolled my eyes. "Anyway, smartass. I was able to talk to the prosecutor, and we're good to go next Wednesday. You'll plead to the misdemeanor just like we discussed, and you'll need to complete the terms of your probation. First, you'll need to—"

Shanda cut me off. "You've gone over it like twelve times already. I got it. Have you heard anything about Jason?" she asked. I could hear worry in her voice.

"No. But I asked the prosecutor to let me know what's happening with his case." I paused. "Have *you* heard from Jason?"

Shanda cleared her throat. "Maybe."

"What do you mean, 'maybe'?"

"Don't be mad at me for not telling you earlier."

I sighed heavily. "Shanda, out with it. What didn't you tell me?"

"Someone left a dead cat at my mom's door," she said softly.

"Did it die from natural causes?"

She scoffed. "Yeah, if having your tongue cut off, your eyeballs punctured, and your intestines pulled out is dying of natural causes."

My stomach roiled, and I fought not to gag. Pity and rage rolled through me as I thought of that poor cat suffering. I was pretty sure I knew who had tried to poison Gary.

"How long ago?" I asked. We both knew who'd done it.

"We found it on Christmas morning."

Rage and sorrow boiled through me. Jason was a fucking pig. "Did you report it and take photos? Do you have any evidence?"

She hummed. "My mom took some photos, and I, uh, talked to a few people at my apartment complex. They said they've seen his car a couple of times in the parking lot."

I bet she'd talked to Walt. "What kind of car does he drive?"

"After he wrecked his last car, I heard he drives a gray Mazda sports car," she answered. "Why?"

I broke out in a sweat. "Do you know the license plate number by chance?"

Shanda started breathing heavily. "The last three digits are SFW. I remember because it also stands for 'stupid fuck wad.'"

I'd been right. That asshole had driven by my house on Christmas Eve. And then he'd left a poor mutilated cat on her doorstep. He really was crazy.

"Why do you want to know what kind of car he drives?" she asked suspiciously.

I cleared my throat and lied. "I want to keep an eye out for him. You've told me a few times he's crazy. And I think what he did proves it."

"Yeah, he is. I just hope he goes to jail and gets raped and shanked there."

I grimaced, but after hearing what he'd done to the cat, I kind of hoped the same thing. "Just be careful, will you? If you see him, call the police."

"Yes, Mother. I have Damien's and Officer Schroeder's numbers too."

"Okay. Good. I'm going to call Schroeder and report it. We need a record of it. And don't call me Mother anymore. It's creepy."

She chuckled. "*You're* creepy. I gotta get back to work. I'll see you next week."

After we hung up, I stared out the window. Jason was escalating his behavior, and I had a bad feeling I couldn't shake.

After calling Officer Schroder and letting her know about the cat, I called Martin instead of Damien. He didn't pick up, so I left him a message and let him know what was going on.

I also asked him to shadow Shanda to try and catch Jason breaking the no-contact order. I didn't tell him I hadn't told Damien. Because I didn't want Jason anywhere near Damien.

Juvenile Drug Court seemed more like a soap opera than drug court that week. None of my clients had relapsed, thank God, but there had been a few serious family fights.

Judge Perez had predicted they might get triggered by their families and the stress of the holidays, and he wasn't wrong.

Roland got into a fistfight with his cousin when he told his aunt he didn't want to be kissed on the lips anymore. He'd also told everyone it grossed him out, which probably didn't help.

Darla also informed her mother she was sick of being cooped up at the house all day when she wasn't at school, and if she wanted to go out and get a job, she would. Darla still had a raging marijuana addiction, so I could understand her mother's worries.

I walked out of the courthouse with Wendy, the DCFS worker, after the review hearing.

She started in about Damien right away. "I heard you've been seeing the dimpled hottie I met a few months ago."

"Huh."

"Uh-huh. Spill," she persisted.

"I'm not sure who you're talking about."

She smirked at me. "You know exactly who I'm talking about. The one who calls you Legs."

"Ah, that hottie. Things are good." I grinned and thought about New Year's Eve. "Really good."

She stared at me. "Wow. You admitted you're seeing someone. And you just smiled. I didn't even know you knew how. It's weird, stop it."

I rolled my eyes. "Quit insulting me."

Wendy smirked. "I'm not insulting you; I'm just describing you."

My phone vibrated in my pocket again. I remembered it had gone off a few times right before court got out.

I looked down at my screen. "Wendy, I need to return some phone calls. I'll catch up with you later." I stopped in the hallway.

"Okay. But I want details. And no more weird grins."

It looked like Shanda had called me twice, and Martin once. My stomach tightened, and I started walking toward the exit again.

I called Shanda back first. She picked up, and I could hear her breathing hard. "Harley, he's here, pounding on the door. I don't know what to do!"

"Shanda, who's at your door?"

"Jason! That fucker, Jason. And it's not my door. I walked Bertie over to the park by my mom's place. And he's pounding on the bathroom door." I could hear loud pounding and muffled yelling through Shanda's phone.

"Shanda, did you call the police?" I asked. I felt panicked now too.

"No, not yet!"

I started running. "What park are you at?"

"The one by my house. Oh, God. The Desert Highland Park. On the side closest to my mom's apartment."

"Okay. Okay." I saw a couple of bailiffs manning the entrance to the courthouse. "Harmon!" I yelled. He was the bailiff who'd told me about the bet.

He straightened when he saw me running toward him. "What d'you need, Harley?"

"Call nine-one-one!" I was breathless when I reached him. "My client locked herself in a bathroom at the Desert Highland Park on the south side of the park in north Palm Springs. A man is trying to get to her and her two-year-old sister. He's unstable and there's a no-contact order against him. Can you call it in while I keep talking to her on my phone?"

He didn't waste a second and pulled out his cell phone. I put Shanda on speakerphone.

I could hear Bertie crying, and Jason yelling through the bathroom door. I felt helpless and sick.

"You fucking cunt! You think you're gonna testify against me?" Jason screamed. "You think you can turn on me and I won't take you and your fucking family out?"

Harmon, the bailiff, got the dispatcher on the line and started quickly and calmly relaying information.

The other bailiff came over. "Tell the asshole the police are on the way."

Shanda must have heard him. "Jason, just leave me alone! The police are coming. They'll be here any minute," Shanda yelled in a scared, shaky voice.

"You didn't have enough time to call them, you stupid bitch." He laughed bitterly. "I'm going to stick a gun under your chin and blow your fucking brains out. After I cut out your tongue."

The bailiffs looked at each other. I knew they were both worried about Jason being armed.

"I'm talking to Harley, and she called them," Shanda said in a shaky voice.

"You stupid little cunt! You can't hide forever." Jason pounded on the door again.

"My investigator's coming too," Shanda yelled back. "He said he'd be here in three minutes, and he used to be a detective."

I froze as her words penetrated my brain.

"No. Please, God, no. Not Damien. Not Damien," I chanted. Then I dropped my briefcase and ran.

Chapter 37

Harmon and the other bailiff yelled after me, but I kept running. I still had my shoulder backpack on me with my car keys in it.

I put the phone back to my ear. "You better leave now!" I heard Shanda yell.

Bertie was still crying, and I could hear what sounded like Jason now kicking the door.

"Harley? The lock is bending. I think he's kicking it," she cried.

I ran harder.

Luckily, I'd worn loafers and a pantsuit, so I made it to my vehicle in record time. My hands were shaky as I tried to open my car door.

I finally got in and backed out, but I knew the courthouse was at least ten minutes away from the park. The police had to get there before the door gave way. And I prayed they'd get there before Damien.

I forced myself to stop being so stupid and useless. Shanda needed me. I tried to picture her locked in the little one-person bathroom and mentally thought of what she could use against him. "Do you have Bertie in a stroller?" I asked.

She paused, probably wondering why in the world I was asking her that. "Yeah. Harley why are—"

"Take Bertie out and put her behind you. If he's able to kick in the door, try to run him over with the stroller as hard as you can."

The kicking continued through the phone. I knew I was going to hear that sound in my nightmares.

"Okay. I need to hang up so I can get her out." She sounded frantic.

"Shanda, try to take his feet out from under him and incapacitate him long enough to get away, or buy you a little time. I'm coming."

"I'll try." Then the line went dead.

I called Damien from my car phone system, but he didn't pick up, so I turned on my hazard lights and sped up. Then I remembered Martin had also left a message. I'd asked him to shadow Shanda until Jason was taken into custody.

I called him and he answered, breathing heavily. "*Now* you call me back?"

"Martin, where are you?"

"In the Desert Highland Park looking for Shanda," he answered.

I quickly relayed where she was and told him about Jason kicking the bathroom door.

"He has a gun. Be careful." My voice broke.

"This information would have been more useful five minutes ago. Okay, I'll find her." And he also hung up.

The remaining five-minute drive was the longest of my life.

When I pulled up to the south side of the park, I saw two police cars with their lights on parked behind Damien's truck. I got out and was immediately accosted by an officer.

He raised his arm to block me. "Ma'am, this is a crime scene. Stay back."

"I need to know if they're okay," I cried.

"Ma'am, I'll try to find out, but you have to stay back."

Martin stood near the bathroom. He turned at the commotion and walked toward me.

"Shanda's okay," he said. I stopped as Martin approached me, and the officer backed off.

"Martin, where's Damien and Shanda?" I took hold of his arm. "I heard Shanda tell Jason she called Damien, and he was on his way over. Have you seen him? Is he okay?"

"Harley, he—"

"Jason has a gun! Please tell me he's okay." I started to break down. "Please tell me Damien's alive. I couldn't live with myself if I got him killed too," I rambled as I grabbed Martin's jacket lapels.

He gently took my shoulders and turned me so I could see Damien and Shanda walking toward me. Bertie was perched on Shanda's hip. I scanned her and Bertie up and down frantically, then turned to Damien.

He looked angry and frustrated. He grabbed my hand, dragging me a few feet away.

I noticed Jason lying on the sidewalk by the bathroom, surrounded by three officers. Bertie's stroller was tipped sideways next to him.

Damien turned me to face him. "Harley, you knew Jason was following her. Why did I get a call from Shanda and even Dickie, but no fucking call from *you*?" He was practically yelling by the time he finished talking.

My hands shook, and I tried to swallow down my residual fear. Shanda and Bertie were unharmed, and he was safe and whole. And glaring at me.

I blurted out the truth. "Because I didn't want you here."

He growled and shook me a little. "For fuck's sake, why?"

"Because it's too dangerous!"

He let go of me and rubbed his face as if trying to find patience.

Fear morphed into anger, and I poked him in the chest. "You can be angry and pissed, and even break up with me. But at least you're alive!"

He narrowed his eyes.

I poked him in the chest again and realized I was shaking. "You'd be alive," I repeated.

He gathered me in his arms. "Harley, baby. No one got hurt. We're okay."

I was past listening to reason. "Every man I love fucking *dies*!" I yelled. "And it's my fault. Oh, God. You could have been shot. Jason is crazy, and he has a gun. I dragged you into this."

He held me to him as I struggled in his arms. "Harley, you are *not* a fucking death harbinger. You don't cause the men you love to die, so get it through your head. That's complete bullshit."

He felt so warm and strong, and I slowly stopped struggling. He was here, pissed as hell, but alive and whole. We stood there for a minute.

Damien stroked my hair, then he chuckled a little.

I stared up at him. "What are you laughing at?"

He brushed a strand of hair back from my face. "You'll figure it out eventually."

Martin finally cleared his throat. "So, I take it you two are an item?"

Damien answered first. "Hello, Dickie. And, yes, we're a goddamn item. Even though I want to shake her half the time."

"Huh. Means you won't get bored." Martin turned to me. "Harley, I'll send you my notes and photos in the next couple of days. Sorry I lost her for a few minutes."

I pulled out of Damien's arms and waved awkwardly. "Thanks, Martin. It wasn't your fault, and I'm glad you're okay too. You sound a lot better, by the way."

"I feel better. Good luck, you two." Martin chuckled, then lumbered off.

I turned to Damien. "I'm never dragging you into my cases again."

"Yes, you are."

"No, I'm not," I shot back. I was so happy he was okay, I hugged him again then turned to Shanda.

She eyed me warily. "Hey."

I checked her and Bertie for signs of injuries again, then gave them both spontaneous hugs. "What happened after you hung up? How are you still alive?"

She jerked her shoulder. "When Jason kicked in the door, I ran him over with the stroller. Just like you said."

I stared at her, unsure if I'd heard her right. "You... ran him over with the stroller?" I repeated.

"Yeah. When the lock broke and he shoved open the door, I pushed the stroller at him as hard as I could. He got caught up in the front wheels, then fell back and hit his head on the cement."

My eyebrows shot up. "It actually worked?"

She looked at me incredulously. "You didn't think it would?"

"Well, no. But I couldn't think of anything else."

We glanced over at Jason, who was handcuffed.

Damien put a hand on my shoulder and squeezed. "She was using the stroller to pin him down when I got here."

Shanda looked a little pale. "He doesn't weigh very much. And he probably expected me to be cowering in the corner."

Damien rubbed my arm. "The police were right behind me. He must have hit his head pretty hard because he still seemed dazed."

"Where's his gun?" I asked. It made me sick thinking about what could have happened.

Shanda looked around. "I stomped on his hand when he fell, then I picked it up and threw it as hard as I could."

Damien eyed Shanda then shook his head. "You need a lesson in gun safety." He glanced at the officers. "I need to tell them there's a gun around here somewhere."

Over the next half hour, the officers scanned the area and found Jason's gun, then questioned Shanda and took her statement.

Bertie was cranky and tired by then, so we drove them over to their mother's apartment. Damien took the stroller up to the second floor, and I carried Bertie. She laid her head on my shoulder and promptly fell asleep.

Shanda looked wrung out and tired as she eyed the little girl in my arms. "I'm tired of worrying about Bertie and looking over my shoulder."

I nodded. "I understand."

She stared at me, her brows furrowed. "Let the prosecutor know I'll testify about the car wreck. About Jason threatening me, and even what was in his backpack. But I don't know anything else. Not about any drug dealers, any other people, or places. Any of it."

I knew she was lying, but I couldn't blame her. She had enough to worry about just trying to live her life and protect her sister.

"I'll make sure the prosecutor is aware. You don't know about anything else," I told her, willing her to understand she could never talk about what she knew to anyone, even me or Damien.

We needed plausible deniability. Shanda was only eighteen years old, but life had already taught her some hard lessons.

Damien smiled at Shanda. "You did well today. You kept your head and were smart to lock yourself in the bathroom and call for help. And taking him out with a stroller was fucking amazing."

I nodded. "You're one hell of a sister. You know that, right?"

Shanda looked at us, and her eyes filled with tears. "You guys are the shit. I don't think I could have gotten through all this crap without you. So, thank you."I finally handed Bertie over to her and gave them both a hug. "If I ever have to represent you again for new charges, I'm going to kick your scrawny little ass."

Shanda laughed. Bertie started waking up and fussing again, so we said goodbye. As we walked away, I sent a little prayer out to the Universe to keep them both safe.

Chapter 38

Damien followed me home in his truck after we dropped Shanda and Bertie off. On the way, I called the courthouse to ask the bailiffs to keep my briefcase in their office until tomorrow morning.

Gary greeted us enthusiastically at the door. Damien fed him while I changed into sweats and an old, thin t-shirt.

When Damien saw me, he looked at my chest and smirked. "I like your t-shirt, sweetheart."

I glanced down and noticed my black lace bra clearly showing through the thin fabric. I shrugged.

His face grew serious. "Why didn't you tell me about Jason?"

I wrapped my arms around his waist and tucked my head under his chin. "I was scared."

Damien squeezed me hard. "You said you don't want me to get hurt. But you showed up at the park less than five minutes after I did, knowing that fucker had a gun."

I thought about what could have happened again and squeezed him back. "You're right, I didn't think. We called the police, and then Shanda told Jason she'd already called you, and you were only a few minutes out, and I panicked."

Damien stroked my back. "It's okay, I understand."

My heart raced, and I felt a little sick. "I can't go through losing someone else."

He hugged me again. "Shanda and Bertie are safe now, and Jason will go to prison for a long time. We're both fine, Legs. Let's forget about it for a while."

I took a deep breath and stepped back. "Okay. That sounds good."

I made margaritas, and we grilled dinner together, then had our meal and drinks out on the back patio around my firepit. Damien finished eating before I did, and he watched me carefully.

I'd turned the heat up on the spool before we started making dinner. When we finished, Damien took my hand and led me over. Neither of us had swimsuits on. We didn't need them.

He put towels on the deck and slipped off my t-shirt and bra. Then he slid my panties and sweatpants down and I stepped out. I stood there while he stripped out of his clothes, then he pulled me over to the spool and guided me in.

"Come here, Legs. You need a little tender loving care." He sat down in the water, then positioned me on top of him, straddling his legs.

His rigid shaft rubbed against me, and he lifted his hips to get a better angle.

I wrapped my arms around his shoulders and smiled at him. "It feels like you need a little TLC too."

"You're right. I swear you take years off my life."

He started tensing beneath my arms. I massaged his shoulders and laid my forehead on his neck. "I was afraid, okay? And Martin is cheaper for surveillance work anyway. I think. I'm pretty sure."

He grunted and ran his hand up my back, then grabbed the nape of my hair. "Who gives a shit about that? This is my case, and you're mine." He pulled my head back.

His firm grip on my hair made my insides tighten, and I rubbed restlessly against him. "I... care about you, okay? Jason dumped a mutilated cat on her doorstep and went after her with a gun. He's unhinged."

He pulled my head back a little more, then leaned in and put his mouth on my neck. His teeth slid down my right tendon, then he latched onto my muscle there, biting down enough to cause a sting.

I moaned and shifted over him. He let go of my hair and brought his hand down to my center. Then he spread me and worked his cock inside.

Having him inside me felt like coming home. My body responded to his, and I sighed softly as he powered into me.

He grabbed my waist and moved me up and down on his cock. "God, sweetheart. You feel so damn tight. Every fucking time. I'm obsessed with your hot, tight pussy."

My womb clenched, and I clamped down on his length even tighter. His mouth found my breasts, and he lapped at my hard nipples, then sucked forcefully on each one. Damien finally stood up with me wrapped around him and laid me at the spool's edge.

He stretched out my legs, then thrust inside me again, getting a better angle and driving even deeper. My neck arched as he bottomed out, and I whimpered softly but pushed my hips up to meet his. He took both my wrists and brought them over my head as he plunged into me.

"That's it, sweetheart, take all of me. Even if it hurts." He punctuated his words with deep thrusts.

His words speared my heart as his body overwhelmed mine. Because loving him did hurt sometimes. And I was so afraid of losing him.

But he also gave me intense pleasure, tenderness, and a sense of belonging. He took care of me and tried to give me what I needed. My thoughts scattered as Damien let go of my hands and brought his fingers down to my swollen, throbbing clit.

He seized it and pinched it softly, then rolled and stroked me. His other hand pulled on my sensitive nipple.

He leaned over and murmured in my ear. "You can't scream out here like you usually do, sweetheart."

"You're the one who screams," I panted. My body tingled underneath his fingers, and my orgasm built.

He chuckled low. When he felt my core start to tighten around him, he bit down on my breast. I threw my head back and wailed into the night as I came.

My mind blitzed out, and waves of pleasure coursed through me. I felt his hand clamp over my mouth, and it only added to my pleasure.

When I stopped crying out, Damien lifted my hips and slammed into me frantically, over and over. Then he rammed inside me one last time, and I felt his hot semen spurt deep inside. I shuddered on his cock, my body still sizzling like I was hooked to a live wire.

When we finally came down, he scooped me up and brought me back into the swirling water. I was wrung out and could barely move.

He tucked my head under his chin and circled me with his arms. "You do scream, Legs. And I fucking love it."

I had a couple of preliminary hearings in front of Judge Conrad on Wednesday morning, and I swung by the bailiff's office to pick up my briefcase.

Harmon, the bailiff who'd called nine-one-one, wanted to know exactly what had happened. He'd already heard Jason had been arrested, but I gave him the details.

He gaped at me when I finished. "Holy shit. She got him with a damn stroller? When he goes to prison, they're going to eat him alive." He smiled meanly and rocked back on his heels.

"My hands still shake every time I think about him having a gun," I replied.

"What made you drop your briefcase and sprint out of here?"

I shrugged sheepishly. "I... uh, got worried about Shanda."

Harmon smirked. "Uh-huh. And you weren't worried about Damien Andreasen at all."

"Who? I don't know what you're talking about."

He patted my arm. "It's okay. We all like him—a hell of a lot more than that slimy prosecutor and a few other assholes who've been harassing you."

I nodded vigorously, giving up any pretense of not knowing Damien. "Me too, Harmon. Me too."

After I finished with my preliminary hearings, I planned to have lunch with Damien. He was waiting for me in the hallway outside the courtroom. He seemed to know I was still a little traumatized from yesterday.

When I spotted him leaning against the wall waiting for me, my heart swelled. I loved his tall muscular body, strong jaw, and beautiful face with his slightly messy, thick, dark blond hair.

I also loved him—his kindness, his wit, and sarcasm. And even that damned dimple. He treated me like gold, and his colleagues and friends adored him. And Gary loved him almost as much as me.

Well, shit. I just realized I loved the bastard. I rocked back on my heels and got a little lightheaded.

He looked up from his phone and noticed me, then grinned. I walked over and stood in front of him. When he straightened, I spontaneously rolled up on my toes and kissed him on the mouth. He put his arms around me and pulled me in for another kiss.

"I guess you win the bet, Andreasen," Trevor, the asshole prosecutor, sneered from behind us. "I'm not sure if you really won though. She seems pretty cold to me."

Damien and I pulled apart, and my mouth fell open. I looked up at Damien before turning around to stare at Trevor. I knew he was a mean snake, but I didn't know he was stupid too.

Damien's face had gone hard and cold, and his jaw locked.

He stepped around me and leaned down into Trevor's face. "If you *ever* harass Harley again, or even look at her wrong, I'll kick your fucking ass," he said softly. He grabbed Trevor's shoulder and squeezed.

Trevor looked up at Damien's hard face and paled. He stumbled back a little, dislodging Damien's hold. "I didn't mean anything—"

Damien cut him off. "Don't give me that shit. She shot you down and made you feel like the mean little prick you are, so you decided to start that fucking bet."

"We were only—"

Damien scoffed. "I didn't win your shitty bet. But I did win the fucking lottery. And I'm gonna let Evan know what you've been doing."

I looked behind Trevor and saw Evan standing in the courtroom doorway, listening to everything. Evan's face was the shade of a ripe tomato, and his bushy eyebrows quivered.

"Trevor!" he barked. "You're *fired*. Your desk better be cleared out in ten minutes."

Trevor turned to me with fury in his eyes. "You did this."

Damien growled, but I quickly grabbed his arm and squeezed. "I've got this. And I love you."

He stopped dead and looked down at me. Then he smiled and flashed me his beautiful dimple. "See? I knew you'd figure it out. And I love you too, Legs."

I leaned into Damien, but I heard the asswipe Trevor scoff and remembered he was still standing there.

I turned to him, and my smile bled away. "No, Trevor. You did this to yourself. And then you dragged a few of your asshole friends into it."

"If you wouldn't have been such a cold bitch—"

Leaning forward, I talked over him. "I wasn't the one who *started* the bet. And now you're going to *victim blame* me for not wanting anything to do with your whiny, pathetic ass? I should just let you run your mouth, so I have more fodder for a sexual harassment lawsuit."

He blanched and stepped back. I could see he finally understood the hole he'd dug for himself. Good, I hoped he suffered even a little of what he'd put me through.

Trevor's face got red. "I don't need this. From any of you. I'm out of here." He turned to the elevator bank and slammed the down button a few times.

He stood there awkwardly in front of the elevators for several seconds, then finally stomped over to the stairwell, pushed the door open, and hurried down the stairs.

The door closed behind him, and I turned to Evan.

He walked over, sighed tiredly, and rubbed his face. "Harley, I'm sorry I didn't do that sooner. I also didn't know there was some kind of bet." He winced. "I'll let human resources know we have a sexual harassment lawsuit coming."

I patted his arm. "I'm good, Evan. You fired him. I think that's a sufficient response from your office."

Evan looked at the door where Trevor had stormed off and shook his head. "It's hard to find decent attorneys these days."

Damien grunted. "Decent and attorneys in the same sentence. Now there's an oxymoron."

Evan smiled as the elevator door finally opened. "Damien, good to see you. Harley, I'll talk to you next week."

When the door closed, I turned and elbowed Damien. "Your girlfriend is an attorney. Are you saying I'm not decent?"

Pulling me close, he smiled. "Sometimes you're decent. And sometimes you're naked."

His thumb rubbed across my lips, and I flicked my tongue out to lick it.

His eyes hooded, and he leaned into me. "I like those times most of all."

Epilogue

I hunched over and wheezed a little as I stared across the net at Damien and Zeke's volleyball team. My teammates were also panting, even though it was a mild fall morning and we'd only been playing for an hour or so. But we'd been playing hard.

I still really wanted to win, but not with the same all-consuming, burning desire I had two seasons ago when Damien had called my team the Walmart parking lot crew. Or even last season, before I found out Frankie had overdosed.

Most of my teammates knew Damien and Zeke well by now, and Jaime had started calling Damien *Hoyuelos* when he found out his nickname was Dimples. We also had a couple of new players this season when Josh moved out of state. But Tiana and Jaime still played on the team.

One of Damien's teammates took the ball back to serve. We were down by two points, and I wasn't feeling very confident this time around. We were tied, and this set would decide the match. And as usual, my team was out of gas.

If we were going to lose, I decided to make it interesting. Before the opposing player served, I quickly pulled off my jersey and threw it to the sideline. My sports bra wasn't a ten-year-old relic this time, but a sleek black one with crisscross straps that held my girls up high and firm.

Damien straightened. Then he glared, his eyes flicking from my face to my chest. His teammate served, and our back line gave Jaime a good bump. He set it for me, and I spiked it between two of their players, earning a point.

"That's cheating, Val," Zeke said loudly. "Effective, but still cheating."

I raised my hands in an innocent gesture. "What? I'm hot and there's no rule saying we have to wear our jerseys the whole time. I checked."

Jaime laughed and whipped off his jersey. His belly hung over his gym shorts a little, but the strange, random tattoos all over his torso distracted even me.

Zeke shrugged. "Well then, fuck it." He pulled off his own shirt and threw it to the sideline. He had the physique of a sleek linebacker, and I heard Tiana whistle behind me.

Then Zeke pointed at Damien. "Off. If she wants to play dirty, we'll play dirty."

Damien stared at me, then he reached up and slowly pulled off his jersey. His pecs and biceps were muscular and perfectly shaped, and his cut abs led down to his beautiful V. Damn it, this was backfiring.

"There's no way I'm taking my jersey off," Tiana called from behind me. "I don't care if we lose or not. But I am enjoying this view."

I turned around and glared at her. She was staring at Zeke's chest. Smart woman.

Then her gaze flicked to Damien, and I growled.

She shrugged. "What? I'm not dead."

We played through the next point, but Damien's chest was distracting. Zeke spiked the ball, and I jumped up to block it. The ball bounced off my hand onto our side, but Tiana didn't even try to reach it.

"Really?" I asked her.

"What? I can only concentrate on one thing at a time." Her eyes were glued to Zeke's chest.

Scowling at both of them, I threw the ball to their server. I fought hard through the next few points, but in the end, we lost when Jaime couldn't return one of Zeke's wicked serves.

I patted Jaime on the back. "It's okay, we'll get them next season."

Jaime shrugged philosophically. "Sure we will. But it might be better to keep our jerseys on."

Damien walked over and wrapped his sweaty arms around me from behind then bit softly into my neck. "Put your damn shirt back on."

I stealthily rubbed my ass against his groin and leaned back in his arms. "You first."

He smiled and nuzzled my cheek. "You started this. And I want to talk to you about something."

Zeke handed us both our shirts. Damien put his on, then started helping me with mine. I rolled my eyes and swatted his hands away.

Everyone had gone quiet, and I looked around. My team was still milling about and giving me funny, amused looks.

"What's going on?" I asked Jaime.

He rubbed his jaw and motioned toward Damien.

Damien stared down at me, then took hold of my left hand and slipped a ring on my finger. "Marry me, Legs."

It didn't sound like a question. I stared at him, not quite comprehending what was going on. Then I looked down and saw the beautiful, hammered gold band with large sapphire stones he'd slipped onto my dirty, sweaty finger.

"Holy fuck," I whispered in amazement.

Tiana laughed behind me. "I think what she meant to say is holy fuck, *yes*."

Damien smirked, and I finally shook myself out of my daze and threw my arms around him. "Yes! Yes, I'll marry you."

Everyone started laughing and talking at once, and Damien whirled me around.

Zeke chuckled and patted Damien on the back. "No kneeling, huh?"

Damien shook his head. "When I kneel in front of Harley, I'm always doing... other things to her. I didn't want to be thinking about that."

Zeke laughed, and I blushed to my roots. Then I took Damien's face and dragged it down to mine for a long, deep kiss.

When we finally pulled apart, he grinned. "I hope you don't mind getting engaged on a volleyball court in front of your team. They brought us together in a way, so I thought it would be fitting."

I shook my head. "It's absolutely perfect. And it almost made up for losing today."

We celebrated with our teams for a few minutes, then walked to his truck after everyone took off.

Before opening the passenger door, he held me close and kissed the top of my head. "I'm not a detective anymore. And your job is probably more dangerous than mine now."

I knew where he was going with this. "I know."

"Shitty things happen. You probably understand that more than anyone I know, and you've lost a lot of people in your life. But I want to go the distance with you."

My eyes filled with tears. "Me too."

He cupped my lower stomach. "I want to put a child or three in here someday and watch you grow. And hear you complain about not being able to play volleyball or drink tequila while you carry them."

My hand covered his, and a tear slipped down my cheek. "I want that too. I love you, and I'll hunt you down if you die on me."

He smiled and gathered me into his chest. "Only you would say you love me, then tell me you're going to hunt me down in the same sentence."

"Only if you die on me," I clarified.

Damien cupped my face and kissed me softly. Then he ran his lips gently across the scar on my cheek. "I love you too, Legs."

A few more tears leaked out, but I kept it together. "Maybe we were meant to find each other in this strange, screwed-up world."

He smiled. "I know one thing."

"What?"

"I'll always have a love-hate relationship with volleyballs."

I laughed and rolled up on my toes to kiss him again.

Four Years Later

My back ached, and my bladder felt like an overstuffed sausage casing. There was nothing wonderful or miraculous about being eight months and seventeen days pregnant.

Except—and then I felt it, that kick to my stomach from the inside. I started feeling those soft flutters in my nineteenth week of pregnancy, and they'd steadily grown into little kicks that sometimes left me gasping.

I rubbed the spot on my tummy absently. "I know, little man. I'm ready to be home with Daddy too."

I pulled into the garage of Damien's house, which was our house now, and parked. His truck was already there. He walked out and opened my driver's side door, then leaned in and studied me.

"Hey, sweetheart. How're you feeling? And how was drug court?"

I smirked and shook my head. "Drug court was interesting. The prosecutor had to explain to the judge what Rastafari is and why my fourteen-year-old client with a serious marijuana addiction shouldn't be wearing Rastafarian colors to his first day of juvenile drug court."

He chuckled and took my backpack, swinging it over his shoulder. Then he held out both hands to help pull me out.

Damien knew I could do it myself, but it would take twice as long. When we walked into the house, Gary greeted me at the door. He moved a little slower now, but he still had a few good years in him.

I gave him pets, then headed to the bathroom where I'd been spending a lot of time over the past three months. Damien was in the kitchen putting a small snack together for me when I came out.

Sliding onto a stool, I leaned my head in my hand. "How was your day?"

He grinned. "Probably better than yours. Is he kicking?" He nodded toward my stomach.

I rubbed my tummy and smiled. "Yeah. It was pretty hard today. He's definitely your son." Reaching around, I also rubbed my aching back. It had been paining me more than usual all day.

He walked around the bar as if drawn to my swollen stomach. He watched it carefully, then laid his hand on the spot where Junior seemed to be pounding on it from the inside.

When he felt the movement Damien froze, like he always did, and studied me with love and naked wonder. "That's fucking amazing."

I crinkled my eyes. He said the same thing almost every time. "He's going to slide out of my vagina, look around, and say to the doctor 'that's fucking amazing' right out of the womb."

He laughed. "Or he's going to come out complaining and saying, 'God, this sucks.'"

"Maybe," I smirked. It had become my favorite saying as I navigated my third trimester of pregnancy.

Damien grabbed my thighs and pulled them apart, stepping between them. My stomach poked him a little, but he didn't seem to care.

"You're fucking beautiful, swollen with our child, and your round, firm tits. I can't get enough of you like this."

I swayed into him. He'd researched all the best sex positions for a woman in her third trimester. And we'd tried them all. He rubbed my lower back, and I placed my hands on his cheeks.

Pulling his face down, I kissed him softly. "I don't think we're going to be able to try the reverse cowgirl tonight."

His lips quirked, and he studied me. "Do you have something else in mind?"

"No, but the baby does. I've been having contractions since nine this morning."

He froze and his eyes narrowed. "And you're just telling me now?"

I rolled my shoulders. "Yeah. Because I didn't know they were the real thing until about two hours ago."

Four hours and twelve minutes later, little Hudson Xavier Andreasen was born. We'd named him after my dad. Damien helped the nurse clean Hudson off and wrap him up, then he brought the little bundle over to me and turned him around so I could see him. I stared into both their faces.

I teared up and lifted my arms. "I love you guys so much, it makes my heart hurt a little," I whispered.

He smiled softly and laid our baby in my arms.

"The little man wants to try out your magnificent, volleyball-sized breasts. I'm jealous."

I let out a laugh, then groaned as my poor stomach muscles cramped in protest. We both looked down as our son latched onto my nipple like a pro.

I smirked. "He's definitely your son."

Damien laid his hand on my cheek. "You two make my heart hurt sometimes too. But it's a good hurt, and I wouldn't trade it for anything in the fucking world."

Afterword

Thank you for reading *Tequila Tuesdays*. If you liked this novel (and even if you didn't) please leave a review on Amazon or Goodreads. Your feedback helps authors share their work and become better writers.

Check out the next book in the Palm Springs Poolside series, *Whiskey Wednesdays*, to be released in early 2024. Amazon.com /author/jlbrannick

To my family and tribe: Thank you for your support. We make a great team.

Thank you to my beta readers and editors, Shelby Nesbitt, Gennifer Ulman, Whitney Tanner, and Susan Keillor.

And to my cover designer at Smart Mouth Publishing LLC.

Follow me on social media and subscribe to my newsletter for the latest news, free giveaways, exclusive bonuses, and new releases!

https://jlbrannick.com/
https://linkfly.to/JLBrannick